For the friends who never let go of each other.
For the friends who never let go of me.

Copyright © 2023 by Lauren Connolly
All rights reserved.

Visit my website at laurenconnollyromance.com
Cover Designer: Cormar Covers
Editor: Jovana Shirley, Unforeseen Editing, www.unforeseenediting.com

No part of this book may be reproduced or transmitted in any form or by any means, electronic or mechanical, including photocopying, recording, or by any information storage and retrieval system without the written permission of the author, except for the use of brief quotations in a book review.

This book is a work of fiction. Names, characters, places, and incidents either are products of the author's imagination or are used fictitiously. Any resemblance to actual persons, living or dead, events, or locales is entirely coincidental.

ISBN-13: 978-1-949794-27-4

FALL BACK INTO ME
HALE BODYGUARDS
BOOK 1

LAUREN CONNOLLY

When a stuntwoman and bodyguard collide, will they heal two broken hearts or leave behind more scars?

Harper Walsh's first reaction to seeing a familiar face from her past is to make the man eat dirt. Fred Sullivan was her best friend until he abandoned Harper in her darkest hour. The guy deserves to get body slammed. But after the slightly violent reunion, Harper can't seem to escape the charming man who could always make her laugh. A meddling sister lands Harper and Fred in a mountain cabin together, and a twist of fate (or poor planning) has the two working for the same A-list actress. Every day spent with Fred reminds her of the boy she used to love and has her prickly defenses softening.

Soon, the burn of her anger transforms into a heat of a different kind…

Fred Sullivan doesn't mind getting tossed to the ground if it means Harper's hands are on him. He still doesn't know if cutting off contact with his closest friend a decade ago was the right choice, but he's had to live with the pain of her absence for years. He's not eager to let her go again. She was his first crush. First love. First heartbreak.

But he never told her the depth of his feelings. Is this his chance to fix an awful mistake? Can he get the words out before the furious redhead breaks his jaw?

Sign up for my newsletter for book news and freebies! All subscribers get a FREE copy of LOVE AND THE LIBRARY.

Get my free book!

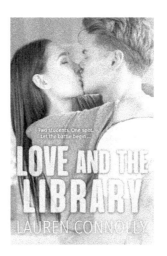

CONTENT WARNING

This book contains scenes with threats used in the form of romantic banter, a vehicular accident, accidental bodily harm, and violent stalking.

This book discusses physical fighting, parental death, ADHD, injury during a house fire, armed robbery, PTSD, and parental manipulation.

PROLOGUE

FRED

SEVENTEEN YEARS OLD

We linger at the foot of the escalator that will take Harper Walsh up to the airport security line and out of my life.

"Don't go," I beg.

"Come on, Fred. Don't do this." Harper stands still in front of me. Quiet. Subdued. Not her. She's been this way for the past month, and now, she's leaving before I can get her—the real her—back.

"Me? *I* shouldn't do this? I'm not the one leaving!" My voice rises with my panic, and a security officer gives me a closer look.

Harper digs her fingers into my arm and drags me to a corner, glaring at me all the while.

Good. This is the first sign of life I've seen from her in weeks.

"That's right. I'm leaving. Stop making this harder than it already is." The cracks in her calm allow anger and desperation to seep through.

Those I can grab on to. Use to change her mind.

"But you don't have to go. You can live with Mom and Phoebe and me. Finish high school here. Go to college here. Your whole life is *here*." And my whole life is her. She's taking my life on a plane to Ireland.

I can't lose someone else I love this soon. This will break me.

"You three have each other," Harper says, and I stifle a flinch at the reduced number. "My mom needs me. And I need my mom." All the fire from a second ago dims, snuffed out by the wetness gathering in her eyes.

Oh no. She can't cry.

I can't take it when Harper cries. I'll give her anything to stop the tears.

"Please, Freddy. Just hug me and tell me to have a safe flight." She slides the strap of her duffel off her shoulder before opening her arms, begging me with her damp eyes.

"Motherfucking goddamn shit!" I mutter the profanities while wrapping her in a crushing hold.

The glorious sound of her laughter brushes against my ear as her strong grip hugs my neck.

Normally, I complain when she uses that annoying Freddy nickname. But what I wouldn't give for her to stay here and call me that every second of every day.

"It's not forever," Harper whispers.

Not forever, but it is for an undetermined amount of time. Do I have to wait a whole year to see the girl I love again when she's old enough to come back for college?

What guarantee do I have that she'll come back at all?

I can't let Harper leave without her knowing how I feel. How much she means to me. That she's my best friend, but every part of me wants us to be more. I should've been telling her all this time. Every day. Starting from when we were five years old and she shoved me off the swings at the playground and I fell for her in every way possible.

"I love you," I growl into the soft skin of her neck.

There. I said it. Now, she can't go because I'm the person she's supposed to spend the rest of her life with, who's going to love her forever. You can't leave that person. You can't just take a plane across an ocean and go to live on the opposite side of the world from your soul mate.

Harper releases her hold on me to cup my face with her hands. Tears trickle in uneven tracks to pool and drip from her chin, and her normally ivory-colored cheeks have gone blotchy red. She's an ugly crier. That makes me love her more.

"I love you too." Her words don't sound the same as mine did. Hers sounds like a good-bye. "I'll call you as soon as I get to my nan's place. And I'll text you the minute I get a phone over there."

She drops her hands to my arms, only to grip my wrists and unwrap my hold from her waist, sliding away from me.

"Please—"

Harper covers my mouth. Her skin is warm and smells like her favorite peppermint hand lotion. She stares me down, determined, even in her sorrow.

"I'm going now. It might be a while, but I'll see you again. I promise."

Harper steps back, grabbing her bag off the floor as she uses the sleeve of her sweatshirt to wipe away her tears. But she doesn't leave. Not yet. Instead, my friend waits, arms crossed, cheeks damp, staring at me with expectation.

I glare back at her. "Soon. You'll see me again *soon*."

The side of her mouth curves right before she plants a kiss on my cheek.

"Good-bye, Freddy."

I catch her hand as she goes to walk past me.

"Not good-bye." The words hurt and are harsh as they leave my throat.

Harper smiles and shrugs one shoulder. "See you soon then."

Her fingers slip from mine. My hand fists, grasping at the bit of warmth that was hers, hoping I can hang on to that small part of her at least.

The escalator carries Harper up and away from me. Just as she reaches the top, my friend turns at her waist to give a final wave. The last sight I have is of her silky crimson ponytail swinging when she turns and disappears from my view.

I wait.

Maybe she'll change her mind. Maybe I'll see her bright yellow

Converse sneakers sprinting down to me. Maybe she'll fling herself into my arms, declaring that leaving me is too painful to bear. Maybe her heart is breaking as much as mine.

But Harper doesn't come back.

She said she'd see me soon.

Apparently, soon means ten years.

PART ONE

CHAPTER 1

FRED

TEN YEARS LATER

Phoebe: Get in, loser. We're going on family vacation.

I grin, reading my sister's text, and crane my head around the arrivals pickup area in the Jackson Hole Airport. The Wyoming airport is tiny compared to where I flew out of in Philadelphia, so locating Phoebe's car an easy task. Especially because my sister is standing by the hood, waving frantically at me.

"Excuse me, strange woman!" I yell out as I approach. "Are you my ride?"

"I dunno. Do I look like the most awesome sister in the world?" She strikes a Peter Pan pose.

Then, without any music, surrounded by strangers, Phoebe Sullivan starts dancing. A weird mixture of the robot and voguing.

"What's this?" I pause, considering backtracking. "What am I seeing right now?"

Unfortunately, I'm too close to pretend not to know her. Plus, we kind of look alike with our dimpled chins and assertive noses—though mine has a bump on the slope from one of the times my face met a drunken fist. Us Sullivans also share the exact same shade of dark brown hair—hers in a neat braid, mine messy and partially smashed against my head because I fell asleep, leaning against the airplane window.

If I try walking away now, airport security will grab me and demand I claim responsibility for the twerking terror I'm clearly related to.

"You, my dear big brother, are witnessing the effects of two grande mochas, consumed in the course of two hours while waiting for your delayed flight." My sister keeps on grooving, only now, she switches over to the routine from the high school dance competition in *Grease*. "I'm high on caffeine and ready for our family vacation! Aren't you excited? Aren't you pumped?"

As I watch her antics, a grin creeps across my face. I can't help it.

I missed Phoebe. That's the whole reason I agreed to fly across the country for a week in the wilderness with her and Mom. Family time. I have a sudden, intense urge to hug her, but her arms are flying erratically in another dance move, and I worry she might accidentally break my nose—again—if I get too close.

And who am I kidding? I'm no more normal than my sister is.

So, I join her.

"Hell yeah, I'm pumped!" My bag flops to the ground as I bust out the running man, followed by a perfectly executed moonwalk, which took me weeks to learn when I was thirteen. Glad I never lost the skill.

I'm just considering if dropping to the ground and doing the worm will win me this dance battle when a car pulls up behind my sister's with a very confused woman at the wheel, gaping at us.

"Okay. I'm officially the airport weirdo. Let's get a move on." I scoop up my bag and toss it into the tiny trunk of Phoebe's eco-friendly rental.

Of course she'd pick the least sensible option for driving the back roads in Wyoming. We're going to get some quality sibling bonding as we both push this thing out of a slightly too-deep mud puddle.

"Mission accomplished." Phoebe slides into the driver's seat and barely waits for me to strap in before she peels out of the airport.

"Your flight got in okay?" I ask.

She flew in from San Jose, which should have arrived within an hour of my flight from the East Coast. Only I had booked with the cheapest airline while she probably flew first class. We're lucky my plane was only an hour late.

"Smooth sailing. I take it as a good sign for the vacation. Everything will go off without a hitch." My sister guides us onto the highway with one hand and reaches over to tug the sleeve of my shirt with her other. "What's with the funky shirt? Is this vacation Fred?"

I glance down at myself, running a hand over the front of my button-up. The thing is the epitome of a Hawaiian shirt. All colorful flowers with big petals, plus a random toucan or two peeking their big beaks out of the foliage.

"A neighbor gave me a whole box of them. You know, after I lost my stuff. They're surprisingly comfy."

When I glance back at my sister, ready for her next joke, Phoebe's face has fallen.

"Crap. I'm sorry. I didn't mean … I'm sorry."

"Hey"—I wave my hand, awkward in the face of her serious shift—"it's not a big deal. You know I'm not tied to my stuff. And I didn't lose *all* of it. It's just hard to get the smell of smoke out of fabric, you know? Besides, I make these shirts look good."

Phoebe's lips twitch up, and then her face gets serious again. "You got the gift cards I sent, right?"

My skin tightens in discomfort. "Yeah. Thanks. Those were helpful." At least, I figure my neighbors found them to be.

"Good. I didn't mean to just, like, throw money at you. And you know you can always move in with me if you need to. Just … you seem to like Philly."

"Phoebe. Stop. Come on. It was a shitty apartment and a little fire. I've got a better place now. And a whole box of kick-ass shirts that, FYI, I wear almost exclusively."

She groans out a laugh, and the tension in the car eases.

I can joke with my sister for hours, but there are some topics—like money and my job and my transient lifestyle—that slip us into an awkward zone. She might be the younger of us two, but despite the occasional wacky dancing, Phoebe is the clear winner in the battle of who has more of their shit together.

Not that I resent my sister's success. Every time I think of how Phoebe is killing it in Silicon Valley with all her tech development skills, I'm so proud that I usually start bragging to strangers on the street. Then, they give me wary looks and back away, but that's probably because they don't have an awesome sister like mine and they're jealous. Sucks for them.

Comparing is the problem. Set my life beside hers, and it's glaringly obvious which one of us has life goals and which one is stumbling through their days.

Not anymore. This time, I think I've found it. What I'm meant to do.

But I keep those thoughts to myself. What's worse than not trying is putting in an effort, getting my mom and sister excited, then watching their faces fall when I inevitably tell them things didn't work out.

I could do without those looks ever again.

"This place is amazing." I gaze out the passenger window at the stretching plains that slam into tall, jagged mountains.

We grew up in the suburbs on the East Coast, and even though I've hopped around a lot since high school, I've never made it out west. Not till now. I thought the Appalachians were mountains, but these …

They're kinda terrifying.

Also, I want to climb one.

"Yeah. I figured the only way to pry Mom out of the lab was to rent a place she couldn't say no to. She's always had secret cowgirl dreams."

Makes sense. Mom loved to watch Westerns on our family movie nights when Phoebe and I were growing up. *High Noon*; *The Good, the Bad and the Ugly*; *Stagecoach*; *Once Upon a Time in the West*; and the list goes on. We'd all groan about how we'd seen them already, but when it was her turn to pick, it was *her* turn. So, no matter the amount of whining, the four of us would pile on the couch and settle in for a repeat.

Phoebe, Mom, me, and … Dad.

I rub my knuckles against my sternum. Ten years, and his absence still hurts, especially in this kind of situation. A family vacation.

"How long do you think it'll be before she buys herself a pair of cowgirl boots?"

My sister chuckles. "I give it a day."

For the rest of the car ride, we cycle between admiring the view, Phoebe trying to explain coding to me—I'm never going to get it, and I trust the robots implicitly—and singing along to the songs we recognize on an oldies station we randomly found after flipping through the local radio options.

At one point, we pass through a town, and I expect us to turn into some nice little neighborhood. Phoebe's boss owns a place here and is letting us use the house for only the cost of the cleaning fee. But my sister keeps driving until we're back out in a wilder area, the road rough on her low-slung car.

The view gets better every mile.

"Turn right in one mile, and you'll arrive at your destination," the GPS says in an Irish accent.

Phoebe claims it's the *best* accent and usually programs all her electronic devices to speak with it.

I keep my mouth shut because the country of Ireland and I have a contentious relationship. It took someone from me, and I never got her back.

That wasn't Ireland's fault. That was yours.

I shift uncomfortably in my seat, only partly because of the axle-rattling bumps in the road. Of course, a family vacation would bring up thoughts of *her*. Ten years later, and Harper Walsh is still a shadow at all our get-togethers. She was family for longer than she hasn't been.

We come around a bend, and when the rental appears through the trees, I huff a breath, the sight an elbow to the gut.

"This is your boss's second home?" I choke out.

Phoebe shrugs. "Probably more like her third or fourth. She's loaded. Which is why I stay on her good side and enjoy the occasional perks."

The cabin—although it seems too big to label it that way—is tucked into its own clearing, roof as tall as the surrounding trees with an entire wall of glass windows. Glancing over my shoulder in the direction the windows face, I realize, inside, we'll have a perfect view of the mountain range across the valley.

"Oh good." Phoebe drums excited fingers against the steering wheel. "They're here!"

I'm so awed by the layout that my mind takes a moment to register her odd choice of words.

"*They're* here?" Returning my stare to the house, I realize there are two cars in the driveway. "Who else besides Mom?"

When I glance at my sister, she's focusing awfully hard on what is a pretty easy parking job.

"Are you dating someone?"

She waves me off with a chuckle. "No. She's just a friend. You'll like her. You've met before."

I sift through memories of the times Phoebe and I hung out with her friends in the past. I'm ashamed to realize I've seen a lot less of my sister in recent years than I used to. I could argue it's because we live on different sides of the country, but I shouldn't let that stop me.

"Is it Macy? Your college roommate?" She was quiet but nice and had a cute dog.

"Not her." Phoebe puts the car in park.

"Uh … Trissa?" She sent her food back twice at brunch. I'd rather not vacation with her.

"*Trista*. Ugh. No. That friendship did not survive, and I'm A-okay with that." She hops out of the car before I can pull another half-remembered name out of the back of my mind.

Once I see her face, I'll probably recognize who she is.

"We're here!" Phoebe shouts.

As I circle around to the trunk, intent on grabbing our bags, I hear the front door open. Rethinking unpacking right away, I abandon the luggage to give my mom a hug first. Been just as long since I've seen her, too, and I'm craving the tight hold of her arms and the comforting pat between my shoulder blades.

"What's all this shouting about?" A husky voice laughs.

A familiar voice.

Not my mother's voice.

No. It can't be. She can't be …

Red hair glows in the afternoon sun, setting the figure on the front porch aflame.

Or maybe that's how she exists in my mind. Burning bright. Painfully so.

Harper Walsh is here.

My heart kicks and writhes in my chest, my rib cage suddenly too small. Sweat gathers in my pits, and I stagger mid-step, sure I've stumbled through time. I must be in the past. The glorious, amazing past. The time when she was in my life and I hadn't ruined everything between us multiple times over.

But, no, this is the present, and she's here.

Ten years have passed since the day at the airport, where Harper walked out of my life and never came back.

She didn't leave your life, an evil, honest voice hisses in the back of my brain. *You shoved her out of it.*

I missed her, but the pain dulled with time. Still there, but bearable. Now, I stifle a groan at the sharp sting of wanting to be near her.

She's so close. Barely twenty feet away. She's looking at me.

Harper Walsh is looking at me.

How can she still affect me like this?

With a heavy, pounding pulse, I wait for another miraculous gift. One of her smiles.

Will it be like I remember?

She has so many smiles. Joyous grins that plump her flushed cheeks. Smirks that claim her mouth and her eyes. Reluctant smiles that wrinkle her nose.

I'll take any of them. I never thought I'd get another in my life.

But Harper doesn't smile at me. Instead, all expression leaches from her face, leaving behind a stony mask.

Even if I deserve the dismissal, the experience still gouges my gut.

Then, she moves toward me, and my hope rekindles.

A decade has changed the shape of her body, but she still walks with the same confidence she had, even as a teenager. I glory in her approach.

Harper raises her arms, and I thank the universe.

She's going to hug me.

I step forward, but then the world tilts off-balance.

No, not the world.

Me.

A second ago, I was standing, but now, I'm flat on my back, gasping for air, staring up into a set of poison-green eyes, sparking with fury.

So much for the combat training I've been through this past month. Roman is going to have my ass when he finds out I let someone get the jump on me.

All thoughts of my buddy's disapproval leak out of my brain as I gaze up into the gorgeous face of Harper Walsh.

Her husky voice caresses every nerve in my body as she says, "Fuck you, Fred Sullivan."

CHAPTER 2

HARPER

Only Fred Sullivan would get tossed to the ground and cursed out and still be grinning.

"Harper." The man has the audacity to sigh out my name, as if in relief. As if my furious face relaxes—rather than terrifies—him. As if I'm not contemplating sitting on his chest and force-feeding him dirt and grass clumps, like when we were six and he had drawn tattoos on all my Barbie dolls.

He deserves that and worse. This man claimed to be my best friend. To *love* me. Then, a handful of months after I moved, he ghosted me.

"Did you set this up?" I continue to scowl, hoping my angry expression will make a dent in his goofy, joyful mood, which he should not be feeling while sprawled on the ground at my feet.

I need him to be groveling and pitiful, so I can stay mad.

But right now, he's all happy and handsome.

Damn Fred Sullivan for not getting ugly over the years. I remember him as tall, kind of gangly, and already shaving at seventeen because the beard puberty had given him was a patchy mess. Now, his body fills out a painfully colorful shirt, and his strong chin has an even coating of scruff. The facial hair frames a charming smile and adds a tantalizing shadow to his Sullivan chin dimple.

"Harper." He says my name again, ignoring my question.

"God, shut up!" I snap at him, stomping away in a very mature display, heading toward the cabin and wondering if I can lock all the doors before he makes it inside.

Phoebe Sullivan waits on the porch for me, wearing a very similar grin to her brother.

The sneaky dots connect.

"You," I growl.

"Me what?" Her innocent act fails immediately when she laughs and launches herself at me, grasping me in a surprisingly strong set of arms.

I wouldn't think working at a computer all day would give her such impressive biceps.

"Harper! Harper! Harper!" She bounces us with each repetition of my name.

Do the Sullivan siblings have a name fixation?

"You're here!"

"Why do I remember you saying this was a *girls'* trip?"

"Because I did say that." Her voice is sweet. Too sweet. "You, me, and my mom. Three girls. Girls' trip."

"Three girls and *him*." I throw a pointed glare at the man climbing to his feet, dusting grass off a pair of well-fitted—too well-fitted if you ask me—jeans.

"Oh, I didn't mention Fred was coming? Oops. Oh well. We're all here now." Phoebe loosens her hold but keeps an arm around my shoulders. "Why don't you put a pause on that murder plot I see brewing in your eyes and show me the house instead?" The pushy woman tugs me toward the house.

My attention flicks toward Fred again, and I find that, yes, he's staring at me, and, yes, he still looks too chipper for his own good.

I clench my teeth and let Phoebe lead me into the house she already knows plenty about since her boss is the one letting us use it. The tour is clearly a ruse to redirect my ire.

Does she have distractions planned for the entire week? Because all

I see is plenty of time to enact revenge on my former best friend. The guy who abruptly cut off all contact with me because …

Well, that's the problem.

I don't know *why* Fred suddenly stopped taking my calls. He didn't bother to give me even the most pathetic of excuses. One day, he simply stopped picking up. Stopped responding to texts. Stopped acknowledging my existence.

At the time, I panicked, sure something had happened to him. But when I called Phoebe, the younger Sullivan told me he was moody, but all his limbs were still attached.

There was no reason Fred couldn't answer my many messages.

Now, he thinks he can smile at me? Act like he missed me?

"Ooh. Look at these high ceilings. And that loft balcony. So cool, right?" Phoebe elbows me in the side, effecting wide eyes as she gazes around the luxurious cabin.

I thought I'd lucked out with a cushy, paid-for vacation with my best friend and her mom, who I love. But I was naive, stumbling straight into her scheme.

I refuse to play her game.

"Why is he here?"

"Is my mom here yet?" Phoebe asks.

"You saw her car. You know she is. She's in the shower. Why is *he* here?"

"Great." My friend wanders to the huge window, basking in the late morning glow that sets off all the warm wood tones in the cabin and makes her brown hair shimmer with gold highlights. "I half-expected her to forget about her flight. You never know with her."

"Phoebe." I let my voice go low and menacing. "If you don't tell me why he's here, I'm going to dump your clothes in that fucking picturesque creek out back."

We hold each other's eyes for a moment, and I try not to think about how her light-hazel set doesn't have the same green starburst around the center that her brother's does.

It's been ten years. Maybe his eyes have faded to a mucky swamp color.

Phoebe huffs a sigh. "He's here because he's my brother, and even though he's a little bit of an exasperating fuckup, I still love him."

"I feel like I should be offended by that," a deep voice says from the front door. And even though Fred is talking to his sister, his attention is on me.

The man being discussed approaches, weighed down with baggage. What a perfect metaphor for our past.

"The last part of the sentence was nice, so that cancels out anything mean I said." Phoebe strolls up to her brother and claims a rolling suitcase from his right hand. "You're in the loft." A quick wave toward the stairs. "Mom is in the king suite through the loft. Harper and I are sharing the queen bed down here." She points to a door past the massive granite-countered kitchen.

"Or—hear me out—we build a giant blanket fort in the living room and all sleep in it like old times." Fred shares a grin between us. "What do you say? Some good ole Sullivan-Walsh bonding time."

The cabin descends into silence.

What. The. Hell?

The idea is so ridiculous that I simply stare at the man with my mouth dangling open for an awkwardly long time.

"I get the feeling Harper would rather not," Phoebe says, her voice dry.

Rather not is an understatement.

Did Fred hit his head and get a concussion that erased the last ten years? Does he think we're still best buddies after a *decade* of silence?

Finally, I find my voice. "I would rather share a tent with an entire family of rabid raccoons," I hiss.

Instead of appearing chastised, Fred curls his lips up with delight. "A whole family? That's harsh. You didn't think one rabid raccoon would get your point across?"

"Obviously not."

Because he's still looking too happy. Too handsome with his too-soft brown hair in a muss around his not-swamp-colored eyes. And too many muscles flexing as he continues to hold heavy bags in the doorway.

Too familiar and strange.

"How about me or a tent with rabid squirrels?" he challenges.

"Squirrels," I declare. And my lips don't twitch up. I frown. Fiercely.

Fred looks thoughtful. "Me or rabid chipmunks?"

Phoebe snorts, and I huff in exasperation, not amusement.

"You're moving into cuter animal territory. Chipmunks, no question."

"You're right." There's a teasing light in his eyes that has my heart rate picking up. "Okay. How about me or rabid ... ostriches?"

"That's out of left field," Phoebe says.

But it's not.

That's exactly the type of joke Fred would have made when we were younger and still talking to each other. Because we went on the school field trip to the zoo together, where an ostrich stole my cotton candy and freaked me out. He knows the big, awkward birds scare me.

He knows me.

No. He knew *me.*

And now, he thinks with a few silly jokes, the last ten years of silence will be forgotten.

I'm done playing this game.

With arms crossed over my chest, I step forward, into the man's space, ignoring how much more of him there is as I stare up into his eyes that haven't changed, watching as his pupils dilate in relation to my proximity.

"Why did you stop taking my calls?" I demand.

The question trips him. My physical aggression, verbal barbs, and angry glares got nothing but his normal playfulness in response.

But this? A simple question that demands an equally simple—yet serious—answer?

Fred's gaze tears away from mine, eyes bouncing around the room, searching for an escape. Under his stubble, I watch his pale cheeks flush as his mouth bobs open a few times.

Eventually, he clears his throat, shrugs, and mutters his response to his scuffed boots. "People lose touch."

Disappointment, stronger than it should be after all this time, pricks and cuts the sensitive places only a few people can reach under my skin.

We weren't just people, I want to say. *We were Fred and Harper. Harper and Fred. We belonged to each other.*

But I keep my jaw clenched shut on the vulnerable words. Fred doesn't deserve them.

I turn my back on him and give Phoebe—who never left my life—the warmest smile I can manage as I hook my arm through hers, leading her to the bedroom I tossed my stuff in. Leaving him behind.

"Okay. Girls' trip."

CHAPTER 3

FRED

There's a possibility I won't survive to the end of this vacation.

Cause of death might be from one of the adventurous activities that Phoebe has planned.

More likely, I'll die from Harper murdering me in my sleep.

Most likely, I'll die from wanting her.

"You were in a movie with clowns?" Phoebe eagerly leans over her plate of pizza, stare rapt on Harper. "I missed that one."

"Yeah. Clowns do some wild stunts. I went to a clown school for training." The redhead relaxes back in her chair, holding a beer in loose fingers, offering my sister an indulgent smile. Her nose wrinkles with the expression.

I'm so jealous.

"You know," Mom says from her spot at the head of the table, "when you told me you were working as a stuntwoman, I couldn't believe it. But after thinking about it for a bit, I realized the job was perfect for you. You're fearless. Always have been." Lori Sullivan reaches over to squeeze Harper's hand, and the casual affection sets off a series of conflicting emotions in me.

My mom isn't exactly a recluse, but she tends to bury herself in her work and lose contact with the world. I bet Phoebe spent some time convincing her to take a week off for this trip. Watching her connect with humans instead of test tubes is a relief.

Then, there's the joy of seeing how well Harper and my mom get along to this day.

But, fuck, I am a jealous asshole.

Because, damn myself to hell, I want to be the one touching Harper's hand.

I want to be the one who *knows* her. All this time, I guess I had in my mind that when I cut off contact with Harper, Mom and Phoebe would lose touch too—maybe not abruptly, but over time, fading out of her life.

Harper always seemed like *mine*.

But that was never true.

Ten years, and she's more glorious than I remember. The light social-media stalking I did over the years didn't do her justice. I've seen pictures and videos of her at her stuntwoman job. I knew about and watched the clown movie—*The Slippery Banana*. Her face was never on camera, so I spent the whole hour and forty minutes trying to identify when she stepped in for the lead actress simply from the way her body moved.

But all those glimpses were at an uncrossable distance. Now, she's on the opposite side of the table from me. I could crawl over it and touch her.

I won't because that's weird.

But I could.

I could shove up from my chair, and in a few steps, I could be at her side. Drop to my knees before her, drag my hands up her muscular legs to the edge of her loose athletic shorts. Stare into her sharp emerald eyes. Wrap her red ponytail around my fist to see if the strands are as silky as I recall. Press my nose against the pale, slightly flushed side of her throat and discover if she still used the same peppermint lotion. A living, breathing candy cane I'd want to suck on.

But Harper is more likely to stab me than let me lick her.

The stuntwoman takes a sip from her bottle, and a drop of condensation beads and drops onto the mound of one boob. Like a creep, I watch the moisture trace down the curve and dip into the cleft of her breast, disappearing in the shadow.

Fuck. I'm just as horned up for Harper as I was when I was seventeen.

Back then, I was too nervous to tell her how I felt.

Now, it wouldn't matter. Because she hates me.

"Maybe you should look into stunt work, Fred."

It takes me a moment to realize my mom said my name, then another moment to comprehend what she said.

"Me?"

"You've always been the adventurous sort too."

She offers me an encouraging smile, and my heart clenches. I know she would support whatever career I chose. She just wants me to *choose* one.

"Oh, yeah. I mean, it sounds fun …" I trail off when Harper grimaces and rolls her eyes.

Did I say something wrong? Or is it just the fact that I'm talking that has her pissed off?

"Mom," Phoebe says, "Harper started when she was in college. Fred is kind of behind. Besides, he's doing that—is it a salesman thing? With the mattresses?"

"That didn't work out." I manage to keep an easy smile and try not to think about my sister's earlier comment about me being a fuckup. She's not wrong, much as it stings to admit it. "But I think I have something else lined up. Been talking to a buddy of mine. He's got a new business, and I'm interviewing for a spot on his team."

I keep things vague intentionally because I already see the tightening in both my mom's and sister's eyes. They're used to this exchange. The question about my job, where I tell them I've moved on to something new. They worry about my inability to hold on to any employment for longer than a few months, and I try hard not to show them how I worry as much as they do.

I could say this time, this new thing, feels different.

But I've said that before too. It's part of the *Fred is a fuckup* script.

Best to keep explanations short and avoid the anxiety of a long back-and-forth.

Hopefully, I'll *show* them this time is different.

Roman believes in me. Or at least, he's investing in me.

"Well, I'm glad you have a friend to call on." Mom smiles at me as she reaches for another slice of pizza.

We decided to do the easy food option this first night—order takeout to eat on the porch while watching the sun set behind the mountains.

Phoebe had floated the idea of us doing a big trip together the past few years and finally decided to make it happen. Only she never mentioned Harper was part of the plan.

But now, I don't want to imagine this evening without her.

My eyes find their way to Harper again, and I flinch when I realize she's staring at me.

Fuck, that feels good.

"Yeah, Freddy is *so* great at keeping up with his friends," she mutters before taking another sip of her beer and performing another round of water-droplet-boob torture. "Bet you guys chat all the time."

"Uh …" I'm having trouble concentrating when half my brain is imagining my tongue tracing the same trail as those drips of condensation. "I guess. Yeah."

Harper's gaze sweeps over me with an air of judgment.

"Bet he doesn't call him Freddy though," Phoebe offers around a mouthful of pizza. "That was always your special nickname for him."

In the glow of the porch lights, I watch Harper's skin flush a deep red, almost as dark as her hair. My hands ball into fists to keep from reaching out to see if there's a wave of heat coming off her.

How am I supposed to survive this?

What is Phoebe's game, inviting both of us?

After a second of contemplation, I decide I don't care.

This is a chance I never expected to have. Never thought I deserved.

Because I don't.

One more area of my life where I thoroughly fucked up was with Harper. First, by dragging her into all my troublemaking antics in high school. Next, by clinging to her after the deaths of our fathers, relying on her to support me emotionally with no thought as to how my neediness might weigh on her. Then, when I realized I needed to back off, I couldn't even manage to talk to her like an adult about it. I just shut down, afraid if I didn't quit her cold turkey, I wouldn't be able to let go.

Turns out, that was a shitty move, and she's still pissed about it, but I don't blame her.

Maybe it's best if she leaves me in the past.

But I'm trying to be different. Trying to be better.

What if I use this week to convince Harper I'm a different man? Not the screwup she remembers. Could I convince her to like me again? Even a little? I'm not good at much in life, but getting people to like me is a skill I've honed over the years.

That, and brawling. Which, after her brutal greeting, I imagine is something else Harper might enjoy.

Maybe I'm making whatever excuses it takes to get Harper back in my life, but with her here, no one can expect me to be entirely reasonable.

I rest my elbows on the table, leaning toward the gorgeous, dangerous redhead, capturing her gaze with mine.

"My name's not Freddy," I growl, pretending annoyance.

Her eyes widen, then narrow.

One thing about Harper hasn't changed. She loves a challenge.

That makes two of us.

CHAPTER 4

HARPER

I *will not look at his butt. I will not look at his butt. I will not …*

My eyes creep up the rock face despite my internal chanting and latch on to the flexing globes of Fred's ass. The climbing harness is the culprit. His cargo pants might have started out loose, but the leg straps cinch the material tight enough that I can see every shift and tensing of his glutes.

Damn Fred and his fine ass.

Phoebe is the one belaying her brother as he sets a route up the cliff face. She's the one who needs to keep her eyes on him as she feeds him more rope, so I have no excuse for staring. Especially with the unbeatable Wyoming wilderness spread out at our backs.

Even his bright orange vacation shirt, covered in flamingos wearing sunglasses, is not a valid excuse for my rapt attention.

Wrenching my eyes away from Fred's behind, I turn to take in the view of sprawling forests and jagged mountain peaks. And as I soak in the beauty of the Tetons, I reluctantly admit a fact to myself.

I'm having trouble holding on to my anger toward Fred.

The problem is, he never did anything to me. It was the lack of doing that ended our friendship.

We didn't have a fight. He just disappeared. It felt like a loss more than anything.

And now, he's here, in front of me, and part of my heart is shouting for joy. The traitorous organ is saying, *Look! Someone we loved returned to us! Hug him hard and never let go!*

Then, I have to remind myself that I never *had* to lose Fred. It was his doing. He intentionally disappeared on me and for no good reason as far as I can tell.

Teenagers make mistakes. That thought comes as my brain starts to play a highlight reel of all my ridiculous teenage antics that got worse and more dangerous after my dad died, and we moved, and I lost my friend.

Should people still judge me for the reckless ways I dealt with my grief?

But I'm different than I was then.

Couldn't Fred be different too?

"That's me!"

I turn at Phoebe's call and realize that while I was having my internal debate, Fred must have already reached the top, set up an anchor, and pulled the rope taut. His sister just let him know the resistance he felt on the rope was her.

Fred's faster than he used to be. How many times has he gone climbing since I last saw him? We'd only just started trying outdoors when tragedy struck our families and I left.

A memory rushes at me, too fast to dodge. One of the three of us, younger, when life hadn't hurt us so bad. Fred, Phoebe, and I used to go to a rock-climbing gym a short drive from our neighborhood with our dads. Robert Sullivan would load us in the minivan while my father would claim the passenger seat and the radio. Us kids would groan when he flipped the dial to the *oldies but goodies* radio station. Their dad would laugh as mine tortured our ears for the whole drive. At the climbing center, Mr. Sullivan would belay Fred, and my dad would rope in with me, so I could race my best friend to the top.

"Show him how it's done, little warrior," Dad liked to say.

"Hell," I mutter as a thickness condenses in the back of my throat. Just the memory of his voice has me choking up.

"Harper?" Phoebe appears at my side, her brows dipped as she takes in whatever expression I'm wearing.

This is why I'm a stuntwoman and not an actress. I have no talent for deceiving with my face.

"What's wrong?"

I clear my throat a few times before I can manage an answer. "Do you remember that last drive we all took to the old gym?"

She immediately gets it. A smile breaks over her face, even as her eyes shine.

"You just got your license," she says.

"And your dad let me drive," I add.

"And Fred insisted on riding shotgun and put on that horrible death metal station."

"Which he didn't even like." I let out a watery snort.

"And Dad pretended to be Fred whenever he pouted. And your dad pretended to be you."

"I never admitted how good those impressions were."

"I was dying laughing in the very back seat," she says.

We're grinning at each other like goofs. Then, I gasp, and the tight hold I thought I had on my tear ducts slips. Suddenly, I'm trying to stifle my sobs, and Phoebe has her arms tight around me as she cries, too, our climbing helmets knocking into each other.

"I'm sorry," I mutter into the now-damp collar of her T-shirt.

"Don't be." Her hands rub my back. "Sometimes, it hits me out of nowhere too. And with us all here? We were bound to think of them."

That's an unavoidable truth. Our memories eternally tie us together. Even if Phoebe and Mrs. Sullivan had written me off, like Fred did, we never would have truly separated.

Not when the worst moment in our lives is a shared one.

After sucking in a shaky, deep, wet breath, I step out of my friend's arms. The woman is a couple of years younger than me—one of the reasons I was closer to Fred when we were all kids. But now, she's one of my best friends—and not only because we lost our dads on the same day, in the same car, when a truck ran a red light and destroyed our lives.

Phoebe held on to me, even when an ocean separated us. She never let too long pass without checking in.

What I'll never tell her is how that loyalty came with a side of pain. Because if Phoebe could hold on to me, why couldn't Fred?

But it doesn't matter anymore.

"Sorry for the waterworks. I'm ready to climb."

"Yeah. Okay." Phoebe uses the back of her hand to wipe away her tears, fills her lungs with a bracing breath, then lets the air go with a dramatic whoosh.

"What's happening? You all coming?" The shout sounds from high above us, and I bend back to see the minuscule head of Fred peeking over the edge of the cliff.

"Keep your pants on!" Phoebe shouts back. "I'm sending Harper your way now."

She smirks, and I roll my eyes. Typical impatient Freddy. He's probably fidgeting like wild, stuck up there by himself.

Soon enough, I'm roped in and mapping my route as best I can from the ground. Since I refused to watch Fred ascend the cliff face, I'm working from scratch. We learned early on that rock climbing is similar to puzzle solving. Only, when you're in a climbing gym, most often, the holds are colorful, making them easy to see. This is all gray, gray, and more gray.

Still, I think I know where to start, and that's the most important part.

"On belay!" I shout to Fred, who's now supporting me from the top of this first leg of our climb. I chalk my hands, using the powder in a sack hitched to my waist.

"Belay on," he calls down to me.

"Climbing!"

"Climb on." His deep voice sends a shiver down my spine.

My fingers gripping a small edge, I wedge my foot into a crack, and then I heave myself upward.

Once my muscles warm up and I get into a steady rhythm, climbing becomes almost therapeutic. One limb moving at a time.

Checking in with the balance and security of my body. Breathing in stone and fresh air and chalk and sweat. I'm so in the zone that I almost overlook the first cam Fred placed. One of the temporary safety devices climbers use to attach themselves to a rock face in case they fall before establishing an anchor. I unhitch the metal piece from the crevice and attach it to my belt, in charge of cleaning up the security pieces as I go now that we have an anchor at the top.

The climb takes me maybe fifteen minutes, which is short when I think of my normal workouts, but my arms are still quivering when I heave myself over the last ledge. Fred holds out his fist for a bump, and I tap my knuckles to his. I could have dismissed the gesture, but I don't want to be *too* petty.

"That was a beautiful climb." He grins while stacking the rope, his gaze running over me.

Instead of answering, I reach for my water bottle, where it's strapped to my waist, and take a long drink and gaze over the Rocky Mountains.

"Harper ..." Fred says my name with a touch of uncharacteristic hesitation. "Were you crying?"

I glance back to find him staring hard at my face.

That's when I remember how my eyes get puffy and my cheeks get blotchy whenever I spring a leak. I guess even the vigorous climb wasn't enough to clear the signs of my breakdown from my face.

"It's not a big deal." *And if it was, does he think I'd want to talk about it with him?*

Even if I admit that maybe I don't exactly ... hate Fred anymore, that doesn't mean we're best buddies. Now, we're just strangers. Sure, throughout the years—after a few too many glasses of wine—I googled him. But Fred hasn't done anything newsworthy, and his social media accounts are information deserts. My guess is, he set them up and forgot about them. Sometimes, he'd randomly check in at a pizza shop or a bar, and I'd be half-sure those were slips of the thumb.

All I know about the guy is that we used to be best friends and he has horrible taste in shirts.

"What's up?" Fred watches me as he resumes pulling up the slack on the rope.

Uncomfortable under the scrutiny, I shrug. "Nothing. Seriously." But when he continues to gaze at me with a puppy-dog stare, I grumble and give in just a bit. "It was just a memory that got me a little choked up. Because we're doing this." I wave at the climbing gear dangling from my harness. "And we used to do this with *them*."

"Oh." A dark cloud drifts over his face, fully blotting out the normal sunny shine from his expression.

A part of me regrets seeing it disappear.

"Yeah. *Oh*. But Phoebe gave me a big old hug, and now, we're good. And we should probably make sure she makes it up here safe and sound."

"I could give you a hug."

My step toward the cliff edge falters, and I turn back to see Fred has abandoned the climbing setup to hold out his arms, offering an embrace as he puts his goofy aloha shirt on full display.

Is he joking?

Isn't he always?

I used to love his constant humor. When we were younger, no matter how bad my day was going, Fred could distract me from the melancholy for a moment at least. And right now, I want that again. I want his hug.

But Fred gave up his role as my soothing presence when he became the reason for my depressed state.

I should tell him no. Protect myself from any future hurt he could casually dole out if I let myself care about him again.

"Maybe later," I say, silently berating myself for leaving even that much wiggle room.

But I was never the one between us who could so completely give up on the other.

CHAPTER 5

HARPER

FIFTEEN YEARS OLD

"What in the ever-loving shit are you wearing?" Fred howls when he sees me.

"Fred! Language!" Mom is quick to scold my friend on his slipup. And slipup it most definitely is.

Fred throws profanities around all the time, but never in front of my mother. Until today, that is.

"Sorry, Mrs. Walsh, but come on. You've gotta cut me some slack. Harper, please tell me this is your Halloween costume or something."

I was in the middle of relating the news to my mom when Fred sauntered into our kitchen, like he often does, and decided to rudely interrupt me. His reaction is so predictable; it's almost comical. Almost.

"That's gonna be a no. Get used to your new reality, Freddy boy." I skip to the middle of the room, twirl in order to get my skirt moving, then land in a power pose with my fists on my hips. "Your best friend is a cheerleader."

He groans.

I grin.

"How could you do this? Who brainwashed you? Was it that super-perky one, Brittany? It was, wasn't it? I'm telling you, that smile she wears all the time is a cover for pure evil!"

I huff a laugh as he attempts to lecture me about my life choices. But then I soften a tiny bit.

"I'm not doing this because some popular girl talked me into it. Don't worry. I'm not looking to replace you with a bunch of prematurely caffeinated powerhouses. This is just something I want to try out. You should see the tricks they do. And in sync!"

My buddy snorts. "I know what cheerleading is. Lots of shouting about being aggressive while clapping and raising your arms at just the right angle. Sounds like a real challenge." Sarcasm drips from his words and heats my blood.

Oh hell, here he goes. If anyone can fire my temper, it's Fred. And the condescending way he's speaking now sounds like he's asking for a punch to the gut.

"More challenging than sitting on a couch, playing Call of Duty for hours."

"Hey! I work hard to develop my video-game prowess."

I roll my eyes at him before focusing back on my mom. She, at least, is proud of me.

"Anyway, as I was saying, there were only two spots, and I got one. I think it was my backflip that really sold me." My hips keep swishing as I talk, loving the sensation of the cool fabric brushing my legs. I didn't need to put my uniform on right when they gave it to me. But I couldn't wait to try it out, and I thought the costume would add the necessary pizzazz to my announcement.

"You mean, the backflip *I* taught you?" Fred still looks put out, glowering at me, as if I just told him I broke his skateboard. Again.

"You taught me how to do one off a diving board," I clarify. "I figured out how to do it on dry land all by myself."

"Like that's any different."

"It is so different! You have to land on your feet and worry about balance."

"Come on." He smirks at me. "You're just trying to make this cheerleading thing sound tougher than it actually is."

All during our verbal sparring, my mom simply sips her tea and turns her head back and forth, like she's observing a tennis match. Now, the subtle instigator decides to speak up.

"Well, my dears, I think there is only one way to settle this."

I have an idea of what she's going to suggest and am not disappointed.

"It seems Fred must show us his standing backflip."

I put absolutely no effort into holding back my snort while crossing my arms and giving him my *whatcha gonna do now* eyebrow raise.

Never one to turn down a challenge, Fred doesn't even flinch.

"What a great suggestion, Mrs. Walsh. Name the time and place."

"Well, it is a lovely evening, and I see no reason to wait. How about in ten minutes, our backyard?"

Damn, my mom can be a hard-ass sometimes. She's never one to let Fred get away with his teasing, especially when he's teasing me. My best friend visibly swallows, but he gives no other indication of nerves.

"Sounds good to me. Prepare to see a perfectly executed backflip." He struts his way out the back door, the very same way he entered our kitchen.

Even though I look forward to him falling on his ass, I suddenly find myself praying we don't have to take a trip to the ER tonight.

FRED

FIFTEEN YEARS OLD

Shit, what was I thinking?

I wasn't thinking—that was the problem. I was doing my best to distract myself from the way that cheerleading outfit hugged Harper's curves.

Why did she have to sway her hips? It was like she was trying to hypnotize me! And I think it worked if her goal was to get me to make a fool of myself.

The warm evening air only adds to my nervous sweating. I've done a backflip off a diving board and on my neighbor's trampoline, but never just standing.

Stop being so nervous. You got this. It's no big deal. Harper is watching.
Shit, that's not the way to make myself less nervous.

When we were younger, having Harper around made me more reckless. I would showboat like there was no tomorrow, craving her awe and approval. Now, more and more, I care about looking cool in front of her. Which is an issue because I still always seem to brag my way into embarrassing things.

But I'm athletic. Coordinated. There's no reason to believe I can't do this.

"Okay! Ten minutes are up! Let's see what you've got, Freddy!" Harper shouts from the deck, still wearing that goddamn outfit.

Then, only adding to the pressure of the situation, Mr. Walsh joins his wife and daughter, looking slightly rumpled with his dress shirt untucked. The man probably just got home from work. Walked himself straight into some prime-time entertainment. He leans in to whisper something to Mrs. Walsh, but she speaks at full volume when answering.

"Oh, we're just waiting for Fred to show us how easy it is to make the cheerleading squad. Whenever you're ready, dear!" The last part is shouted even louder for my benefit.

This isn't the first time Harper's mom has called me on my bullshit, but there's an understanding that I always need to at least try to live up to my bragging if I'm to sustain her approval.

Mr. Walsh grins and leans on the porch railing, not looking to give me any assistance. If I hesitate any longer, he'll probably duck inside to grab a camera. So, yeah, time to put up or shut up.

I bend my knees a couple of times, as if this will somehow give the dirt beneath me more spring. I figure my best option is to push off even harder than I would on a diving board. That should get me far enough off the ground to get all the way around. And swing my arms really hard—that should help.

In my head, I count, *One … two … THREE.*

My legs rocket me off the ground, and I'm airborne. The momentum of my arms pulls my body backward. My knees tuck into my chest, and as if in slow motion, I watch the sky pass before my eyes, then the horizon, then the ground.

This is actually happening!

I'm doing it!

But the ground doesn't give way to the sky again. It simply rushes up to meet my face.

Oh fuck.

The tight ball I held my body in collapses quickly as my arms flail and my knees seek to take the impact of my landing. Unfortunately, that job has already been filled by my skull.

The soft grass does little to pad my cheek as it smashes into the dirt. When my chest follows next, all the air bursts from my lungs. I gasp out a groan.

Goal of not embarrassing myself? Failed.

After a moment of lying facedown in the Walshes' backyard, I roll over onto my back, panting in halting chokes of breath.

A gorgeous face interrupts my view of the sky, grinning down at me with an interesting mixture of concern and glee.

"That was a backflip, huh?"

I still haven't gotten my lungs to function properly yet, so I just nod.

"Funny," Harper says. "When I do mine, I tend to land on my feet. And I inflict less bodily harm on myself."

I shrug but find her smile is catching. She chuckles and wipes a large clump of yard off my face.

"You okay?" Her hands give my neck and shoulders a brisk check-over, which makes my heart beat harder.

I nod again, breathe in deep, and clear my throat. "Maybe … I was wrong."

"Ah. I love hearing you say those words." Laughter sparks in her eyes. "So, are you going to come see me cheer?"

"Cheer for the cheerleader?" I let out a mock moan.

Harper keeps on smiling.

"Yeah. Okay," I sigh. "I'll watch you do your wild flips."

The thought of her dancing and cartwheeling in her uniform

invades my mind, and I make a mental note to try not to die from how much I want her.

"That's a good Freddy."

She leans in, and I hold the breath I just regained, barely daring to hope.

She kisses me.

On my forehead.

A big, goofy, smacking kiss, and then she meets my eyes again, grinning all the while.

"You're forgiven."

CHAPTER 6

HARPER

PRESENT DAY

The Fred I knew couldn't hard-boil an egg without giving himself a second-degree burn. Now, through the sliding glass door, I watch him effortlessly flip burgers on the gas grill. Patties of ground beef he seasoned and formed himself. Not that making a decent burger is some challenging feat, deserving of a grill master award.

But this skill, this bit of growth, serves to remind me that Fred might have changed in more ways. Maybe this man is different from the reckless boy who broke my heart.

So, why didn't he ever reach out?

The simplest answer is, he didn't want to. I glare at the hardwood floor between my bare feet.

Was staying friends with me really that taxing? Did I demand too much?

I hate having these thoughts. The same ones that kept me awake at night after my best friend ghosted me. The doubt that had me wondering if it was *me* who had done something wrong. If I was the reason our relationship ended.

"People drift apart," he said.

One thing hasn't changed. Fred is still a terrible liar. We didn't drift. He pushed me over the edge of a waterfall. But I'm tired of drowning in this resentment. Tired of letting the callousness of a teenage boy affect how I interact with the grown man.

I push the glass door to the side, joining Fred on the porch. When he glances over his shoulder and sees I'm the one approaching, I watch his spine straighten and a happy smile curl the corners of his mouth.

This version of Fred is happy to see me at least.

"Hey there. How do you want your burger cooked?"

"Medium well." I lean a hip on the porch railing, cross my arms over my chest, and hold his gaze. "Are you sorry you stopped talking to me?"

Fred's eyes widen, his entire body tensing. Maybe preparing for another attack from me.

But when a moment of inaction passes between us, without me saying or doing anything more, he relaxes a touch and gives me an answer. "Yes."

Simple. A lot less words than Fred normally uses. Which somehow lends the admission more weight.

I nod and turn my attention to the darkening woods around the clearing, considering if I want to press for more. The answer is as simple as his.

Yes.

I want to know why. What happened? What spurred the change? Was it him? Was it me?

But I'm not the same girl I used to be. The one who would pester my friend to reveal his secrets until we were exasperated with each other and got into a shouting match.

So, even though just the presence of Fred has me wanting to be childish, I choose to take the mature route.

I let it go.

"Okay. You're forgiven." Because that's what adults do, right? They forgive people, even when nothing gets fixed?

The doubt, lingering like the sting of a splinter under my skin, eases a touch when Fred grins wide, the expression entirely too charming.

"Friends?" he asks.

"Sure." Not like we were though. I don't think I can ever trust him like I once did. But I have friends who aren't ride or die. Fred can be one of those.

Then, a terrible, jealous part of me catches on the protruding bit of an aching splinter.

"Who's your best friend?"

Fred blinks. "Best friend? Um, I guess …" He goes thoughtful.

Is he scrolling through a whole Rolodex of people he's known and loved these past ten years?

Stop it. You forgave him. Besides, he's probably going to say Phoebe, which is a super-sweet thing to say—

"Roman. Roman Hale." He flips a burger and throws me a rueful smile. "Got into a bar fight with him. Not against him. This group of assholes was giving the guy a hard time for being Army Special Forces and wanted to go a round. He probably didn't need me, but I couldn't stand by when it was four against one." He shrugs and rubs a thumb against a bump in the bridge of his nose that I don't remember being there ten years ago. "Been close with him ever since."

"Huh." I shove my hands in the pockets of my sweatpants, hopefully hiding my clenched fists. "Roman Hale."

Fred nods, a fondness in his expression. "You'd like him."

"Would I?" Oof, that came out with a bitchy twist.

Fred's brows dip as he stares at me. "I think you would. He's down-to-earth. Can hold his own in a fight." He smirks. "And he thinks I'm hilarious."

"Sounds like he has terrible judgment. Like clinically bad."

Fred pretends to be affronted. "How dare you? I am an amusing delight."

"I bet that's what all the ladies say. In the bedroom. After you pull your pants down."

Instead of blushing or blustering, Fred lays his spatula to the side and saunters over to me. The way he moves, playful yet smooth, mesmerizes me for a moment, which is the excuse I use for how close I let him get. Right in front of me. Hands on the railing on either side of my hips.

Looming.

Since when did Fred learn to loom?

And to smolder?

"Harper Walsh"—he purrs my name—"have you been imagining what I look like with my pants around my ankles? Standing next to a bed?"

Here's another change the years have wrought: Fred Sullivan has turned into a dangerous devil.

Good thing I have strong defenses.

"I don't have to wonder," I whisper as my finger trails down the front of his colorful shirt, ticking against buttons as I go and enjoying the way he sucks in a deep breath. "Remember the day after that hike we did on my fifteenth birthday? I walked in on you putting ointment on your ass to help with the poison ivy rash you had gotten from using the wrong leaves as toilet paper."

Finally, I get a blush. In the porch light, I watch a delicious red spread from the collar of his Hawaiian shirt up to his five o'clock shadow, fully engulfing his cheeks. Even his forehead flushes.

"I did my best to forget that," he mutters.

"Don't worry." I pat his chest. "I never will."

Fred sighs, letting his dimpled chin drop to his chest. "I promise the rash cleared up." He raises his head with a wicked grin. "Want to see?"

Yes, please. The words sit just behind my teeth, caught the moment I realize what's happening.

I'm flirting with Fred Sullivan.

We always used to tease and goad and good-naturedly mock. But this is different.

These jokes carry an air of anticipation. The possibility of more, if only we keep going. Keep hinting until our hands brush and our clothes become uncomfortably tight and our lips feel lonely.

Flirting with Fred Sullivan? I can't do that. Not when I've *just* forgiven him.

Totally and completely forgiven. No lingering resentment at all.

"No thanks." I duck under his arm. "I trust you've got yourself a perfectly pale ass. Speaking of, maybe you should focus on the color of those burgers."

One patty seems to have caught on fire. Maybe the man hasn't improved in the kitchen as much as I thought.

While Fred curses and tries to regain control of the grill, I head inside the house. Not running away.

"Did Fred tell you how long it'll be?" Phoebe asks from the kitchen counter, where she's opening a bag of buns.

Mrs. Sullivan is at her side, dumping a bag of lettuce into a large bowl. None of us are culinary experts.

"Should be any minute now. Some might be well done."

Phoebe snorts, and her mom wears a smile that reminds me a lot of her son.

"I'm sure he's doing better than I could have managed," Mrs. Sullivan says. "I can work a Bunsen burner fine, but a grill has always baffled me."

"Maybe we should try that sometime." Phoebe grins. "Bunsen burgers. It's genius."

The Sullivan women chuckle together. Their easy banter has a mixture of love and homesickness mixing in my stomach. Not for a place so much as a person. My mom, as much as we get into it sometimes, is a constant in my life I haven't seen lately. She's still living in Ireland, and my schedule is often too hectic for an international trip.

I miss her. I should find a way to visit her soon.

"Let's eat outside again. Harper, want to take this out to Fred to put the burgers on?" Phoebe hands me a platter, and I try not to let on how reluctant I am to be alone with her brother again.

The flirting has left me all …

Off-kilter.

Just think about his poison ivy–covered ass.

"No problem."

After I'm sure I have complete control over my errant thoughts, I head back outside with the serving tray cradled in my arms. No burgers are on fire when I arrive at his side.

"Here." I offer the tray. "I think this'll be big enough for your meat."

Fuck.

My.

Life.

What demon on my tongue made me say *that* to *him*?

Fred turns slowly, a ridiculously huge grin on his face. "Do you think so?"

I grit my teeth and almost retreat into the house. Then, I decide I'd like to see that cockiness deflate.

"Yep. Actually"—I hold up the platter with a thoughtful expression—"I think this might be *too* big of a plate for your meat. When your meat is on it, there's going to be a lot of extra room. In fact, if we serve your meat on this platter, your family will be confused. They'll ask why your meat looks so small. Everyone will stare at your lack of meat and assure you it's okay that there's not much. Only—from the way you bragged—they thought there would be *a lot* more."

The goofy smile disappears as Fred's jaw drops. I half-expect him to cover his junk with his hands to protect himself from my monologue. Instead, the strange man lays his tongs beside the grill, then sinks to his knees before stretching out flat on the patio, lying prone on the ground.

"What are you doing?" I take a step back.

"I'm dead," Fred announces. "You've killed me. On my tombstone, please write, *Here lies Fred Sullivan, perished at the age of twenty-seven due to a mortal wound to his ego. Please note: his penis was an acceptable length.*"

Don't laugh. Don't you dare laugh.

I clear my throat and glare down at him. "Hmm, no. I think I'll write, *Here lies Freddy, more dramatic than any diva in Hollywood.*"

He blinks, then drops an arm over his face, effectively hiding his eyes. "You keep calling me Freddy."

I can't read the tone of his voice. Does he like that I use that old nickname? Does it frustrate him, like it used to?

When he clambers to his feet, I turn my back to hide the smile that's overtaken my face.

I missed this. I missed him.

Now, he's here, as goofy as ever, and I don't have to miss him anymore.

And that—one less person in my life I have to miss—is an amazing thing.

An intoxicating thing.

CHAPTER 7

FRED

Horseback riding was Mom's choice of activity. She was so excited when we arrived at the farm that she actually bounced in her seat and clapped.

A horse girl at heart.

Me? I have a healthy respect for horses, tending to keep my distance and offering a nod of recognition whenever I cross paths with one. A nod that says, *I know you could bludgeon me in the head with one of your hooves, and I will do my best not to give you a reason to.*

Safe to say, I'm the least graceful of us four in the saddle.

Doesn't help that we're riding in a line, and I'm behind Harper, her hips swaying in perfect time with her animal's steps. The movement keeps hypnotizing me, and I barely catch myself from sliding sideways out of my saddle and face-planting in the middle of this beautiful aspen wood forest.

"How are you doing back there?" The redheaded temptress turns her torso enough to glance back at me.

"Me? I'm doing great. Sugar Cube and I have a tight bond now. Considering becoming a cowboy."

Harper smirks, and I want with every *bad at horseback riding* cell in my body to lasso her and drag her into me. Maybe do like the hero in one of those historical movies, where the man pulls a damsel in distress into his saddle and they ride off into the sunset together.

Realistically, I'd be the one in distress, and Harper would have to share her mount with me. But whatever gets my body pressed against hers.

Or even better, if *I* were the one she rode. Gripping tight with her thighs …

"Didn't you do stunt work for a cowgirl movie?" Phoebe calls out from her place in front of Harper.

Yes, she did, I think to myself, *in* Lady Outlaws.

"Yeah. I get most of my work from doubling for Shelly Lovegrove. She starred in *Lady Outlaws*. But I mainly handled bar-fight scenes. There are stuntwomen with better horse-handling skills than me who came in for that shoot."

"Your work is fascinating," my mom offers, better able to converse with us as we condense on a switchback in the trail. "Did you ever tell us how you started with it? I thought your degree was business."

I watch the muscles in Harper's shoulders shift as she shrugs.

"It was, but that's because I wasn't sure what I wanted to do. When I got to college in California, I joined the cheer team. Then, I learned about martial arts clubs on campus and tried a few of them out, loved them, and stuck with it. There was a director who was shooting an action movie, and they needed a lot of extras who could fight—a lot of women extras. So, they came to our campus and invited us to be in the background. That's when I saw some professional stuntwomen working. They were"—her voice goes dreamy, and I wish I could see her face as she talks about her passion—"amazing. I talked to a few afterward. They gave me tips, and I found a mentor. That was the start."

"I want to hear more later!" Mom calls out as the trail straightens and she gets ahead of us.

I want to hear more too. I want all the details I've missed from Harper's life.

Like, why did she go to college in California? Her plan was to come back to Pennsylvania when she graduated high school. At least, when we were talking that was what she wanted.

Am I the reason she went to school so far away?

Guilt sits heavy in my gut until I remind myself that Harper could have chosen California for plenty of reasons, and even if it was because of me, she found her passion there. She likely wouldn't have become a stuntwoman if she'd followed the original plan.

"We should wrestle," I announce, loud enough that Phoebe overhears and scoffs.

Harper throws an unreadable look over her shoulder. The fact that I can't interpret the expression on her face shoots a pang of discomfort through my gut. I used to know what every subtle shift in Harper's mood meant. Now, there are parts of her—more than I want to acknowledge—that are unknown to me.

"We did," she says. "I won."

"That doesn't count." I think of the easy way she threw me to the ground on my arrival. "It was a surprise attack. I wasn't ready."

Harper's body sways in a lovely dance as her horse navigates a small stream. I try not to topple to the ground like a bag of bricks.

"Never expect me to fight fair, Freddy," she calls out. "Not with you anyway."

That sounds like a threat, but weirdly, it makes me feel special. As if I get different rules than everyone else in Harper's life.

But she's also right to deny me a bout. I should've anticipated her attack—or at least recovered from it faster. Roman would have been disappointed if he had seen how easily I gave in. Or maybe he would have laughed. Probably a combination of the two.

Harper is not an enemy, I silently point out. *She's not the type of person Roman and his team are training me to anticipate.*

Also, I'm only a few weeks into working with my friend. At first, I thought Roman's demand for me to train for a year was excessive. But after Harper thoroughly knocked me on my ass, I can admit, I've got a ways to go. I'll try not to complain about it in the future.

If I told Harper about my job prospect, I wonder if she'd help me. If the badass stuntwoman would give me some pointers. Some hands-on training.

Fuck. Let's just be honest.
I want her hands on me.

I guess I haven't changed much since I was seventeen. Harper still has me ready to fall to my knees and beg for a taste of her sassy mouth. And just like when I was a teenager, I don't deserve a second of her consideration. She's so far above me that I can't even joke about it. But that's all I do.

The jester trying to catch the attention of the warrior queen.

Was there something in her eyes last night? When I was in her space, trying to flirt, did I catch a flash of heat? Or was it the normal exasperation?

And why the hell didn't I lock the door all those years ago when I was slathering that ointment on my ass?

I've made many mistakes in my life, and a lot of them seem to have happened around Harper.

"You're falling behind!" The shout comes from farther away than I expected, and I glance up from the pommel on my saddle to see a large gap between Sugar Cube and the rest of our riding party.

Harper has stopped her mount and turned in her saddle, waiting for me as stray crimson hairs, loose from her ponytail, flutter in the breeze against her smooth cheeks. When we meet eyes, she rolls hers, smiling all the while.

That smile. It does things to me. Sets off explosions in my chest. Batters me with wanting, the pain piled on over the years slamming into me all at once right now as I'm faced with her. The woman I never expected to see again.

"You're forgiven."

She shouldn't forgive me. I don't deserve it. There's no taking back the things I've done.

But there's also no turning away from Harper when she's here, looking at me with …

Not love. I lost that.

But affection maybe.

Attraction?

You don't deserve that either.

And still, I click my tongue at Sugar Cube and try to urge her faster, worried what might happen if I lose sight of Harper.

This is the second chance I don't deserve. I won't let it slip away.

CHAPTER 8

FRED

The day after our horseback ride, I find my mom in the kitchen, hugging a jar of pickles, silently crying to herself.

Panic mode activated.

"What's wrong? Are you hurt?" I already have my phone out, searching for the closest hospital.

"Oh, no. No, I'm fine." Mom grabs a paper towel from the roll on the counter and attempts to blot away her tears. "Not injured. I just grabbed this, and it brought back memories." She holds up the jar, as if that should explain everything.

"You remember a time when pickles … hurt you?"

Mom lets out a wet chuckle. "No. I love pickles. Did I ever tell you how your father and I met?"

"Wasn't he working at a sandwich shop near your college? And he wrote his number in your takeout container, right?"

Speaking of sandwiches, lunch sounds good, and Mom doesn't look like she's up for the task of making her own. I search through the cabinets and find two plates.

She leans against the counter, her smile trembling, arms still hugging the condiment. "That's the short version. The truth is, I hated your father when I first met him."

"Seriously?" I pause in the middle of pulling deli meat out of the fridge.

Mom nods with a watery giggle. "I did. He would always tease me when I came in. Because the first time I went, I asked for two extra pickles with my sandwich."

As she talks, I get back to sandwich making, even as I listen closely to the story.

"He called me Pickle Girl. Every time I went into the shop, there he was, grinning behind the counter, saying, 'Hey, Pickle Girl!' And, 'How's my Pickle Girl doing?' And, 'Got some fresh pickles, just for you!' Months of it. I wanted to shove a pickle up his ass."

A memory comes back to me—of my father kissing my mom's cheek and affectionately calling her Pickle. I always thought it was a funny endearment, but I never knew there was history behind it.

"How'd he win you over?" *And where can I get some of that magic, whatever it is?*

Her expression is wistful. "I marched into the shop one day and told him I didn't appreciate being mocked, and if he called me Pickle Girl one more time, I'd find another sandwich shop to go to." Mom wraps her arms tighter around herself, hugging the jar closer. "You know how your father always had those ruddy cheeks of his. Well, I watched all the blood drain out of his face. Pale as a ghost. The man looked horrified! And I'm thinking, *I'm just one customer. What's the big deal?*"

The big deal was that he was in love with you. Helps that I know the ending to their story.

Helps and hurts.

Trying to ignore the painful reminder that my mom's love story ended in tragedy, I carefully spread mustard on a slice of bread for each of us.

"The next day, I went in, ready to storm off if he pulled out the silly nickname again. But your father gave me a sweet smile and said, 'Hello, Lori. I hope you're having a good day.' And then he rang me up for my normal sandwich. I left, and when I was walking back to my office"—she sighs—"I realized I wasn't mad so much about being called Pickle Girl. Really, I just wanted the handsome sandwich maker to see *me*. To say my real name. To stop teasing me for just long enough to get to know me."

A man who can't stop teasing a woman long enough to tell her how he really feels. Why does that sound so familiar?

Oh. Yeah. Like father, like son.

"That's when I opened the lid of the takeout container and saw his phone number." Mom sidles up to me and sets the jar down next to our plates. "Much later, I found out the extra pickles I kept asking for cost another ten cents. Your dad never charged me for them. He'd been covering the cost from his own pocket. Treating me to my pickles."

Smooth move, Dad.

The story doesn't surprise me. My dad loved to do that for us. Find out something small we enjoyed and surprise us with the treat at random times. For Phoebe, he'd always have peanut butter cups, and for me, he'd randomly toss me a bag of beef jerky.

Then, Harper would immediately try to steal it because she claimed the dried meat gave me bad breath. We'd wrestle over the bag until one of us came out the victor.

And now, I'm wondering if most of my craving for jerky was only partly about the taste, but mostly about having Harper pin me to the ground.

When I think about it, Dad usually gave me the snack when Harper was nearby.

Did Dad know about my crush?

More than anything, I wish he were here now. I want to talk to him about Harper. Ask his advice. Bemoan my abysmal flirting abilities and listen to his booming laugh when I list all the ways I screwed up.

I want my dad.

"I miss him too." I mutter the confession as I stare down at the lunches I made for Mom and myself.

Dad was always the one who assembled the sandwiches when I was growing up. He proudly claimed he had professional experience. That no one could put meat on bread the way Robert Sullivan could.

"We were lucky to have him as long as we did. At least, that's what

I tell myself when missing him gets unbearable." Mom's lower lip quivers, and my gut wrenches at the idea of her trying to survive the pain all on her own.

She's not alone now though, and I gather her up in a tight hug, like she used to do with me when I scraped my knees or woke up from a nightmare. Mom's shoulders shake, and her cries are muffled by my chest. I swallow a few times to keep my own tears at bay.

That's when Phoebe and Harper come in from the deck, catching us in the middle of a grief storm. My sister's eyes go wide at the sight of our normally subdued mother crying. Before she can panic, like I did, I stretch out one of my arms in invitation.

"We're remembering Dad. Gotta hug it out."

Understanding calms the worry on Phoebe's brow, and she strides across the room to plaster herself against my side, helping to encircle our mom in love.

Clasping my sister close, I seek out Harper's gaze.

She stands still in the doorway, watching our family hug with a lost expression.

"Hey," I say softly, and her green eyes flit up to meet mine. "Got a spot for you right here." I extend the arm not holding Phoebe and wait.

The next move is hers.

CHAPTER 9

HARPER

Joking with Fred is one thing.

This is more. So much more.

Accepting comfort in a vulnerable moment will give him a certain kind of power over me.

But that spot at his side looks appealing. Especially when I'm remembering things. An endless reel of moments flashing through my mind from my childhood. Scenes with my dad and my mom and the Sullivan family.

So much of my life was made up of those six people, two of them now gone forever.

Suddenly, it's impossible not to move forward. I need to grab hold of the people who are still here.

I don't register crossing the room. One moment, I was separate, and the next, I'm nestled into Fred's side, my arms around his waist and Mrs. Sullivan's back, hands clasping Phoebe's elbows. We've formed ourselves into a bundle of misery and supportive love.

Before I consider if the move is smart, I bury my face in Fred's shoulder, breathing him in.

Hell, I missed them. Missed *him*.

I'm not sure how long we stand there, wrapped up together, but at some point, Lori lifts her head, face blotchy from crying. Our arms drop, and we detach, giving her room to breathe.

Fred's hand lingers on my lower back half a second longer, and then he steps away.

And I miss the warm press of his fingers.

"Who wants a sandwich?" His question comes out in a rasp, and he grabs more plates before getting an answer.

"I could eat," Phoebe announces, sliding onto a kitchen stool.

"I'll be back. Going to splash some water on my face." Mrs. Sullivan wanders out of the kitchen toward her bedroom.

Fred opens a jar of pickles and sets three on a plate with an already-made sandwich, then pushes it to the side, presumably for his mother. As he continues with food prep, I debate on making an escape.

That was … a lot.

And not just the emotional weight of the memories.

That hug might have acted as emotional support for the Sullivans, but I came away with a different result.

My body is thrumming everywhere I was pressed against Fred.

What. The. Fuck?

Something must be wrong with me—to take a touching moment and turn it into … whatever this is.

What is this?

My eyes follow Fred as he moves through the kitchen. When we were younger, I only ever thought of Fred as a friend. When we were sixteen, we shared a silly kiss that set off some sparks, which I quickly extinguished because it was Fred.

Then, I left for Ireland, and that distance had me seeing him differently. Wondering if I should've explored more.

But then he cut off contact, so once again, I demolished those feelings.

At least, I thought I had.

He's handsome. That's it. My libido is responding to his face and his body.

I haven't slept with anyone since my last breakup. This is just horny Harper at the wheel, looking for the closest viable person.

Not Fred. Do not go down that road.

"You still like BLTs?"

Fred's question has me refocusing on the present moment, and I realize he already has a package of bacon open and a pan on the stovetop.

"Don't worry about it." I move to his side. "Everyone else is having lunch meat."

"It's not a problem." He offers me a sweet smile that has me noticing the scruff of his five o'clock shadow and how the dark hair emphasizes his chin dimple. "Promise I won't burn the bacon."

I want to kiss him.

I barely stifle a groan. Then, he lays strips of bacon in the pan, the savory scent of cooking meat filling the kitchen, and Fred becomes almost impossible to resist as he carefully makes my lunch.

The bastard bites his lower lip as he concentrates hard on his cooking.

The sight gets me wet, and I back up out of sheer self-preservation.

I do not want to kiss Fred Sullivan. Or lick him. Or unbutton that gaudy aloha shirt and bite his bare chest.

But when I settle on a stool beside Phoebe and continue watching him prepare lunch for all of us, I worry that I'm lying to myself.

Why else would I watch his fingers flex as he slices a tomato? Or map the tensing of his shoulders while he washes lettuce? Or imagine what he'd look like in nothing but an apron when he slides the expertly crafted BLT across the counter to me?

"Thank you," I murmur, unable to form a joke or a scathing comment in the face of his simple act of generosity.

"Anything for you, Harper."

When I glance up to meet his stare, I see the heat in my belly reflected in his hazel eyes.

Damn it. I want to fuck Fred Sullivan.

CHAPTER 10

FRED

SIXTEEN YEARS OLD

The thumping of music vibrates the stairs as I head up them, searching for my best friend in the middle of an increasingly rowdy house party.

In *her* house.

I find Harper at the end of the upstairs hallway, leaning against a wall, palm pressed over her eyes. Worry turns the cheap beer in my stomach into acid.

"Hey. You okay?"

She starts, unaware of my approach. Normally, she's not so easy to sneak up on.

Harper rips her hand from her eyes and lunges forward to cover my mouth with it. The scent of her favorite peppermint hand lotion fills my nose as I suck in a surprised breath.

We've known each other long enough to be able to communicate without words. Apparently, I need to shut up.

With a single eyebrow raise, I ask, *What's got you acting so weird?*

Harper slowly uncovers my mouth before pointing at the bathroom, then uses her hands to give the clear sign of penetration.

My other eyebrow shoots up to meet the first, and heat pools in my gut. And my armpits. I start sweating way more than necessary.

"You want to have sex in the bathroom?" I ask, voicing my secret fantasy, but also a major fear because I'm pretty sure I'd be terrible at sex and Harper would never want to see me again afterward.

She gasps and slaps her hand back over my mouth.

Seems I overestimated our nonverbal communication skills.

In a harsh whisper, she clears up the misunderstanding. "God, no! I'm trying to tell you, there're some people—"

Her explanation is cut off by a distinctly feminine moan. I glance from the door to Harper, finally understanding.

Someone *else* is having sex in the bathroom.

Lucky them.

My friend removes her hand and finishes with a whisper. "What she said."

Then, she snorts. Next a chuckle. Soon, Harper is struggling to choke back laughter, probably worried about giving us away.

I pretend to be the mature one in our duo, giving a disappointed shake of my head before taking another swig of my beer.

"Thought you had the mayhem under control." I keep my voice down.

My words are enough to halt her complete descent into hilarity, but she still wears a broad grin that makes my heart all achy and heavy.

"Bathroom is better than bedroom." She shrugs. "Just remind me to bleach the sink counter. Why are you up here anyway?"

I roll my eyes. "Some wild pack of girls is looking for an innocent victim, and they had their targets locked on me before I made my narrow escape." I glare at Harper. "With no help from the hostess, I might add. If it hadn't been for my quick thinking, there'd be an unfortunate amount of red lipstick smeared over half my face by this point."

The group tried to drag me into a game of Seven Minutes in Heaven, and Christy Jackson had her eyes on me. I knew she was going to find a way to maneuver the both of us into a closet together. But that's not my idea of heaven.

Heaven is standing in front of me, wearing a smirk and yellow Converse.

"Seriously?" Harper asks, oblivious to my hopeless crush. "You turned down the opportunity to make out with a bunch of girls? Why?"

I shift on my feet, not meeting her eyes. But that only makes my best friend more curious.

"Tell me." She pokes my chest and recaptures my gaze. "I want to know." She stares up at me, green eyes clear and inviting.

Shit. Harper was always the one I spilled my secrets to. Recently, I've started keeping things from her. Secrets I'm too scared for her to find out about.

But now, she knows there's something going on, and she'll pester me all night until she gets an answer. So, I just give her a taste. A small chunk of my issue.

"I've never kissed anyone before, okay?"

I physically brace myself, ready for her mocking. That's how our relationship is most times—us ribbing each other.

But then there are moments, like now, when Harper shows me she really does care about my insecurities.

"Oh, Fred." She slips her hand into my free one. "I'm sure there are loads of guys at school who haven't kissed anyone yet." Her fingers give mine a reassuring squeeze. "So, you didn't want to make out with those girls because … you didn't think you'd do it right?" Her voice gets high at the end, like she's not sure of her interpretation. "Because if that's the case, you've got nothing to worry about. Trust me. I'm no expert, but neither are the guys downstairs. I don't think anyone would be judging you."

"What's that supposed to mean?"

She smirks. "It means, they're crappy kissers. Bryan licked my entire cheek one time, and Sanjay kept his lips so puckered that it was like trying to make out with a soda straw." Harper shrugs. "We're all just a bunch of teenagers, stumbling our way through intimacy."

The wisdom of her words is lost on me as I imagine her swapping spit with our classmates. I want to charge downstairs and introduce their offending mouths to my fist.

Those fucking pricks were lucky enough to get the chance to kiss her, and they didn't even do it right? If I get to kiss Harper …

No. She's my friend. I shouldn't be thinking about what it would feel like to have her soft, warm lips press against mine.

"Well, thanks for the reassurance. But performance anxiety isn't the issue."

When Harper cocks her head to the side, a wave of shiny crimson hair spills over her shoulder. I know if I leaned in close to bury my nose in the strands, I'd get a strong whiff of peppermint. All of her products—shampoo, conditioner, lotion—carry that delicious, fresh scent. Sometimes, I ask to borrow some lotion, just so my hands smell like her.

"Then, what's the holdup, Freddy?"

I give her the glare she expects, pretending I don't like her little nickname for me when, really, my heart beats harder every time she says it. If this were anyone else, I wouldn't answer the question, but Harper is special. She means more to me, and so I give her more of myself.

"Don't laugh."

She drags her finger in an X across her heart in a silent promise.

With a sigh, I relent. "I don't want it to be some empty throwaway kiss. Just a dare some girl's friend gave her. When it happens to me, I'll be thinking about it for the rest of the night. Probably remember it for the rest of my life." I thank the universe for the dim lighting because I know my face is hot and red from embarrassment. "So, yeah, it doesn't have to be some huge deal or anything. But I don't want to regret it."

We're both quiet for a moment. I keep my eyes locked on my beer as I wait for her reaction.

"Wow."

I meet Harper's stare to find her smiling at me, but not like she's laughing.

"I never realized you were so romantic."

"I'm not romantic," I grumble, my face flushing darker. "I just care about things."

"Okay. Okay." She purses her lips and studies me. "You do want to kiss someone though, right?"

Hell yes.

"Just … this seems like it's weighing on you," Harper continues. "Wouldn't it be better to figure out how to have your meaningful kiss, and then you can relax about the whole subject? Maybe even move on from the kissing stage."

Swiftly, she pokes me in the exact ticklish spot on my stomach. I keep ahold of her hand as I evade her other.

"Not sure a house party is the best place to look for a meaningful connection," I point out.

A male groan filters through the door behind Harper, and I indicate with my head toward it to prove my point. She smirks, but then her face fades back into contemplation. Not good. Harper's plans vary so widely in hijinks and success rate that I have no way of predicting what might come out of her mouth next.

"Would you want to kiss me?"

Oh fuck.

Her words are a punch to the gut.

No, more like a stroke over my groin. The second my mind latches on to the image, I get half-hard, now even more grateful for the darkness.

"Wh-what?" I stutter over the question, expecting her to give me a shove, laughing that I actually believed her.

But Harper keeps looking up at me with her open, inquisitive gaze.

"I'm sober. I care about you. Oh!" Her gaze sparks with actual interest, and I can't keep the air in my lungs. "After my unfortunate tongue bath with Bryan, I watched a few videos online, talking about how to kiss properly. I think we could do this thing right. Do you want to try?"

I should say no. Or I should tell her how I really feel. How she's the only one I want to kiss. How I want more than just friendship.

But could that be what Harper is doing? Is that why she wants to be my first kiss? Because she wants me just as much as I want her?

This night could change everything. Monday morning, I could walk into school with my arm around her waist, not just as her best friend, but also as her guy. How many hours have I spent daydreaming about Harper and me together?

Too many to count.

This is my chance.

"Okay, ye—"

The bathroom door swings wide, and a senior—I think her name is Margaret—stumbles out with a guy I don't know. Both are laughing, obviously wasted, and they don't notice us until they almost plow us over.

"Oh!" Margaret gasps, then giggles into her palm. "Um, bathroom is free!"

The couple maneuvers past us, and the guy throws me a wink.

Once they're down the stairs, Harper snorts. "No way am I going in that bathroom without a pair of rubber gloves."

That's it, I think. *Moment is over.*

We'll rejoin the party, and I'll have to wait until I'm home in my own bed to fantasize what it would have been like to actually get to make out with Harper.

My moping is interrupted by the click of a key in a lock.

"Come on. Time to pop your kissing cherry."

While I was lost in my thoughts, she unlocked the door to her bedroom, and now, she's pulling me inside. Letting go of my hand, she shuts and locks the door behind her.

I've been in Harper's room plenty of times, but tonight is different.

Unable to move in case I break the spell, I stand by the door and stare at the familiar yet strangely new space. The delicate white furniture has never matched her powerful personality, but apparently, the bedroom set was one of the first things her mom purchased upon moving to the States from Ireland, so Harper has never had the heart to ask for another.

My friend stands a foot in front of me, running her gaze from my feet to my head.

"You had another growth spurt, didn't you? You've got at least four inches on me now." Her voice is accusatory, and some of the tension holding me tight drains away. Leave it to Harper to get mad at me about something I have no control over.

"Sorry. I'll stop drinking so much milk."

That earns me a snort as she walks over to her dresser. "We

shouldn't have to strain our necks. I think if I sit up here, we'll be on level with each other." Haphazardly, she pushes aside the makeup that clutters the surface, leaving an empty space. She promptly hops up to sit on the dresser. "Okay, I'm ready."

Oh fuck.

I don't know if I want to run to her or away from her when she beckons me closer. I give in to the former, clutching my empty beer can to my chest like a lifeline. When I stop just a couple of inches from her knees, Harper spreads her legs open, giving me space to stand between them. I stifle a groan at the invitation.

"I'll take that." Harper lifts the drink from my hand and sets it on the surface next to her. When I hesitate to move closer, she cocks her head to the side. "Do you want to do this? We don't have to if you don't want to."

The threat of losing my chance propels my feet forward until I'm nestled between her thighs.

"Yes. I want this."

"Okay, cool." Harper settles her hands on my shoulders, grinning as she meets my eyes, which are now perfectly level with hers. "So, the videos I watched said it's best if we go slow. There's no rush. You tilt your head a bit this way." Her palms cup my cheeks and gently move my head into position. "And I tilt the other way." Harper tips the opposite direction and leans toward me. "Don't worry about tongues. We'll just focus on lips first. We can do tongues later."

Later. Holy hell, Harper is planning for a later. My heart, which is pounding like a snare drum, beats with happiness.

I'm going to kiss Harper Walsh.

I cross the distance left between us and try not to mash my face into hers. *Go slow, she said.*

Her lips are soft and plush beneath mine. She waits until my mouth is fully in contact with hers before she starts moving.

We set a leisurely pace, gentle presses, caressing each other with only our lips. I do my best to follow her rhythm, new to all of this. I'm encouraged when she doesn't pull away from me. Time passes slow or fast—I can't tell because I'm finally tasting Harper.

She's sweet, probably from a fruity drink she was sipping on earlier. I want more.

I'm about to pull away, just slightly, so I can ask her about tongues when her hands shove my chest. I stumble backward, ripped away from pure bliss. Only adding to the shock is the horrified expression on her face. My stomach clenches.

Was I that bad?

"Shit! Shit, shit, shit!" Harper launches off the dresser, racing toward the door, dragging my heart along with her.

"Wait! I'm sorry! Whatever I did—"

"You'd better run! Your parents will kill you if you get caught!"

What? My kiss-drugged mind tries to make sense of her words. Then, I realize the room isn't dimly lit by Harper's old night light anymore.

Instead, there's a riot of flashing red and blue spilling through the lacy white curtains.

"Time to deal with mayhem I didn't plan on."

With that frustrated statement, she wrenches the door open and sprints down the hall, leaving me with a craving for her that has only increased after getting a taste.

CHAPTER 11

HARPER

PRESENT DAY

"Cheers to an audience who loves badass women fighting vampires." Phoebe extends her flute of champagne to me across the hot tub, and I clink the lip of my glass against hers.

The sky is dark above us, filled with stars unobscured by the bluish illumination from inside the tub.

After I got the call from my agent an hour ago, letting me know that the show Shelly acts in and I stunt for has been renewed for two more seasons, Phoebe insisted we soak and drink to celebrate. The relief of steady work is more relaxing than this hot water against my muscles.

"I still don't totally believe it." My body eases lower, every joint loosening with relief. "There's this disconnect between making the show and when it eventually goes on-screen. You think it's amazing, but will anyone else?"

"Well, they did." Phoebe smacks her lips after a deep sip. "I did too.

I was quoting it to all my coworkers until they either watched it or refused to talk to me anymore."

I bark out a laugh. "Thanks for the persistent marketing. If you ever get tired of that tech stuff, I'll connect you with the show's PR team."

Phoebe fluffs her hair and tops off her glass, then starts trying to dig season two spoilers out of me even though I keep insisting I haven't seen a script yet.

Yet another reason I wanted the show to continue. The writers left us on a cliff-hanger, and I'm as eager as the fans to know what happens next.

"What's all this cackling and drinking about, and why am I not in the middle of it?" a deep voice says just over my shoulder, and I try not to jump at the realization that Fred snuck up on us. Or at least, snuck up on me.

Phoebe is facing the house and gave me no indication of her brother's approach.

Sneaky witch.

"Harper's show got renewed. We're celebrating by getting drunk!" Phoebe extends a mostly empty champagne bottle.

"You know I've only had half a glass, right?" I hold up my barely touched flute.

My friend frowns in an overexaggerated pout. "Then, where'd all the bubbly go?"

I snort. "You are going to have a bitch of a headache tomorrow."

"Any left for me?" Fred comes around into my line of sight.

He's got yet another aloha shirt on, this one covered in piña colada glasses, plus a bathing suit with an equally gaudy palm tree pattern. He somehow looks both ridiculous and hot.

Maybe I did have more than half a glass …

"Is Mom coming out too?" Phoebe asks.

"She headed to bed. She said—and I quote—'I have no interest in becoming human soup.' " He shrugs with an indulgent smile.

"Her loss. Soup is great." Phoebe sinks lower in the tub until her chin brushes the water.

During the day, this heat would've been uncomfortable and stifling.

But these mountain nights get cool, and I love the contrast of warm water and fresh, frigid air.

Living in LA seems like it should be paradise with endless sunny days. But it also means breathing in a whole lot of car fumes and smog. I didn't recognize it until I visited a place like this, where there are more trees than cars. I could get drunk off the clean air alone.

"You coming in?" I watch Fred where he stands, lingering just outside of the tub. Since he's wearing his suit, I assume soaking was his plan.

"Yes. Definitely." He blinks, glances down at himself, frowns, then sets the towel he's carrying on the bench that sits a few feet from the hot tub.

The Jacuzzi sits a short way from the house, a stone path making the trek to it easy, yet far away enough to keep it out of the light spilling from the large windows. I rest my head back on the lip of the tub, gaze at the stars, and try to search out the few constellations I know. The Big Dipper peeks out from the tops of the trees, and I follow its scooping direction to the North Star.

It seems like years since I've been able to fully relax like this. No need to stress about hustling for another stunt gig. No early shoot to get up for tomorrow, and my body isn't beat up from one today. I'm here with friends, and after all these years, there's a kind of truce between Fred and me.

A splash to my left has me turning my head in time to see Fred sink into the water. He lets out a groan that does unwelcome things to my body, like tightening my nipples and curling my toes.

"You didn't do too bad on that horse today." Phoebe tilts her glass toward her brother. "I half-expected you to fall off."

"So glad I exceeded your expectations. Let's see if I can handle myself as well if we run into a bear."

Phoebe snorts. "There're no bears in Wyoming."

Fred and I exchange a dubious glance before both turning to look back at Phoebe.

"Are you serious?" he asks.

"What?" She glances between us. "There aren't."

"There most definitely are," I say. "You do know we're, like, *right* next to Yellowstone, right? Pretty sure there're black bears *and* grizzly bears."

"How did you not know there are bears here?" Fred stares at his sister.

"I thought they were all in, like … Montana or something." Phoebe throws furtive glances toward the dark woods.

"Well, they're here too," Fred says carefully, as if truly scared for his sister's mental state. It would be kind of sweet if her gap in knowledge wasn't so hilarious.

"God, Phoebe." I snort. "You're the smartest person I know. How could you not know there are bears here?"

"Because bears aren't *everywhere*, Harper," Phoebe snaps. "Some places exist without bears."

An owl hoots, and she yelps, then scrambles from the hot tub.

"Nope. No way. Mom was right. I'm not making myself into human soup for some hungry grizzly. I'm out." Phoebe snatches up her towel and sprints back to the house, holding the champagne bottle like a weapon as she goes.

When the glass door slams behind her, Fred and I both start chuckling, then full-on belly laughing.

"No bears," he mutters while wiping a stray tear from his eye.

As our laughter fades, the situation clarifies for me.

Fred and I are alone in a hot tub, surrounded by darkness, wearing nothing but swimsuits. And I've been feeling things about him. Or my body has. Odd, pleasurable tingles.

"Congratulations on your show," he murmurs. "You all deserve it. *House of the Huntress* is amazing."

"You watch it?"

He nods. "Mainly to see if I can pick you out, wearing leather pants."

I splash his grinning face with water as I sort through how to feel about the possibility of Fred watching the show I'm in, even before this reconciliation trip. He could be joking. That's the problem with him—sometimes, I think he's being serious, but really, it's just the setup for a laugh.

I decide not to investigate further. I don't want to lose my relaxation by stressing over a past relationship and conversation subtext.

"Are you dating anyone?" Fred's question lands heavy in the space between us.

Dating talk. What are you thinking about, Freddy?

"Not right now," I admit. "I broke up with my girlfriend a few months ago."

She was talking about moving in together, and when the suggestion annoyed rather than excited me, I realized I'd checked out of the relationship at some point.

"Your girlfriend?" Fred stares at me with wide eyes. "You're …"

I let the silence grow between us, partly because telling him the truth feels like it leaves open a possible door I'm not sure I want to step through with him. But I also enjoy the flabbergasted expression on his handsome face.

"Bi," I finally say, letting him off the hook.

"Oh. Okay." He tilts his head back, staring at the stars, like I was before, appearing thoughtful. Then, he suddenly slaps the water and points a finger at me, eyes narrow, lips smirking. "You made out with Christy at the homecoming game junior year, didn't you?"

I pretend innocence. "Who, me?"

"You still expect me to believe you two were all breathless and flushed because you were *showing her some cheer moves* under the bleachers?" Fred shakes his head in mock disappointment. "You used my poor, unimaginative straight-man brain against me." He throws me a rueful smile. "Now, I need to add *another* person to the list of all the people I'm jealous of. Damn you, Christy Jackson."

That shrivels up the response on my tongue.

Is he serious? Once again, I can't tell. *Is Fred flirting for real or playing a game?*

Suddenly, I'm not in the mood for hints and guesses and will-he, won't-he. It feels too much like high school. We kissed once back then, the experience almost immediately interrupted by the cops shutting down my house party. I was grounded for two months, and when I saw Fred at school, he acted the same he always had with me.

I'd felt the start of sparks when his unexperienced lips brushed mine, but I snuffed them out, assuming my friend wasn't interested in me that way.

Now, I'm almost positive he is.

And if I listen to my body rather than try to ignore it, I'll have to admit that I'm into him too.

Only physically, of course.

What if we've both matured enough to go a little further? Have some fun?

I've forgiven Fred. He's an attractive guy. And the only thing that would relax me more right now is an orgasm.

This could be the worst idea I've ever had.

There's the future to consider. The days after this trip ends. We're not in Vegas—what happens here could follow me around long after I fly away from Wyoming.

I'm flying to LA, and he lives on the East Coast. Easy enough to avoid him if things get awkward. Another ten years could pass by without me ever seeing his face again.

A strange ache pulses through my chest at the thought, but I don't linger on it. Time to live in the moment.

"Are you seeing anyone?" I ask before making a move.

Fred slowly shakes his head, holding my gaze as he does.

Good.

I press myself off the underwater bench and float the few feet separating us. Fred's brows tick up as I approach. Instead of slipping in beside him, I mount his lap, caging him in with my arms, taking control before I lose mine.

"Why would you be jealous of me kissing other people?"

His thighs are hard under mine and clench as I speak.

Fred clears his throat. "Because I want to be the one kissing you."

He keeps his hands at his sides, not reaching for me. Just watching.

"Hmm." I pretend to be thoughtful. "What if I don't want to kiss you?"

He frowns, his stare dropping to my mouth, then sliding off to the side. "I wouldn't blame you."

The confession is quiet, but I'm close enough to hear.

"Right?" I keep my voice low and sultry. "Kissing is a kind of art form. Last time we tried, you were a little sloppy, sorry to say."

He whips his head around to meet my eyes, his narrowing. But I also see the way his lips twist and tighten as he fights a smile.

We were so young then, at that party. Felt old enough at the time, but I had no idea. And with my friend standing there, awkwardly confessing about his lack of experience, I would never have mocked him.

But now? I don't mind being a touch ruthless.

"You think I still kiss like a sixteen-year-old virgin?" he asks, tone offhand, as if he doesn't care about my answer.

I shrug and let my arms rest on the top of his broad shoulders, casually draping myself over him. "Yes."

This back-and-forth banter between us takes no effort. Flirting with Fred is as easy as breathing, every part of me slipping into this scenario like a well-worn sweatshirt.

A sexy sweatshirt.

"Want me to prove you wrong?" There's a deep, husky note in his voice now, which has me shivering despite the heated water cradling us.

"If you want to try kissing me again …" I hedge, sliding my hips forward an inch on his lap. "I'll need proof you've learned something. Worked on your craft, so to speak."

Fred's gaze holds mine, searching. Then, in a swift movement, he wraps his arm around my waist and stands, exposing both of our torsos to the mountain air. I yelp, not expecting the move or the next step, which involves Fred settling me on the wide lip of the hot tub before letting go and sinking into the water in front of me. His palms land heavy on my knees, guiding them open.

"I'm happy to demonstrate my improvement," he offers from between my splayed legs.

"Oh." *Oh fuck.* "I—I meant, like, kiss my neck or something."

Fred freezes, his mouth a breath away from my inner thigh. His eyes flick to mine. "I could do that."

The warmth of his exhale is the worst and best kind of tease.

"No. Um, this shows … initiative."

Holy shit. Fred is ready to dive face-first into my pussy like a scuba champ.

"Good job. Please continue with your demonstration."

He shoots me a goofy grin and still wears the broad curve when he presses his mouth against my skin, imprinting his joy on me.

I brace my arms on the ledge behind me, not minding the sudden exposure to the elements when Fred is promising to heat me up from the inside out.

"Now"—Fred speaks between kisses—"I might not"—kiss—"possess the same"—kiss—"skills as"—kiss—"Christy Jackson …" He pauses at the edge of my swimsuit bottoms to gaze up at me. "But I swear there's no one on this planet who wants to taste you more than I do. So …" He trails off, as if searching for even more profound words after that statement. Fred settles on a rueful shrug, a lopsided smile, and, "Here we go."

"Here we go?" I laugh and then gasp when he tugs the crotch of my suit to the side and gets to work.

He was right. Christy knew what she was doing under those bleachers.

But I'd always preferred the awkward lip lock with Fred.

And I find it's the same with this moment. I've been with plenty of people across genders, many with amazing cunnilingus skills. Being with Fred is somehow different. He's not an expert, but damn is he enthusiastic. My former best friend eats me out like he's been hibernating all winter and I'm the first berry bush he found outside his cave.

Okay, yeah, calling my pussy a berry bush is weird, but whatever. He's ravenous for me, and I feel like a fucking goddess as I listen to the slick, kind of sloppy noises he makes, alternating between delving his tongue inside me, licking along my intimate lips, and sucking on my clit.

"So fucking good," he moans at one point, his lips never losing contact, and the praising words get me right there.

I just need that final push—

Two fingers slip deep as Fred tongues the bundle of nerves.

Past lovers have told me that, sometimes, when I orgasm, I'm silent but violent. The description holds true now as I clench my teeth together and shudder, curling around Fred's head, reaching for his bare back and digging my nails into his skin just for something to hold on to. He groans deep, the vibrations against my pussy dragging out the pleasure until I'm panting and ready to topple either into the water or onto the bare ground.

Fred keeps me steady though with his arms locked around my thighs.

Don't let me go.

CHAPTER 12

FRED

That just happened. That was real. Her taste is on my tongue.

Harper's quivering aftershocks vibrate in her thighs. I want to hold her tighter, press myself deeper, but I restrain the urge, worried about bruising her soft skin.

Soft, at least, where there aren't any scars.

In the dim blue glow of the hot tub, I can pick out the puckers in her skin that show where she was hurt once and healed in rough, little patches. Letting my hand slide up, I brush a scar near her hip.

"Crawling under barbed wire," she says, and I realize Harper is watching me trace the evidence of her injury.

"Why did you go and do that?" After the question, I kiss the silky skin of her inner thigh, unable to help myself.

Harper, the girl—woman—I've secretly longed for since I was a teenager, is splayed before me, her chest flushed from the way I licked her. Under the water, a raging hard-on tents my swimsuit, but I do my best to ignore the demand. She's already given me more than I ever hoped for. Now, the goal is to figure out how to have her wanting my face between her legs for the foreseeable future.

Probably pointing out her scars is not the way to go about it. It's no wonder I'm only ever good for a handful of hookups. Partners find me fun, and then they move on to someone they can take seriously.

I don't blame them. I can't even take myself seriously most of the time.

"Not movie-related, if you can believe it." She gives a dry laugh. "Most of mine are, but that was from sneaking onto an abandoned property with some kids I hung out with in Ireland. Not the best crowd. Got my first official tetanus shot."

"Look at you. Living that criminal life." I kiss her other thigh and wonder about the years we spent apart from each other. How the evidence is written on her body.

Mine too.

And I should've known that Harper would notice and not keep quiet about it.

"You have burn marks on your back."

"I do."

Her belly is soft where I nestle my face, and I tongue her belly button.

There's a tug at the back of my head, on the verge of uncomfortable. Harper has her fingers in my hair, fisting the strands and tugging my head back so I'm forced to look at her.

"Tell me about the burns," she demands.

My lids lower halfway as I enjoy the firm grip she keeps on me. Being held by Harper, even with a hint of violence in the hold, is my happy place.

"I was living in an old house with bad wiring. Something sparked one night a few months back, and the place went up."

Her face narrows into a fierce frown, as if she's pissed off at the flames that hurt me.

I drag my hands up her legs and settle them at her waist, kneading my fingers into her sides. "But I got out okay."

"You have scars. I know a third-degree burn when I see one." Her voice has a hard edge I want to tease away. Get her gasping again.

I shrug and try to move my head forward, maybe kiss her collarbone or the plush curves of her boobs, where they press at her suit top.

Harper holds me firmly in place.

"Some pieces of ceiling fell. Gave me some love taps." I smirk.

Harper continues to frown.

I don't want to talk about the fire anymore. I want her panting. I need more of her on my tongue.

I need the weight of the past to go away, especially the parts where we weren't together.

"You never said if my kissing improved." My thumbs slip into the waistband of her swimsuit, playing with the stretchy fabric.

Tell me to take them off. Tell me my mouth is the best you've ever had.

Harper's fingers loosen in my hair, releasing my head. I'm about to lean forward for another taste when her palm spreads flat against my chest, pushing me back.

"You were adequate. I'm going to bed." With that abrupt dismissal, Harper removes my hands from her waist, adjusts her suit bottom so it covers everything it's supposed to—damn you very much—and maneuvers out of the Jacuzzi.

I'm left floating, very horny and confused.

"Do you have any tips?" I ask, trying to keep my voice light. Teasing.

Not desperate. Not pathetically wondering if Harper learned some acting skills while working in Hollywood and just gave an Oscar-worthy performance of a fake orgasm.

She pauses, foot on the path back to the house, then slowly turns back to me, her face unreadable in the shadowy night. "Don't wait so long next time."

Don't wait so long?

Is she talking about tonight? This trip? Or is Harper referring to the space of time between our first kiss and this hookup?

The words throw me off so much that I miss her continuing on to the house.

She's almost too far away, so I shout my question. "So, there's going to be a next time?"

Because whatever the first part of her advice meant, the second was clear.

I didn't completely screw things up.

"Fuck you!" she yells back, the words loud in the calm mountain air.

I grin. "Anytime! Anywhere!"

I'm not sure, but I think she scoffs. I sink into the heated water, chuckling to myself. My fingers rub against my lips, as if I can capture the sensation of Harper's intimate taste and hold it there forever. Then, my hand sneaks over my shoulder to the deadened patch of skin on my back. It finally stopped itching last month, and the doctors told me the area healed as well as could be expected.

I've used a mirror to get a look, and I know the sight of the twisted, puckered skin isn't attractive. But I don't regret the actions that resulted in the injuries. That night changed my life in more ways than leaving marks on my body. The fire revealed something about myself.

And maybe, if I don't fuck things up again, I could be someone worthy of Harper Walsh.

CHAPTER 13

HARPER

SEVENTEEN YEARS OLD

I wait until we get home from the funeral to cry. During the service, I held my mom as she tried to stem her own flood of pain with a handful of fragile tissues. But nothing could stop the heart-wrenching sobs, not her gritted teeth or the press of her hands against her mouth.

How could I pile on top of that with my own devastation?

But now, Mom is in her bed with Nan checking in on her, and I can finally sneak away and curse at the universe on my own.

Why him? Why my *dad?*

He was funny, and loving, and good.

Why do good people die? It's not fair!

How do I live the rest of my life without him?

As I pace around my bedroom, I clutch a pillow against my chest and ignore the tears soaking my cheeks. The salty evidence of my pain drips down my chin and my neck, soaking the high collar of my black dress.

The material is stiff yet still clings to me, itchy and stifling. Suddenly, the thing I hate most in the world is this dress. I need it gone.

Chucking my emotional-support pillow to the ground, I proceed to bend and reach my arms behind me until I find the sneaky zipper attempting to hide in my hair. As I wrench the tab down, I hear a tear.

Who cares? I've been to two funerals in two days, and that's enough mourning for an entire lifetime. I never want to put this outfit on again. Destroying it sounds like the perfect plan.

"Fuck you, you ugly, itchy dress," I growl as I stomp on the offending material, then kick it the length of my room and back.

There's a thump, then a grunt behind me, and I turn in time to watch my best friend heave himself through my open bedroom window. It's a move he's done plenty of times, but never in formalwear.

And never while I'm only in a bra and underwear.

Fred straightens, and his eyes go wide when he takes in my lack of clothes.

"Oh shit." He turns his back. "Sorry. Didn't realize you were changing. I can go."

"No. It's fine."

We've known each other since preschool. He's seen me in bathing suits skimpier than this.

"Stay. It was more like rage stripping anyway." I catch my breath, winded by the childish attempt to take my hurt out on a floppy, inanimate object.

Fred is still wearing his suit. The same one he wore yesterday to his own father's funeral. The pant legs are half an inch too short and show off socks with green and blue stripes.

The sight has me wanting to smile, but I don't think my mouth curves that way anymore.

"Your pants don't fit." I point the fact out mainly because I don't want to talk about anything sad. That's what this whole week has been.

Can't I forget, just for a moment, that my life has been destroyed?

"Yeah." He rubs his hands down his thighs, as if the pressure would add more material. "I'd take them off, like you, but I forgot to do laundry. Ran out of underwear this morning."

A weird bark comes out of my throat. The closest sound to a laugh I can currently manage. "You were commando at my dad's funeral?"

Fred glances over his shoulder, a grimace on his normally smiling mouth, his face turning cherry red. "Sorry."

In that instant, in the middle of the swirling pit of despair that is my grief, I experience one soothing breath of reassurance.

My whole world isn't gone.

Fred is still here.

In two strides, I'm across my bedroom, flinging my arms around his waist, hugging him from behind so tight that I might break a few of his ribs.

Fred doesn't complain. He reaches back to give me an awkward reverse hug, which I find more comforting than any expression of sympathy I've received so far.

"It's okay that you don't have any clean underwear," I murmur against the fabric of his suit jacket.

"Thanks." Fred continues to hold me, forearms pressing against my bare back. "What can I do? What do you need?"

I'm glad he didn't say any of the normal consoling phrases.

He's in a better place.

This won't hurt forever.

He's smiling down on you.

You'll be okay.

Fred knows those words are useless. He probably got them all yesterday multiple times over.

Maybe that's the silver lining of us losing our dads in the same car crash. We know exactly what the other is going through.

That's a fucked up thing to think. I'm a mess.

And if I were given the option to bring Mr. Sullivan back from the dead even if my dad couldn't come too, I'd do it for Fred. And for Phoebe and Mrs. Sullivan.

But my torn-apart heart clings to the bit of comfort I can find, knowing Fred is hurting the way I am, that we're going through the same thing together.

"Just keep doing what you're doing. Be my friend. Don't …" My voice catches, and a new flood of tears spills from my eyes. "Don't leave me alone."

I couldn't stand it. Losing someone else in my life … losing Fred.

The world sees him as a goofy screwup—which he can be sometimes—but I know he's got the heart of a golden retriever. He's kind and loving, and despite his world falling apart the way mine is, he's still here to comfort me.

I don't know how I'd survive this aftermath without him.

Fred releases his hold, but only long enough to turn in my arms so he can hug me against his chest.

"I'm not going anywhere, Harper," he mutters the promise into my hair, his voice raw with emotion. "I swear."

I believe him.

CHAPTER 14

HARPER

PRESENT DAY

I can't forget his mouth.

Ever since I left Fred in that hot tub last night, my mind has been playing his top-tier oral skills on repeat like a sports highlight reel.

Adequate was a blatant lie. That was phenomenal.

But then he told me about the fire. Or more accurately, I forced him to tell me about the fire, and still, he only reluctantly gave me details. But there was enough in what he did say for me to tell it was a big deal.

The man had gotten *burned*. And not a small spot either. At least half his right shoulder is scarred, and I wonder if I would've found more if my hands had gone on an exploration.

What if it was worse?

The crushing wave of emotions that came with that possibility had me running from him. The idea of one day getting a phone call from Phoebe out of nowhere, telling me that Fred is gone...

I turn abruptly, and the man on my mind almost plows into me.

"My bad." He grins. "Forgot the meaning of personal space."

I glare at him, furious that he could've died and my last memory of his face would've been at the bottom of an airport escalator when he was seventeen.

Then, I blush because, now, I have the memory of his face cradled between my legs.

Fred's hazel eyes with their green sunbursts drag over me from under the brim of a worn baseball hat. Then, he glances over my shoulder.

"I'm going to go take a piss!" he yells to the other two in our group. "A long one!"

Phoebe chuckles from up ahead.

Well, there go all my sappy, sentimental feelings.

"No need to wait for me," he adds.

This, ladies and gentlemen, is the guy I let eat me out yesterday.

"Glad to hear you're staying hydrated, honey," Mrs. Sullivan calls back from farther down the trail, sounding distracted.

But that's how she's been all day—with her binoculars glued to her face, leading our trek through the Wyoming woods. Lori really wants to see a moose before the trip is over. The woman seems to love anything with hooves.

"Uh, Harper?" Fred stops me when I'm about to follow his mother and sister on the trail. "How are you feeling? Need to take a pee break? A *long* one?"

Flabbergasted, I stare at a blushing Fred, who wears a hopeful smile.

"Excuse me?"

"Just wondering if you might want to hang back with me and *use the bathroom*?" He wiggles his brows suggestively for the last few words, and I finally understand.

"Oh my God," I whisper-yell at him. "Are you trying to convince me to hook up with you in the woods, and you're using the cover of us *peeing* together so your family doesn't realize what we're doing?"

"I knew you got me." He boops my nose before I can swat him

away. "Harper needs to use the facilities too!" the man shouts for all the woods to hear.

"Mom," Phoebe calls out as she trudges away from us, "Harper and Fred are going to take a dump together. They'll catch up."

"Okay," Mrs. Sullivan responds. Then, at a lower volume I'm sure we're not meant to hear, she says, "Those two are much closer than I thought."

The two women disappear around a bend, and I'm left with a grinning Fred.

"They'll never know," he assures me.

"I can't even articulate how bad you are at subterfuge. I should leave you here, all horned up, just on the principle of the thing."

"Please no." His smile turns to a pout. "I've been hiking behind you all morning, and your ass *will not* quit. Have mercy."

I eye him in his hiking pants, paired with yet another colorful button-up—this one with huge purple and yellow flowers. He would be the easiest person to find if he got lost in the woods.

"Define mercy," I say, reluctantly admitting to myself that I want to rip that eyesore of a button-up off him.

Fred's joy explodes across his face, and he grabs my hand, leading me away from the trail, into the woods. Not too far, but deep enough that if other hikers were to pass by, they wouldn't see us. We haven't passed too many people today, opting for one of the less popular trails that still has some beautiful views.

"Mercy," Fred explains, gently guiding me back against a tree, his body pressing flush against mine, "is giving kissing another go. As long as my demonstration last night proved I'm not a total failure?"

It did. I still feel the stray tingle between my legs when I think about his mouth on me. But I'm only here for a few more days, in this strange vacation land, where Fred and I are good again and I can have more with him than I did before.

More than kissing.

I slip a finger under the strap of his backpack. "What kind of supplies did you bring with you?"

His brow twists. "You mean, like, food?"

"Hell, Fred. I'm supposed to understand you're talking about making out when you say wanna 'take a piss,' but you don't get I'm talking about condoms when I say 'supplies'?"

His eyes go wide. "Fuck. Wait. Really? Here? You would, and me, I'd be there, and we—shit." He steps back abruptly and slips his backpack off, slamming the thing on the ground and wrenching the zipper open.

I then watch a grown man tear through a daypack, frantically searching for prophylactics I'm almost certain he didn't think to pack.

The sight is kind of … endearing.

Fred really just wanted to make out with me. Doesn't make me any less horny, but still, there's a stirring in my heart.

Wait, what? No. No, don't do that, heart. Get out of here. I just want to climb his bones.

"I have nothing," he says, momentarily dejected. Then, he gives me a wicked grin from his spot on the ground. "But I don't need a condom to taste you again." His focus drops to my shorts.

I scoff. "I've been hiking for two hours."

"Pull them down," he coaxes, voice dropping to a low rumble. "Just let me look."

Whoa. And I thought the Jacuzzi was hot.

I slide my backpack from my shoulders and try not to shiver when I see Fred lick his lips.

"Fun fact," I say as I tug on the zipper of a side pocket. "Last time I used this bag was at Burning Man, which was kind of a fuckfest. Which is why I might have … yep." I pull out a small box. Three Trojans. "As long as you're not packing some mythically large dick in your shorts, these should work for us."

Fred pops to his feet, smile wide, eyes on fire. "Nope. As established, I have a perfectly acceptable-sized tool. Good for universal use, no special equipment needed."

I smirk. "Not sure I've met a man so proud of his average-sized dick."

"Ah"—he holds up a finger as he saunters toward me—"but if I had a ginormous, meaty dong, what incentive would I have to get good at using it?"

"Not to mention, just the words *meaty dong* have my vagina setting up a *warning: trespassers will be shot* sign."

That breaks Fred, and he scoops me up in his arms, burying his face in my neck as he laughs. "Hell"—he chuckles—"you're so fucking sexy when you're mocking me."

And he's irresistible when he laughs. Now, I'm the one feeling frantic to tear into something.

"Put me down and start taking some clothes off," I demand.

Fred does as he was told, letting my feet settle on the forest floor, and then he releases me and moves his fingers to the top button of his flowered shirt. But I don't want some striptease. I want to see the bare chest I only got a shadowy version of last night. The hot-tub lights were too dim to take him all in.

I toss the condoms onto my backpack. "Don't bother with buttons."

Since I'm only a couple of inches shorter than Fred, I have no problem helping him drag the material up his arms. But when the shirt collar reveals his mouth but catches on his slightly crooked nose, I get the evil urge to pause. Which is how Fred ends up with his arms in the air, sleeves bunched around his biceps, unable to see because of the shirt I haven't fully removed.

Grabbing his wrists, I turn us quickly and cage them against the tree, holding *him* in place.

Then, I swipe my tongue over Fred's lips before kissing him deep. From the way his hips thrust and his shoulders wiggle, I can tell he's fighting a battle between lust and frustration. When I break off to kiss down his neck, his chest heaves with pants.

"Harper." He whines my name, which is even more hilarious in this situation, not to mention the fact that he's a grown man who should not be sounding like a petulant child. "You can't kiss me when I can't see you. That's not fucking fair."

Briefly, I'm glad his eyes are covered. Otherwise, he might spy something I don't want him to see. Like how this goofy situation entices an affectionate portion of my heart to wake up and admire the man in front of me.

This is just a hookup, I remind myself.

"If this is how we have sex for the first time, I'm going to be *so* pissed," he grumbles.

Which only sets me off laughing. I bury my head against his neck, letting my hands drop away, pressing my mouth against his hot pulse, and try to remember that I should be seducing him rather than finding him adorable.

Free from my restraints, Fred jerks the shirt the rest of the way off and tosses it to the side. He cradles the back of my head, coaxing me to tilt up until our eyes meet.

"Perfect," he murmurs, the word a breath before his lips touch mine.

Fred kisses me tenderly.

Too tenderly. I need this rough, like a battle. All I want with Fred is a fight, and sometimes, that comes in the form of aggressive fucking. I drag my teeth across his lower lip and dig my nails into his exposed back, loving the way he groans in response.

"We can't take forever," I chide him as I shove down my shorts and underwear, managing to tug them over my hiking boots, which I refuse to remove because I'm not about to get a sharp rock in the sole of my foot, no matter how bad I want to get laid.

I reach for my T-shirt, but Fred's hands stop me.

"No, leave it."

"What? Something wrong with my boobs?" Last I checked, they're a nice handful even if a sports bra has been mashing them down all morning.

"Never doubt that your boobs are fantastic. But if you take your shirt off"—Fred turns us until I'm flush against the trunk I recently pinned him to—"this tree is going to tear your back to shit."

His comment has me thinking of Fred thrusting into me … and how that'd be more pleasant against soft sheets or a smooth wall than rough bark.

"That's … thoughtful of you?"

He grins at the questioning note at the end of my statement while he undoes his pants, letting them sag around his thighs. Fred's cock is already hard, and when he grasps the base and gives a squeeze, a touch of pre-cum beads at the tip of the head.

My insides clench in response.

Fred plucks a condom from where I dropped them on top of my bag and rolls the rubber onto his length. Then, he grasps my thighs and boosts my legs up to circle his waist, my back braced against the trunk.

"Can't be Prince Charming if you don't know the gallant way to fuck your princess against a tree," he says.

I dig my nails into his shoulders and lock my ankles together behind his hips. "If you start calling me princess, I will bite your ear off."

"Fuck, that's hot," he groans with a grin, the hard head of him teasing against my entrance.

Then, the asshole pauses, the humor fading from his face as he stares at me, gaze dipping to the space between us, where he's so close to sinking deep and giving me the pleasure I crave.

"What are you waiting for?" I growl.

Fred shakes his head. "To wake up, I guess."

There's too much in that innocent confession. Too much longing, and disbelief, and awe.

I can't handle it. What I can handle is a hard fuck in the forest.

"You're not the princess in this scenario, Sleeping Beauty. Get in me, or I will make this your goddamn nightmare," I hiss.

Fred chuckles, the sound morphing into a grunt, then a groan as his hips rock forward and he slides into my core.

And of course, when he's seated deep, firmly buried in me, Fred doesn't start pounding away. He grips me close, one palm grasping my thigh, the other cradling my head against his shoulder, his chest pinning me back against the tree.

"You have to know that your threats of violence only make me harder. Make me want you more." His voice is guttural, murmuring in my ear. "You cursing at me is the best foreplay."

"Fuck you," I mutter as I rotate my hips to grind my clit against him. Finding the right angle, I dig my heels into his back, holding him in place. "Right there," I breathe. "Oh God, right there."

"Hell, Harper. You gonna come on my cock?"

Fred does the best thing he could, which is stand perfectly still as I work myself on him. With him inside me, I'm deliciously full and achy, small pulses of pleasure hinting at the ecstasy hovering within reach.

"I-I am." I bury my face against his throat, sucking and nipping at his hot skin as I continue to rock and use him as my own personal pleasure device.

"Do it," he grunts. "Please. Fuck, I want to feel you come again. You left scratches on me last night, you know? When I saw them this morning, I wanted to crawl into your bed and worship your pussy again. Hell, Harper, I can still taste you on my tongue, and I love it."

"Damn it!" I choke on the curse as I come, score my nails across his back as I scrabble for purchase, something to keep me steady while the orgasm wrecks me.

"That's it," Fred whispers, finally starting to move, short thrusts in and out of my pulsing body, which draw out my waves of pleasure. "That's it. Just like that. You did good. So good."

His rate picks up, and I gasp with each long slide.

"Fred," I pant, and he mutters his own curses, mixed with praises.

I shouldn't get off on him whispering how I'm a good girl. I shouldn't.

But, fuck, I do.

"Harper." Fred's voice wraps tight around my name as he drives deep and stays there, his body quivering and jerking with his release. And all throughout, he repeats my name.

This was more than a fuck in the woods.

I ignore the thought as Fred eventually slips out of me and carefully lowers my feet to the ground. He stands still, staring at me, face unreadable.

I cross my arms over my chest, knowing I look ridiculous in a T-shirt and hiking boots and nothing else. "Quit staring at me, weirdo."

Fred grins wide, then deftly slips the condom off his flagging dick and ties a knot at the opening. Instead of tossing it into the woods for some poor squirrel to stumble upon, Fred crouches—naked—by his backpack and fishes out a ziplock bag. He double-bags it and tucks the used condom into his pack.

"Leave no trace," he announces, clearly proud of himself.

I roll my eyes and fight a smile. "Good job. I'm sure the park rangers will give you a merit badge." I scoop up my bottoms and trudge deeper into the woods.

"Where are you going?" Fred calls after me.

Away from you, so I can remind my heart not to get attached.

"For a *long* pee," I shout back.

CHAPTER 15

FRED

"Fred!" Phoebe's shout, colored with worry, has my breath locking up in my chest.

After a quick glance back at Harper to make sure she's close and heard it too, I break into a run.

"Phoebe!" I yell to let her know I'm on my way.

Up ahead, I catch sight of her pink tank top. She's bent over, and when I get closer, I spy our mother on the ground.

"Mom!" If I was panicked before, this multiplies that by one hundred.

Please tell me she's okay.

Not my mom. Please not my mom.

"Stop shouting so much. You're going to scare the animals off."

The glorious sound of Mom's grumpy scolding allows me to finally suck in a full lungful of air.

Skidding to a stop beside them, I find my sister with a worried frown and my mom sitting on a rock with one foot bare.

"What happened?" I ask just as I feel the weight of a hand on my shoulder.

Harper's at my side, brow creased in concern.

"Mom's hurt," Phoebe says.

"I stepped on a root wrong," Mom explained. "My ankle went one way; my body went the other. But I don't think it's a break. Just a little tender."

Shit. We're already a few miles into this hike, and the thing is a loop. There's no shortcut to getting back.

"Do we call the park rangers?" Phoebe asks. "Get her helicoptered out?"

"Oh God." Mom looks aghast. "No. Don't do that. I just need to sit for a bit."

But even as she protest, I watch her ankle flush an angry color. Even if nothing is broken, that thing is going to be sore. Too sore to put weight on for more than a step or two.

Phoebe looks to me, then back to our mother, and I spy the shine of tears in her eyes. She's tough, but like me, anything that threatens the health of our remaining parent terrifies us.

"Here. I have a wrap." Harper steps around me and kneels at Mom's side, then starts rummaging through her backpack.

Damn, this woman is prepared. If I wasn't worked up about my mother, I'd be turned on right now.

The stuntwoman grins as she holds up the bandage. "Can't work in my profession without learning some basic first aid. Let's get this ankle braced."

As Harper wraps the injury, despite her gentle movements, I see the strain on my mother's face.

No way is she walking out of here.

Not on her own legs anyway.

"Well, Mom," I say, making up my mind, "looks like you're finally getting a return on all those times you lugged as around as kids." As I talk, I slip my backpack off.

"What are you talking about?" She narrows her eyes at me.

I give Mom my *aren't I the most lovable son in the world* smile.

"You're riding piggyback."

I pass Phoebe my bag. "Why don't you take that? Harper can get Mom's bag. And I'll take Mom."

Harper shuffles out of the way, and I crouch down in front of my mother.

"I'm too heavy," she argues.

"Come on, Mom." I pat my upper back. "Climb on. Spider monkey–style."

"You don't need to."

Glancing over my shoulder, I give her a conspiratorial smirk. "Work with me here. I'm trying to impress Harper with my muscles and endurance."

That's only partly true. Mainly, I want to get my mom out of these woods and to an emergency care facility as soon as possible. But if it means Harper gets to see my biceps flex during the process, who am I to complain?

"Oh." My mother glances at the redhead a second too late to catch Harper's eye roll. "Well, if it's to woo Harper, I guess I could help with that."

"There's the wingwoman I need. Now, climb on. I know I've got nothing on a horse, but you're stuck with me."

Mom chuckles, and I take that as a good sign. She wraps her arms around my neck, and I hook my grip under her thighs. Lori Sullivan is an average-sized woman—aka much heavier than a daypack—but luckily, the training I've started with Roman involves weight lifting and long stretches on the treadmill. This might be a challenge, but I can handle it.

Plus, it's my mom. I'd run myself ragged if it meant she didn't have to suffer.

"We good?" I face the rest of the group and find my sister and Harper watching me.

Phoebe still looks anxious, but not near the level of when I came upon them.

Harper smiles with a teasing edge. "Consider me thoroughly wooed."

Despite her sarcastic tone, I'm almost certain I catch a hint of heat in her gaze before she turns to take the lead on the trail.

"You're welcome," Mom whispers in my ear, and I chuckle.

"Thanks. But don't go injuring yourself again just so I can get a date. My flirting has improved some since high school."

"All right, honey. I believe in you." She pats my shoulder. "Let me know if you see a moose."

"Of course," I murmur, once again distracted by Harper's ass, which refuses to quit.

Mom believes in me. Harper forgave me and admitted she's attracted to me.

This trip is my chance to make an impossible dream come true. To convince Harper to give me a shot at something long-term between us. Something permanent.

And as my boots crunch on twigs and dead leaves, crossing miles with the weight of my mother on my back, I try to ignore how the days are slipping away.

CHAPTER 16

HARPER

EIGHTEEN YEARS OLD

"If he picks up this time, I'll tell him." The old wallpaper in my new bedroom doesn't seem to care about my declaration. "I swear."

It's been four months since I moved to Ireland and said good-bye to Fred. Three weeks since we last talked.

Used to be that we were on the phone every day even if it was for five minutes, just to say *hey*.

Now, he won't pick up. Or return my texts. Not even to let me know he's alive. After a week of silence, I texted Phoebe, asking after him. She said her brother was fine, just quiet.

Which leaves me here, pacing in the smallest bedroom of my nan's house, an ocean away from my best friend, wondering why he won't talk to me.

"He's going to pick up this time," I say with all the confidence I can muster.

He has to. I have something I need to tell him. Something I didn't realize until we were so far apart and I lost the chance to see his grinning face every day. Without his constant, amusing, comforting presence, my mind finally caught up with my heart.

I love Fred.

Not the way I said the words to him in the airport. As a friend to a friend.

I love Fred, like I'm having trouble breathing without him. I love Fred, like I want to hug him hard, then get even closer.

I love Fred, like I want to kiss him again. And touch him. And have him say my name with heat in his voice.

If only I'd known I would love him like this during that first kiss, I would have ignored the cops and kept on tasting him. Would've locked the door tight. Would've made him promise to climb in my window that night and every one after.

"I'm not going anywhere, Harper. I swear."

That's what Fred said to me after my dad's funeral, and he wouldn't lie to me.

He's going to pick up this time, and when he does, I'm going to ask him to …

I groan and flop back on my bed.

This is the murky part for me. What exactly do I want Fred to consider?

Saying I'd like to date him sounds too tame for this craving that's grown inside me. I want to tie myself to Fred even if that rope has to stretch across an ocean.

Could he love me like that? Even a little bit?

This idea is wild. Asking him to be mine when we don't see each other anymore.

But I submitted college applications to schools all over Pennsylvania. One of them will accept me, and next year, we'll be in the same country again.

Maybe just ask him to wait for me? Or to consider the idea of us together at the very least?

No. The very least is asking him to pick up his goddamn phone when I call.

"He'll pick up this time."

Please pick up this time.

I scroll through the names on my phone and click on the one that matters most.

The line rings.

And rings.

And rings.

After the fifth, Fred's voice mail answers for him, and my battered heart punctures, oozing toxic pain and anger into my body.

The beep sounds, indicating I should record my message.

Say it now. Tell him you love him.

"Fred …"

But I can't.

The only way this abandonment could hurt more would be giving him all the pieces of me, letting him see every vulnerable angle, and watching as he still turns his back.

So, I stomp on my love for Fred. Ground it into the dirt of my soul with my heel until all that's left is crumpled resentment.

"This ignoring me shit is a dick move," I say into the phone. "If you change your mind about being an asshole and want to call me, don't. I'm done."

I hang up and toss my phone to the side, shoving up from my bed to pace. But there's no room to move in here. And I don't want to go downstairs because I might have to talk to the emotional shell that is my mother or I might get interrogated by my stern grandmother if she sees my red eyes.

"Stop crying," I chide myself, hot tracks trailing down my cheeks. "He's not worth it."

Only I think he is. Thought he was.

Why the hell can't he just tell me what's wrong?

My phone buzzes, and despite the dismissive message I left, I lunge for it.

The name flashing on the screen snuffs out the tiny spark of pathetic hope.

Anna: Pub tonight? Johnny was asking after ya.

Her name shouldn't disappoint me this much. Anna befriended me the first week I got here. She's brazen, she curses like a sailor with a stubbed toe, and she likes to get into trouble.

My kind of girl.

But … she's not Fred.

Neither is Johnny, the handsome bartender who sometimes slips me a free shot of whiskey.

What they are is here. And interested in spending time with me. Right now, that counts for a whole hell of a lot.

Anna: He's a fecking fine thing.

Her comment on Johnny's looks has me snorting, and the almost laughter decides it for me. I'm done with this pity party.

"Fuck it." With rough hands, I wipe the tears away.

My dad is dead.

My mother walks around like a ghost.

And now, my best friend won't talk to me.

What's the point of staying in this house that'll never feel like home? Why should I sit quietly in this cramped bedroom, contemplating the other ways my life can fall apart without my say so?

What I want more than anything is to forget. Forget my dad is gone, and my mother is depressed, and Fred doesn't love me, even a little bit, like I love him.

"Maybe Johnny will love me."

But he doesn't have to. All he needs to do is help me feel good again.

For as long as he can.

And if Johnny doesn't do the trick, I'll find someone or something else that can.

CHAPTER 17

HARPER

PRESENT DAY

We're sitting at the breakfast table, Mrs. Sullivan icing her ankle, and I'm trying to pretend like I don't enjoy how Fred is playing footsie with me under the table when my phone rings. I see Shelly's name on the screen and decide that I can't ignore my LA life anymore. Not that I was fully ignoring it. Only, the past few days, I've tried not to let my mind drift too far out of what I now think of as Wyoming World. No thoughts about the future. No thoughts about the future with Fred. No thoughts about the future without Fred.

"It's Shelly," I tell the table. "Shelly Lovegrove. She might be calling about work. I should take this."

Fred smiles at me, but the expression feels more like a frown. Maybe I'm not the only one who is trying to ignore the days that will come after us leaving this cabin.

I have no idea what will happen next. What I even *want* to happen next.

When I start thinking too much, important questions come up. Like, where does Fred even live? I know it's on the East Coast, but that's a big place.

The realization that I have very little understanding of the current Fred has me hurrying away from the table faster. Aiming for the back door, I step out into the sunny day and wander into the backyard as I focus on my phone.

Maybe Shelly called at a perfect time. Other than Phoebe—who is biased—Shelly is my best friend. True, she's also kind of my employer. Shelly doesn't pay me, but she's the one I often get jobs through. Still, all of that working together, training together, acting and stunt work together have formed a yearslong friendship between us. A true one that I rely on. One that is deep enough that I would never let work issues come between us.

If Shelly were to choose another stuntwoman over me, I would ask her why, I would listen to her answer, and I would get over it. Because Shelly means a lot to me. And there're few people in my life that I can say that about.

So, after whatever work news she has for me, I decide to ask her about this Fred thing. Because it is a *thing*. And if anyone knows how to deal with complicated relationships, it's a famous actress.

"Hey, Shelly. How's it—"

"Harper," she cuts me off, and the ragged way she says my name sets off every internal alarm in my head. There's fear in her voice. Desperation and a sense of loss.

Something happened. Something happened to my friend, and I need to know what.

"What's wrong? Tell me what's wrong," I demand, then remind myself to rein in the intensity.

When Shelly relates the events of the past twenty-four hours, all I can do is press a hand to my mouth and try to keep tears from falling down my face. It takes her a while to get all the details out. They're mixed up, thrown at me out of order. But in the end, I understand one thing.

Shelly needs me. And not over the phone. My friend needs me to be where she is. She needs my arms around her, and she needs me to tell her that it's going to be okay.

"I'm coming home." I try to speak as calmly as I can manage with my heart tearing open for her. "I'll be on the next flight. I'll be there within the day."

"Harper," she whispers, my name the only response she can seem to manage now that her story is told.

The fact that she doesn't argue with me—doesn't try to convince me that I should stay on my vacation for the last couple of days—tells me how much she needs me. Shelly is not the type to impose upon someone else. She rarely asks for help. And I think a lot of the times, she's self-conscious about how much space even her fame takes up. Even though she wants me by her side, she hasn't asked. But I can tell.

"I'll be there. Soon," I promise.

After making sure that she's as safe as she can be, I hurry back into the house.

I do what I can to keep the worry and panic off my face, but when I try to smile at Fred and Phoebe and Mrs. Sullivan, they must see that something has changed in me.

"What's up?" Fred stands from his chair, approaching me with the familiarity born of a childhood friendship and a few days of intimacy.

That's over now.

I step back.

I have to leave him. I have to leave the magic of this place, and it will be easier if Fred doesn't touch me. It will be easier if I forget the last couple of days happened.

"I'm sorry," I say to the room as a whole. "I'm heading back to LA a few days early. Something came up." Glancing at Phoebe, meeting her confused gaze, is easier than looking at Fred. "This has been an amazing trip. Thank you for inviting me. I wish I could stay longer, but I need to go. I'm going to pack my things and rebook my flight."

Not waiting for a response, I hustle through the kitchen, focus on the doorway to my shared bedroom.

I should've known he'd follow me. Fred lingers in the doorway as I tug my empty suitcase from the closet and shove my shoes into it. He waits until I start pulling open drawers to speak, as if needing proof I'm truly on my way out.

"I don't understand. One call, and you're leaving?"

"I have to go." I duck into the bathroom and come out with my toiletry bag, adding it to my suitcase.

"We've still got two more days," Fred argues.

"Shelly needs me."

"Shelly Lovegrove?" He huffs out a disbelieving breath. "The A-lister actress who probably has a whole staff at her beck and call? What does she need you for? Did the starlet have a bad spray tan?"

"No. It's not a fucking spray tan," I mutter as I toss clothes from the dresser into my bag, not bothering to fold things.

Pack, then book new flight? Or book flight, then pack?

I don't know what order is best. I've never had to make hasty travel plans before, and I can't stop hearing the tears in my sweet friend's voice. And as much as I want to, I can't fully ignore Fred standing near, wanting me to stay.

But stay for what? Another couple of rounds of sex?

Or is he asking for more?

Either way, it doesn't matter because it's Fred, and that would never work.

"Then what?" he presses. The man I want so badly to ignore steps into the room and closes the door, as if he thinks a private word will change my mind. "She didn't get the romcom role she wanted? Some A-lister broke up with her? Hairstylist shaved her head? What's got you running out of here like your ass is on fire?"

"Oh my fucking God!" I snarl, wheeling on Fred, my worry turning into rage. "Could you stop with the jokes for once in your life? *This* is not funny." I hurl my belongings with more force into my rolling bag and zip the thing so aggressively that I snap off half of the plastic tab. "She's my friend. And some shit went down in her life, so I'm going to go be with her. I'm going to comfort her and support her, like friends should do."

The toxic sludge of our past boils up between us because he couldn't keep his mouth shut. Couldn't help me instead of turn on me.

"You probably think it's fine if I ghost her, right? Things are hard, so it looks like it's time to bail ship, huh? That's your MO, isn't it?"

Fred flinches. "Harper—"

"You haven't changed," I hiss and snatch the keys to my rental car off the dresser. "Ten years, and you haven't matured a day."

"I'm sorry." His voice has lost the mocking edge. "What happened?"

Too late. Too fucking late, Fred Sullivan.

"Don't worry; you'll probably get to read about it in the tabloids." I choke on my next breath as I imagine Shelly picking up one of those news rags. "Hell, *she'll* have to read about it on every magazine cover for a month. Fucking pieces of shit motherfucking cocksuckers …"

Fred probably thinks I'm referencing the magazine editors, but I've got some other cocksuckers in mind.

"Please, Harper." Fred's voice goes low, pleading. "Just let me—"

"We fucked, okay?" I snap but manage to keep my voice down. I really don't want Phoebe and Mrs. Sullivan listening in. "You got to live out your teenage fantasy. I got a few orgasms. Now, we're done. I have no interest in looking after a man-baby who can't take *anything* in life seriously." I slam my suitcase on the ground, honestly surprised when no wheels pop off with the aggressive move. "You're hilarious, Fred. Got a joke for everything. But I don't need a comedian in my life. I don't expect you to stick around. So, don't."

I glare into his hazel eyes one final time and realize that I'm a liar.

I told him I forgave him, but I didn't.

I still don't.

Maybe if he were a different person, I could have. But all I see is the same boy who broke my heart and never thought I was even worth an explanation.

"We're something," he insists, voice raw and desperate.

"Not anymore." I shove past him and wrench open the door, schooling my face in time to meet Phoebe and her mom at the front door.

They hug me, tell me to have a safe journey. Phoebe instructs me to call her when whatever my secret drama is calms down, and I promise to because she's been there for me my whole life. She'll get the truth from me. She'll hear from my lips what happened to Shelly.

I can feel him at my back, waiting for me to turn around.

But I don't. I stride out of the cabin and climb into my car, and I leave Fred Sullivan in my rearview, where he belongs.

CHAPTER 18

FRED

Hollywood Sweetheart Held at Gunpoint in Own Home!

As I stand in the ticket counter line at the Jackson Hole Airport, I stare at the news article headline on my phone screen and curse myself.

Desperate to understand how badly my thoughtless words had screwed things up, I did what Harper had said. I checked the tabloids. There was nothing yesterday, so I just paced and stewed and tried to figure out if I could follow after her and fix things. Turned out, the media was only slightly behind the juicy gossip. Now, forty-eight hours later, the world has learned how two armed men broke into Shelly Lovegrove's house and cleaned the place out as best they could. As of now, the assholes are in the wind, and this woman is traumatized, and I tried to make her friend feel bad about dropping everything to go to her side.

Look up *piece of shit* in the dictionary, and you'll find a full-color photo of me.

No wonder Harper blew up at me. Even if we didn't have the past we do, I still would have deserved to get reamed out by her.

"Can I help you, sir?"

At the sound of the no-nonsense customer-service voice, I realize I've made it to the front of the line.

"Oh, yeah. Sorry. I, um, have a bag to check." I slide my ID and ticket across the counter, then set my duffel on the scale.

A wild, desperate idea comes to my mind.

"Also, could you tell me if you have any flights going to LA? And how much it would cost to change my destination?"

"Let me see." The woman tucks her hair behind her ear and starts typing at an impressively rapid pace.

I don't want to get on a plane, flying in the opposite direction of Harper, leaving things angry and broken between us. This trip was our second chance. Even Phoebe admitted that was the point of her subterfuge.

"It was long past the point where you guys should've talked," she said once Harper was gone. "So, I forced the issue. But I can't fix everything for you."

I thought I was fixing things. Harper and I were becoming *something* again. Becoming more than we'd ever been before.

Or maybe it was all exactly as she said. Me playing out a teenage fantasy and her getting a few orgasms. What did I really do to show Harper I was different from the boy she used to know?

Am I different?

I envision my not-really-a-plan playing out. So, I'll what? Show up in LA, try to win Harper over while she's focusing on supporting her friend? Why should she give me another moment of her time?

All I'm doing is existing in my fuckup state because what have I even done with my life? Odd job after odd job. Crappy apartment after crappy apartment. Too many nights sitting at a bar, drinking a beer and talking to strangers just so I don't have to go home to my empty place and face the fact that my next day will be just as pointless.

Do I drag all that nothingness with me to LA and ask Harper to take a chance on me? Take a chance on what?

A disappointment.

Even if she threw out all her common sense and said yes, I'd eventually end up hurting her the way I do with Mom and Phoebe.

The way I hurt Harper when we were younger.

Despite what I claimed, about people drifting apart, there's a reason I stopped taking her calls. A reason I cut off all contact.

I'm better left in the past.

Harper would never have moved on from her dad's death with me dragging her down. Especially when I was the reason our fathers were in that car in the first place. I had no right to hold on to her.

I refuse to be that kind of drain on her again.

"There is a flight to Los Angeles leaving at five twenty p.m. It would cost just over six hundred dollars for the change. Would you like to adjust your flight plan?" the desk worker tells me, eyes on her screen.

I give the woman a smile, hoping it comes off as grateful and not full of despair.

"Thank you for checking. I think I'll stick with New York."

After paying for my bag and grabbing my ID and ticket, I wander slowly toward the security line, lacking any sense of urgency.

So, I'm not going to bother Harper with my presence. But still, I wish I could *do* something. Ease Harper's stress after our rough parting.

What does she need?

My best guess is, Harper wants more than anything to help her friend.

And I bet what Shelly Lovegrove wants most in the world is to feel safe.

"I can do that," I mutter to myself, an idea forming.

Pausing by a giant wall mural of an eagle, I slip my phone from my pocket and dial a familiar number. He picks up on the second ring.

"Hey, man." Roman Hale's voice slides through the speaker, deep and daunting. "How was vacation? You heading out soon?"

"Hey. It was great." *At least until I messed it up.* "At the airport now, about to head through security. But I wanted to talk to you about something as soon as possible."

"Of course. What's going on?"

I clear my throat and hope I'm doing the right thing.

"Have you ever heard of the actress Shelly Lovegrove?"

PART TWO

CHAPTER 19

ROMAN

ONE YEAR LATER

An unfortunate part of running a successful security company is dealing with overly demanding clients.

"I set her up in the conference room." Felicity, Hale Security's office manager, sticks her head through my doorway, even as her body looks ready to keep walking.

Her. Shelly Lovegrove. One of our Hollywood A-lister clients and possibly our first client lost if I can't figure out why none of our bodyguards meet her needs.

I steeple my fingers together as I lean back in my office chair, the ergonomic seat letting out a soft sigh with the movement.

"How'd she seem?" I ask.

Felicity pauses her retreat, tilting her head in thought. "Quiet." That's all I get before the manager disappears.

Well, I guess it's good she's not shouting in rage, making demands. I've had a few clients like that, like businessmen with millions to spend. They want something one way, and if you can't deliver precisely what they anticipated, then they take that as permission to go off on you.

Doesn't happen often. Not to me anyway. Mainly, I have to step in for my employees. Something about my former military status tends to make those blustering guys go googly-eyed. They prefer to treat me like a life-sized G.I. Joe doll that'll tell them war stories if they pull my string.

With a sigh, I shut down my computer, push away from my desk, and get ready for the customer-service part of my job. With a few tugs, I have my suit straight, the expensive material lying perfectly in the tailored fit. I didn't used to be a suit kind of guy, but my sister gave me a talking-to about image and what I wanted to convey.

When I described the company I envisioned, with me at the head, she told me, "Fill your closet with suits."

Her advice hasn't steered me wrong.

After four years of hard work, Hale Security now takes up the entire fifty-sixth floor of this New York high-rise. We have high-profile clients all over the country, and my team is constantly growing to meet the demand.

But I know one wrong word from someone with the right influence could destroy our reputation and put us out of business. Hopefully, that's not what Shelly Lovegrove is here to do.

The windows I stroll past reveal an overcast day, spitting the occasional rain down on the sprawling cityscape. Dreary. But then I step into my conference room and find the sunshine the sky is missing, waiting for me in the form of a woman.

Shelly Lovegrove is a household face, especially here in New York, where her profile regularly appears on billboards. I knew, theoretically, she was an attractive woman.

But this blonde in a yellow trench coat is living, breathing, and stunning.

My hand rises to my hair, and I have to remind myself that checking it will probably ruin the careful styling I applied to the red-blond strands this morning.

"Ms. Lovegrove," I greet her, extending my palm to her, reminding myself that she's a client and not a beautiful woman in a bar I'm attempting to pick up.

Problem is, I'm struggling to remember how I treat my other clients when she flicks her eyes to mine and offers a tiny, apologetic smile.

"Mr. Hale. Thank you for seeing me." She rises from her chair and takes my offered hand.

Hers is smooth and cool, and I wonder if my offices are too cold. I'll have to talk to Felicity about that.

"Of course. We want to do everything we can to make this partnership work." I unbutton my suit jacket and settle in the chair across from hers.

When other clients come in with issues, I maintain an understanding but firm air. That's how I need to be now, and I try to strike the right balance while not letting my attention stray to the collar of her rain jacket.

"But I'm struggling to grasp the issue we're running into with your protection detail."

The actress grimaces, and the twist of her lips is endearing. And distracting.

"I want to apologize," she starts. "I know I must come off as a spoiled brat."

True, but I'm not about to say that. Not to her face anyway. I might think she's the most gorgeous woman to step foot in my office, but that doesn't mean she's going to be easy to work with. Shelly has requested more personnel changes than any of my other clients.

"Maybe if you told me what you found lacking in the guards we'd assigned to you, I could make the necessary adjustments," I offer.

None of my employees could give me an explanation.

Strangely though, none of them had anything bad to say about Shelly herself. Just that she was quiet with them. Standoffish was the worst report I got back.

"Oh, no. They aren't lacking." The actress presses a palm to her chest, wrinkling the shiny lapel of her coat. "*I* am."

Not what I expected.

"How so?"

Her fingers slide together to fiddle with the single pearl hanging from the slim gold chain around her throat. After a pause, she meets my eyes, her irises a light-blue color that reminds me of sunny days.

"What I've found is that your security team all seem to have a military background," she says. "Is that correct?"

I nod. "Military training establishes many of the skills required to be a successful member of a protection detail."

She smiles, but the expression is tight. "I don't doubt that's true. The problem is, I've had some … bad experiences with members of the military."

I sit straighter, spine rigid, all my attention homing in on the slight tremble in her voice. "Bad in what way?"

Shelly lets the pearl drop and clasps her hands in her lap, out of my view. "In a painful way."

Someone hurt her. But I already knew that.

"Does this have to do with the men who attacked you last year?"

Michael Braydon and Jed Morris. Two lowlifes who thought an actress would be easy to rob. And she was. Back then. My job is to make sure she's never anyone's prey again.

The two men were eventually apprehended and are both in jail now. As far as I recall, neither served our country in any branch.

"No." Shelly huffs out a sigh, her brow crinkling in frustration. "I'm not explaining this well."

She spears me with her eyes again, holding steady as I stare back, though her pupils are dilated in a sign of stress.

"Take your time."

If I need to push my afternoon meetings, I will. I want to do whatever we can to keep Ms. Lovegrove as a client.

Because that's good business, of course.

Not because I have a sudden urge to circle this table, kneel next to her chair, and take her hands in mine, rubbing them until her skin is warm.

"A person in my past hurt me." Her confession, laid so bare, fills every inch of empty space in the conference room. "He was in the military. And I'm not saying that's *why* he hurt me. I'm sure it wasn't. But he carried himself in a way—his body, how he spoke, even the way he cut his hair …"

She waves toward my head, and I'm suddenly conscious of my high-and-tight style, my fingers flexing to comb through the strands.

"Other military members often exhibit similar traits to him. Habits and mannerisms. It's glaringly obvious to me. For my job, I tend to observe how people interact with the world. It helps me play different roles. Anyway, what I'm saying is, even though I logically know your employees are there to keep me safe, my physical response"—she clutches her hand in front of her chest, as if trying to grab hold of a racing heart—"is fear."

Understanding dawns. "You're scared of your protection detail?"

Shelly grimaces. "Not because of anything they *did*. Like I said, I'm the one with the issue. But it's hard to feel safe when I see a Hale Security guard out of the corner of my eye and panic. I know it's odd."

Before she's done, I'm already nodding.

Shelly claims this is her issue, but I wouldn't say that means she deserves the blame she's heaping on herself. The panicked reaction to something or someone that brings up a bad memory is behavior I'm familiar with.

I've been around enough people who were in combat to understand the signs.

Shelly Lovegrove has post-traumatic stress disorder. Or something like it. I'm not a psychologist, though I've warmed up to therapy over the years.

"That's not odd. It makes sense."

The woman's shoulders relax a touch, but there's still an element of strain around the corners of her eyes and mouth. Her attention flicks to me, then away, and back again. Her fingers clutch at her little pearl.

And I recognize the stress signs.

I spent six years in the Army Rangers. Even in a suit, I look like former military.

Right now, Shelly's mind and body are telling her to be scared of *me*.

The knowledge has me wanting to mess up my neatly styled hair.

"When I went through everything last year," she says, "I found a security guard through another actress friend of mine. Delia, my guard, was a former MMA fighter. She never served. I don't think I realized how rare that was in your profession. When she went on maternity leave last month, I asked around to find a replacement. Multiple people pointed to you. And I remembered how Cleo—you remember Cleo Vox? She gave me your card soon after the break-in. Said you'd reached out to her to get in touch with me. I appreciate that. If I hadn't found Delia, I would've called you then."

My friend Fred asked me to reach out to the actress, and maybe it's cold, but I saw her situation as a good business opportunity. A chance to expand Hale Security further into the celebrity market. We had a handful of actresses and actors at the time, but I wanted the name Hale on every A-lister's lips when the subject of security came up.

Still, I pride myself on caring about more than just my bottom line, and I know how much trust must matter after all of Shelly's power was taken from her by strangers. Which is why I reached out to Cleo Vox, a client, and asked her to pass the offer on. I figured if Cleo was happy with our guards, which she seemed to be, then she'd talk to Shelly. That way, the actress would have the word of a friend and coworker to trust rather than a stranger.

I'm glad Shelly kept our information even if she went another route at first. And I'm pleased to hear Cleo thought well enough of my employees to advocate for us.

"I'd like to keep working with Hale Security," Shelly continues. "But I'm not sure how."

Pushing aside my disappointment at realizing I scare her simply by existing, I consider the problem.

Shelly wants a bodyguard whose body language doesn't scream, *I used to be in the military*.

A face pops into my head, and I mull over the idea before presenting it to her.

"I do have someone on my staff who could work for you. He's only received training from our firm, no military background. Everything we threw at him, he's done great with, and the guy is loyal to a fault. But he's only worked on a team. You would be his first solo assignment."

Strange bit of coincidence that he's the same man who pointed me in Shelly's direction in the first place.

"Other than him being new, do you have any concerns?" she asks.

"None. I would trust him to guard my sister, and that's the highest compliment I can give."

Her smile, when it comes, has my tie feeling too tight and my suit too restrictive.

"Then, I trust you."

CHAPTER 20

HARPER

ONE WEEK LATER

The gym smells like sweat with a hint of the synthetic covering of the floor mats.

Smells like choreography day.

I roll my shoulders as I stroll through one of my favorite buildings on the studio lot, starting the process of loosening up my muscles as I head to the locker room. We've had it easy these past couple of weeks. All the actors went out on a press tour to promote *House of the Huntress*'s new season, and us stunt folk hung back in LA, already mapping out the action scenes for season three. But that's a lot of talking and blocking. Now, with the stars of the show back in town, we'll get into the nitty-gritty.

I'm ready to get tossed around.

"Hey, Harper," a familiar voice calls out.

I turn to see Serenity perched on a bench, tying up her sneakers.

"How was your weekend?"

I shrug and toss my bag into a free locker. "Boring. Cleaned. Went on a run. Ate too many empanadas from a food truck that decided to park within walking distance of my house."

"Damn. Empanadas sound good right now. You should've texted me. I would've eaten too many with you."

Serenity Yu is a fellow stuntwoman, and after two years of working together, I'd call her a friend. *House of the Huntress* has three female leads, played by Shelly, Cleo Vox, and Mai Turner. Serenity is the stunt double for Mai, both of them sharing a heart-shaped face, dark eyes with folded lids, average height, and long, silky brown hair. I have to put on a wig to imitate Shelly's short, sharp platinum-blonde bob. Or I will when we start filming. Today, there's no point in hiding my red ponytail.

"Next time," I promise her. "Maybe I can convince the producers to hire the truck to stop by and serve lunch one day."

"Do it." She grins with finger guns.

We go back and forth about our favorite food trucks around LA while I change from sandals to sneakers, and then Serenity leaves me on my own as she heads out to warm up. After clicking my lock into place on my locker, I follow her back to the main exercise area.

Where I immediately stumble to a stop.

I love a good scary movie, but I've never been one to believe in ghosts. Still, for a moment, I doubt myself. Because a ghost seems like the only plausible explanation for what I'm seeing.

Fred Sullivan.

At my job.

In a suit.

I haven't seen the man in a year, and now, he's just … here?!

He died, and they buried him in this fancy attire. Now, he's back to haunt me because walking out on that heavenly Wyoming sex was a sin that condemned my soul to eternal torment.

Just as I'm coming to terms with my damnation, Shelly strolls up to my ghost and starts chatting with him, ruining my theory and forcing me to face reality.

But reality makes no sense.

"What in the actual fuck?" I mutter, stalking across the gym.

When I'm halfway to him, Fred's gaze lands on me, lingers, but then returns to Shelly.

My stride falters, but then I grit my teeth and power forward.

Is this asshole seriously going to ignore me? The fuck?

If Shelly wasn't here, I would toss him to the floor all over again. But since she is, I save all my aggression for my voice.

"Fred," I snap. "What the fuck are you doing here?"

His attention returns to me, and he offers a small, apologetic smile. "Hey, Harper."

"Don't *hey, Harper* me," I hiss. "How did you get in here? Did you climb a fence or something?"

His smile widens. "I don't know if I should be offended because you think I broke in or flattered because you think I could've made it past lot security."

"I ..."

Is he saying he has permission to be here?

"Harper"—Shelly captures my attention, and I find my friend wide-eyed and worried—"do you know Mr. Sullivan?"

Mr. Sullivan?

Suddenly, I'm oscillating between the urge to laugh or cry. All because of that simple title.

The idea of Fred being called Mr. Sullivan reminds me of all the times we were escorted to the principal's office to get a talking-to about some mischief we had gotten into.

Mr. Sullivan and *Miss Walsh*, they called us, as if reminding us that we'd be adults one day would have us acting like them sooner.

But then my mind goes to the *real* Mr. Sullivan. Fred's dad. The guy who used puns every chance he got, who would make sure to have a box of Orange Julius pops in the freezer because he knew I liked them, and who was always the loudest one cheering me on at football games because he had this booming voice no one could match.

Mr. Sullivan.

"Harper and I were friends, growing up," Fred responds when I let the silence stretch too long. "Lost touch though. Sorry, Harper. I should've found a way to call you and let you know. I'm Shelly's new bodyguard."

That snaps me out of my nostalgia freeze.

"Her *what*?"

"My bodyguard." Shelly stares at me, and I can tell my response to finding Fred here is freaking her out.

But seriously?

"You, Fred Sullivan, are a bodyguard?" There's no way to keep the disbelief out of my voice.

Any moment, he and Shelly are going to break. They'll start laughing and yell, *Gotcha*, and life will begin to make sense again.

But that doesn't happen. Fred offers me another smile, only this one seems strained at the corners.

"I am."

Whirling on Shelly, I try to reason with my friend. "I know you haven't been meshing with the guys from Hale, but that doesn't mean you can just grab some rando off of Craigslist!"

"Mr. Sullivan works for Hale Security." Shelly glances between the two of us. "I asked for someone unconventional."

Holy hell.

"Well, they fucking delivered," I snap, my glare at the man, not my friend.

"Um, okay. Harper, can I talk to you for a minute?" Shelly gives Fred her publicity smile, wraps a vise grip around my arm—*when did she get so strong?*—and tugs me across the gym, where he can see us but can't hear us. When we're far enough away, she turns to me. "What is wrong with this guy? Should I get him escorted off the lot?"

"What? No. God." Great. Now, I've got Shelly scared of the most chill guy in existence. "He's not dangerous. But ... that's the point!" I throw my hands in the air, getting dramatic as I try to compute this unpredictable start to my day. "The Fred I know isn't bodyguard material."

He's distracted. Hyper. Goofy ... sweet ... sexy ...

Hell no. Reroute.

I shake my head to get rid of the complimentary descriptions that don't support my point.

Shelly nibbles on her thumbnail, the way she does when she's thinking. "I met with Roman Hale when I was in New York. He said

Mr. Sullivan is new, but he's gone through all the training, and he's worked with teams and performed well. Could he be different from the guy you knew? How long ago was that?" Her blue eyes hold mine, open and concerned. "People grow up, right? They change."

I grit my teeth to hold back my immediate denial. My instinct is to tell her that Fred could never change. He'll always be the irresponsible boy who breaks things on accident.

But the truth is, I don't really know him. Not anymore.

That doesn't mean I'm suddenly comfortable with this situation.

"I just want you to be safe," I tell her, which is the truth.

But there's also the selfish part of me that just wants Fred gone because of the weird, achy way he makes me feel.

Shelly wraps her arms around my shoulders, pulling me in for a tight hug. "Thank you. For looking out for me." She releases the hold. "I promise to let you know if I think he isn't up for the job. But he's the first guard who doesn't have me flinching every time I get a glimpse of him."

Shelly grimaces at the confession, and I silently imagine wailing on her asshole father, the military man who thought his daughter needed a firm hand when it came to the rules of his household.

"If he lives up to Mr. Hale's praise, I think he might be the best fit," she continues. "Do you think you could give Mr. Sullivan a chance?"

I close my eyes, compose my emotions as much as I can, then glance back at my ex–best friend to find him watching us.

"On one condition." I scoop Shelly's hand in mine and draw her back across the room toward the waiting bodyguard.

A fucking bodyguard. That is going to take some getting used to.

"What's the verdict?" he asks, tone steady without a hint of defensiveness. If anything, he sounds resigned.

"Do you need to go by Mr. Sullivan?" I ask.

He blinks. "No."

"Good." I turn to the woman at my side and wave between them. "Shelly, this is Fred."

My friend wears a curious smile. "Your condition is using first names?"

"Yeah. For … safety. One syllable. Easier to say." I cross my arms over my chest, refusing to explain further. "Now that that's all settled, time to work."

If Shelly wasn't watching me, I'd shoot another glare at Fred. He deserves it for springing this on me.

What was he thinking? What has he been doing this past year that landed him this job?

Phoebe and I have talked plenty, and she's never mentioned it. Although I did establish soon after the Wyoming trip that I didn't want to hear anything about her brother.

It hurt too much.

This hurts too. Time to distract myself from the pain by making every other part of my body hurt.

Ah, old coping mechanisms. The only friends I need.

CHAPTER 21

FRED

"I get the feeling you don't wear suits very often."

I glance to the passenger seat of my company car to find Shelly watching me, and I realize I'm tugging at my collar. Again.

Great. Way to be super professional.

Roman is giving me a shot with this gig, and I really want to not screw it up for a whole list of reasons.

In the past, I would've made a joke. Possibly about stripping. But I like to think I've matured—slightly—in the past year.

"Maybe not. But I'll get used to it."

"Is there a reason you all wear suits?" she asks.

Roman's voice plays through my mind and comes out my mouth. "A suit conveys a sense of professionalism. So we can move around with the client and not stand out too much, but stand out just enough that people think twice before approaching you."

Another glance to the side has me catching a soft smile from the actress. Shelly really is a gorgeous woman, and maybe if I hadn't been obsessed with Harper Walsh since I got bludgeoned with the puberty stick, I might be attracted to her.

But I am a taken man—even if said woman refuses to take me.

"If you want to keep wearing suits, go for it. But I'd rather you be comfortable. And I'm not looking for a bouncer." A tinge of a darker emotion enters the actress's voice. "I just want someone to have my back. If something were to … happen."

The meaning under her words hangs heavy in the air between us.

"You can count on me," I tell her. And I mean it.

A year ago, I wouldn't have said those words. For most of my life, people couldn't count on me for anything other than a laugh. But I'm not that man anymore.

"And I'll consider a more casual look."

If she brought it up, it must matter in some way. Roman gave me a briefing on how military types unsettle her. Maybe suited guys fall in the same category.

We crawl forward through traffic. I thought driving in New York was bad, but LA traffic is atrocious. I'm just about to ask Shelly if she wants to listen to some music or maybe an audiobook when she comes at me with the observation I should've been expecting.

"So, you're in love with Harper."

Not a question, and I stop the car a bit too abruptly in response.

But Shelly only huffs out a laugh. "Sorry. I have no tact. At least, not when I'm off script."

Since we're not moving, I'm able to give the starlet my full attention. She's got curiosity vibrating off her.

"I'm right though," she presses. "Right?"

"Am I that obvious?" What's the point of lying? Especially when an important part of my job is maintaining Shelly's trust.

"Yes. But in a very sweet way." Shelly frowns. "How'd this all come about? Seems like too much of a coincidence, you both working with me."

I smooth my thumbs over the steering wheel. "Harper was on vacation with my family when you called last year." She appears confused, so I add, "After the robbery."

Her blue eyes go wide, then blank, as if she's trying to stuff away every emotion related to that event.

"Harper didn't tell us anything," I assure her. "Just that she was coming back here to support you. I saw on the news what happened." I shrug and accelerate, finally able to merge onto the highway. "I'd just begun training with Hale Security, and I'm friends with Roman. I suggested he get in touch with you. You were the kind of client he was looking for, and I thought you might want"—I throw her a rueful grin—"someone at your back."

The car falls quiet again as Shelly absorbs my explanation. In the past, this situation would've had me fidgeting and trying to think of a joke to break the tension.

But my training involved more than just combat and observation. When I thought I'd have to drop out—say *thanks, but no thanks* because I couldn't fucking concentrate on even the most important task for longer than a few minutes—my buddy told me to talk to a professional. Said there might be something undiagnosed that I was—or more like wasn't—dealing with.

Intelligent bastard.

"Why is Harper mad at you?" Shelly asks as we cruise past a line of palm trees.

Ouch. That stings, even when coming from a different source.

"I think …" I hesitate, trying to find the best way to phrase what I want to say. "I think Harper would be the best person to ask." Not because I don't know, but the idea of talking about her when she's not here feels weird to me. "And I give the full go-ahead for her to talk all the shit on me she wants. I deserve it."

"Interesting."

"And if you talk to her and anything she has to say makes you change your mind about having me as your security, I won't hold it against you to ask for a replacement."

No matter how much that would suck.

"Noted." Shelly reaches for the radio dial but lets her hand drop before she turns it on. "You said you went through training for your job. Could you tell me about that?"

From the corner of my eye, I catch her camera-ready smile.

"Might come in handy if I ever audition for the role of badass bodyguard."

"Sounds like my kind of movie."

We share a smile, and for the rest of the drive to her house, I detail the months of training Roman and his team put me through to get ready to protect another person.

And I try not to think about how one word from Harper might send me packing back to New York.

Give me more time with her, please.

Shelly's phone buzzes, and she pulls the device out while we pass through the gate of her neighborhood. The actress told me she bought a house here after last year's incident. I can see why she'd want more barriers between her and the rest of the world.

When we pull into her driveway, one of the smaller homes among a row of mansions, I turn to find Shelly giving me an odd look.

"Something wrong?" I ask as I park in her garage.

She taps a thumb against the side of her cell. "I just got a text from Harper."

"Oh?" And look at that, my heart is pounding double time.

"She wants me to give you her number."

"Really?"

There were thousands of times I wished that I'd had it. And a few drunken times I was later glad that I didn't.

"Yeah." Shelly types something on the screen of her phone, and a moment later, I feel mine buzz in my pocket. "Sent it. And now, I'm left wondering why you don't already have it." She holds her palms up in surrender. "But I won't ask." Her hands drop. "I'm just really hoping you all get things straightened out, so I can hear the story."

"Me too," I murmur to myself, proud I don't give in to the urge to pull out my phone and stare at the string of numbers that will connect me to Harper.

My job is not done for the day.

With Shelly at my side, we enter her house. She waits for me in the kitchen as I check the place over, making sure there's no one hiding in any of the rooms or the closets. For someone else, this might be overkill. But Shelly arrived home from an awards show last year to find two armed men lurking in her house.

She has reason to be cautious.

I end my circuit at the security panel in her front hall, checking to make sure everything is working and no alarms were tripped while we were out.

"All clear," I tell the star, finding her where I left her in the kitchen, mixing herself a drink. "Meghan is on call if you decide you want to go out." I name the backup guard assigned to Shelly. "Text or call me if you run into any trouble, okay?"

"Thank you, Fred." She toasts me with what looks like a dirty martini—I bartended for a handful of months years ago—and takes a sip. After she swallows, Shelly gives me a hopeful smile. "Good luck with Harper."

"Thanks. I'm sure you'll hear how it goes."

I leave her then, knowing my charge is safe. And I'm off the clock after another successful day at a career I never imagined for myself, but find I kinda love. I don't know how deep Shelly's fear runs, but whenever the actress feels uneasy during the day, she can always glance over at me and know I'm in the room to keep her safe. Providing that peace of mind for another person gives my working hours meaning.

I've found my calling.

Now, if only I could figure out my love life.

I drive out of Shelly's neighborhood and pull into a strip mall parking lot, wanting a place I can linger. Harper's phone number adds weight to my phone, pressing the device into my palm as I stare at a different string of numbers than she had as a teenager.

In a familiar sequence of moves, I navigate to my saved voice mails, tapping on one I archived eleven years ago.

"Freddy. Frrrrredyyyy. Why won't you pick up your phone? Did you drop it in the toilet again? I thought you'd learned not to put it in your back pocket anymore.

"Or did you lose phone privileges because you got detention or something? Tell your mom you want to talk to me. She loves me more than you anyway, so you'll at least get your cell back for my calls.

"I'm so freaking bored here. And I don't know anyone. And Mom is making me go to church. Catholic Church. I never did my First Communion or whatever, so when they hand out the Body of Christ, I sit alone in the pew while everyone else goes up to get their crackers. This one old lady keeps making the sign of the cross when I'm around, and I'm pretty sure she thinks I'm the spawn of Satan. I want to get black contacts and pop them in every Sunday just to freak her out."

A big sigh sounds through the speaker.

"Don't think Mom would like that. So, I need you to come here and do it for me. Or just come and don't pretend to be the devil. I don't care, just come. I'll take you out for fish and chips. We can have a whole truckload of crack.

"Ha! Bet you thought I meant drugs. Nah. I'm talking about C-R-A-I-C. Craic is what Irish people call fun."

Another sigh.

"I miss having craic with you, Freddy. You are the master of craic.

"Don't let it go to your head."

Long pause.

"Guess I'll head to bed now. Just wanted to say hey. Talk to you later."

That was the last message she left me with a note of hope. The last one where she wasn't truly worried about me abandoning her. The ones after that hurt to listen to, but I still kept them.

And now, I have the chance for more.

I dial the number Shelly sent me.

CHAPTER 22

HARPER

When Fred strolls into the bar, he's gotten rid of the tie and the suit jacket, but he still looks entirely too presentable in his crisp white button-down and dress pants. He resembles a businessman, done with a long day of crunching numbers and ready for happy hour. A five o'clock shadow tries to hide his chin dimple, unsuccessfully. He must've run his fingers through his hair at some point. The neat arrangement sits in a mussed yet still attractive mess.

Damn you, Fred Sullivan.

"If you glare at me any harder, my clothes are going to catch on fire," is his way of greeting me as he settles on the stool at my side.

"Don't worry. I'll douse it by dumping my beer over your head." I wave at the full glass sitting on the bar top by my elbow, waiting to be chucked at a cocky man. "I could do it preemptively."

Fred snorts, eyes sparkling with too much good humor for the mood I'm in. But that's Fred. Silly when everyone else is serious.

"Explain," I demand. "What the hell are you doing here? Working with *Shelly*, of all people."

He takes a moment to order a beer while I wriggle with agitation in my seat.

"I've been training with Hale Security since you last saw me. I told you a buddy of mine started a company, and that's the one. Shelly is a client."

Fred Sullivan, working security? Even if he'd told me he was a mall security guard, I would've had a hard time believing it. The guy I knew didn't mesh well with authority.

"Yeah, I got that. What kind of standards does this Hale Security have?"

From what Phoebe mentioned in the past, Fred tended to work as a delivery guy, a ride-share driver, or a bartender. Not exactly top bodyguard material.

Fred smirks. "Normally former military. But it's not a requirement, and Roman didn't hold my delinquent past against me."

God, does he think that makes this better?

"Of course. Your best buddy, Roman, hands you a job, and you say, *Sure, why not?*" I pound my fist on the bar. "This isn't some dress-up game, *shoot for the job you want, not the one you're qualified for* bullshit. This is Shelly's safety we're talking about. Why in the hell do you think you're the right person to protect her?" I growl the accusation, still able to picture the fear in my friend's eyes when I arrived at her hotel room a year ago.

She refused to go back to her loft after that day, saying she could still hear the click of the safety coming off the gun. Apparently, one of the robbers kept fiddling with his weapon like it was a fucking fidget spinner.

Fred's mouth loses its playful curve, but he doesn't drop his eyes from mine, and when he speaks, the man actually sounds serious.

"I didn't put my name up for this. And Roman doesn't hand jobs out as favors. He assigned me to this role because, in his professional opinion, he thinks I can handle it. I've always been good in a fight"—yeah, I remember the brawls under the bleachers in high school—"but I've gone through training this last year. I'll easily admit, I'm not the best bodyguard in the business. But I'm capable, and I'm someone Shelly is comfortable around." Fred leans toward me, hands braced on his knees. "I also know how much she means to you. Alone, that would have me jumping in front of a bullet for her."

"Don't joke about that," I hiss.

He straightens in his seat. "I wasn't."

And I don't know what upsets me more. The idea of someone shooting at Shelly or the idea of Fred flinging himself into the dangerous path to protect her.

Trying to ignore both images, I take a deep swallow of my beer, then wipe the foam from the top of my lip.

"And you just happened to end up guarding my coworker?"

Fred focuses on his thumb as he traces the digit through a puddle of condensation on the bar top, all the while detailing what he did the day after I left Wyoming.

Read the tabloids. Worried about Shelly. Contacted Roman Hale. Tried to give my friend something that might make her feel safe.

At the end of his recap, I sit still, struck quiet by the explanation I did not expect.

Even after I yelled at him—told him I was done with him—Fred did what he could to help me.

My righteous anger fizzles, barely a guttering flame in my chest. We sip on our beers in silence for a stretch, which is another new thing. The Fred I knew couldn't abide the quiet.

I'm the first one to break it.

"So, you're living here now, in LA?"

Fred rests his elbows on the bar. "Yeah. Renting an apartment not too far from Shelly's. Not in that gated paradise though. Just because I know the boss doesn't mean he pays me *that* much."

He grins my way, his hazel eyes playful, and I catch a hint of green starburst in the dim bar lighting.

"You're going to be with Shelly every day?" Soon after the incident, Shelly hired protection and has a guard with her most of the time. "How does that even work?"

"I'm her primary bodyguard during the day, Monday through Friday. Then, Meghan, another of Roman's based in LA, is on call for the evenings and weekends. Shelly can also call me, and I'll show up if I can. It's just billed as overtime."

Fantastic. My inner voice is pure sarcasm.

Sounds like I'm going to be seeing a lot more of Fred. Which he must have known when he agreed to take on this role.

He outlined the connection between Shelly, Hale Security, and him, but that doesn't explain why he agreed to take the job. If Fred is good friends with the boss, he could have said, *Thanks, but no thanks.*

Yet here he is. Back in my life in a big, unavoidable way.

"And what were you expecting from me? To pick up where we left off in Wyoming?" I say this in a defensive tone, as if I haven't been mentally stripping him in my mind since he walked into the bar.

But just because my vagina wants a heavy dose of Fred shenanigans doesn't mean he can stroll right into my pants. I don't owe him anything.

The exact opposite really since he still hasn't given me a good explanation for our friendship breakup. And as demonstrated by my meltdown last year, saying I forgive someone doesn't mean I *actually* forgive them.

When I asked my question, Fred was in the middle of taking another sip of his beer, which he promptly snorts up. The once-distinguished-looking bodyguard is now hacking beer out of his nose and throat, and I find this messy display comforting in a way.

"No," he gasps. "God, no."

Well, he didn't have to say it like that.

I raise my brows. "That was vehement. Sounds like I was terrible in bed. Or against a tree, I guess."

Why am I fishing for compliments?

Fred slams his glass on the bar and leans toward me, serious eyes again. There's no avoiding the intense hold of his stare. "You're the best I've ever had, Harper. And I suspect the best I ever *will* have. Never doubt that." Abruptly, he leans back, smile sheepish. "But I know that was a vacation thing for you."

A vacation thing. He's right. That's what it was.

"Exactly." I nod in agreement. "So, you and I are supposed to be colleagues now?"

The man lets out a sigh, so large that his shoulders droop at the end. "If you tell Shelly I'm not a good choice, I won't hold it against you. You've seen some of the worst of me, and you're her friend." His sad eyes meet mine again. "She's got a loyal friend in you. Shelly's lucky, and I want her to be and feel safe at all times. Even if I'm not the one doing that for her."

Damn Fred. He's not giving me any of his past petulance. The immaturity that I could point to and go, *See? You can't handle this because you're a man-child!* It's especially hard to stay mad at someone who won't fight with me.

He's too damn agreeable, and it makes me want to tie him to my bed and choke him a little bit. Then do other things …

Fuck you, libido! Think about something else!

Shelly. Her safety. Her peace of mind.

"She didn't even have anything worth stealing," I blurt.

Fred gives me a curious look.

He might already know. Hale Security probably has a whole incident report. Still, I feel the need to explain.

"I don't know what all you were told about what happened last year with Shelly. But those assholes broke in because of a necklace she wore on the red carpet. The thing was coated in diamonds, and they thought she'd have it with her when she got home. But it was a loan from a jewelry store—a bit of publicity—and she returned it immediately after the event." I grit my teeth, thinking about how skittish she was for weeks afterward. "Maybe nothing like that'll happen again. But she's famous. People expect her to have things. To *do* things."

Success has a curse sewn into the seams. Shelly needs to perform well to keep working, but the more well-known she becomes, the more people with bad intentions take notice of her.

"And I'm here to make sure no one takes something from her she doesn't want to give," Fred says, sincerity in his low voice.

It's exactly the right thing to say.

And it's making me feel all the wrong things.

Making me feel like I could trust him with precious parts of *me* too.

"Good talk." I chug the last few swallows of my beer and toss some cash on the bar. "See you around."

"Harper—"

"Night!" I call too loud, so I can drown out whatever might come out of his mouth next.

Because this Fred might mean safety for Shelly.

But he's dangerous for me.

CHAPTER 23

HARPER

I thought I could handle Fred at my job.

But that was before he showed up, wearing another one of those gaudy, god-awful aloha shirts. The thing is bright turquoise with little surfer dudes riding waves across his chest, sporting tiny neon-pink bathing suits.

Is this how he plans to protect Shelly? Burn out the retinas of anyone who approaches her?

"You're glaring."

Speaking of my too-sweet friend, the actress stands at my elbow, offering me a curious smile.

"I'm not glaring," I say. "I have resting *fuck the world* face."

"Ah. Of course. And this particular iteration of *fuck the world* face would have nothing to do with my bodyguard? The one dressed in the fun vacation button-up?"

"Of course not."

"I admit, when I said he could dress down and he told me his wardrobe consisted of Hawaiian shirts, I would've sworn he was joking." As Shelly speaks, her smile blooms into a full-blown grin.

I groan. "You like him."

My friend blinks, her head jerking back. "I don't want to date him."

"No, I mean, you like him as a person. You think he's funny. And charming. Everyone does eventually. Even the guys he got into fights with at school would be his buddies the next day." My shoulders droop on a sigh. "He's impossible not to like."

Shelly hooks her arm through mine and leads me to the mat in the center of the gym. "You seem to have a firm handle on it."

Only I don't. Last night at the bar, I was practically sliding out of my chair to get closer to him. And now, I'm just … picking at things. I feel petty and frustrated.

And I can't ignore Fred when he's a walking tropical billboard.

"Come on. Show me the choreography from the last scene in episode one again. I still don't have that spin kick down," Shelly coaxes.

"Fine," I grumble as I snatch up some protective gear, so I don't accidentally concuss one of the stars of the show. "Let's be responsible adults."

For the rest of the morning, it's a show-and-tell of fake fighting. Once my muscles warm up and Shelly and I sink into our usual instruction banter, I can pretend there's not a sexy ghost from my past leaning against the far wall.

Then, lunch comes around, and Shelly waves her new buddy over. Fred strolls up to us, wearing an expression that does things to me. And, no, I will not be elaborating on *things*.

As he approaches, I realize another change in the man I thought I knew. The Fred from high school would have been bored to the point of murdering innocent passersby if he had to spend hours on the sidelines, simply watching someone. My ex–best friend was constantly moving, even when it got him into trouble in class. There was barely a day that went by where a teacher wasn't telling him to go back to his seat. Most of them knew to let us sit next to each other or else Fred would wander over to where I was. Partly because we were best friends and always looking to spend more time together. But also because the guy could not sit still and just needed somewhere to move to.

Have the past ten—no, eleven now—years worked that constant buzz of energy out of him?

"You two are amazing," Fred says, reaching us. "I mean, I'm here if something goes down. But you all could probably lay a few assholes out without my help."

Worried how his comment might be received by Shelly, I glance over to find my friend with a wide smile and a flush on the top of her cheeks.

"Thanks, Fred. But that's all Harper. I just do the steps she shows me." She turns her attention to me. "I kind of want to see you and Fred go at it."

I'm taking a swig from my water when she makes that comment. Mistake. I do a picture-perfect spit take, spewing my water on myself and the person I'm facing.

Which is Fred.

His eyes drop to his water-and-spit-speckled clothes, then flash up to mine, twinkling with humor. "You could just say you don't like my shirt."

I'm too busy coughing up water to snap back at him.

Shelly stares at my messy state, eyes and mouth wide. "Gosh, Harper. I meant, go at it on the mat. Like a fighting demo. Not … *that*."

"You mean, you're not setting your coworkers up for your secret voyeuristic kink?" Fred says, all teasing. "Wow. Movie stars are more boring than I imagined."

Shelly smirks. "Normally, I wait till week two to give my protection detail the rundown on my kinky lifestyle. Which, sadly, Harper refuses to be part of. Not sure why I'm still friends with her."

"I hate both of you," I rasp, dividing a searing scowl between them, then walk in a completely dignified and not-at-all-petulant way toward the exit.

When did Shelly start making jokes like Fred? Or has she always?

Oh no. Do I like Shelly because she reminds me of Fred?

That can't be. Shelly is Shelly, and Fred is the bane of my existence.

I push out the front door into the studio gym parking lot and deeply breathe in the fresh air that doesn't smell like sweat.

On gym days, the producers are usually good about getting a food truck to come to the lot, so we can grab a quick meal during our break and get back to things. Today's has every type of falafel a heart could hope for.

With my plate full of tahini- and hummus-covered perfection, I settle at a table with Serenity, Mai, Cleo, and Cleo's stuntwoman, Kimani.

"This afternoon, we're going to go through everything with the minions." Heather, our stunt coordinator, settles her tray across from me and tosses a thumb over her shoulder at a group of people at another nearby table.

We don't normally refer to the extra fighters as minions, only that's what they are in episode one of season three. A bunch of evil minions, serving a vampire sorcerer. The big bad of the whole season. Also, Shelly's character's evil ex.

It's a whole awesome, complicated thing. And, yes, I watch *House of the Huntress* because I love it as much as everyone else.

"Sounds good." Shelly slips into the space at my side with her own collection of food.

Fred sits down across from her, a plate in his hand as well.

I expect him to start with his silly, maybe flirtatious comments. Win over the whole table until they think he's the most charming man in Hollywood. Maybe even offer him a role on the show.

Instead, he keeps his mouth shut as his eyes scan the area, and I get the sense he's counting the people present. And something else …

Identifying their threat level?

Suddenly, I'm rabidly curious to learn exactly what that year's worth of bodyguard training entailed.

Finished with his observation, Fred's eyes clash with mine.

Great. Now, he knows I was staring at him. He gives me a wide smile, then turns his attention to the group.

It's not exactly a dismissal, but I have the urge to snap my fingers in his face and get his focus back on me.

Wow, and I thought he *was the immature one.*

I fight the blush trying to creep up my cheeks when I realize just how weird I've been acting while Fred has kept any unprofessional feelings close to his chest. Maybe I can be forgiven, seeing as how I didn't expect to see him here while he did expect to see me.

Still, I've had time to deal. Now, it's time to make a decision.

Am I going to let my Fred grudge continuously unbalance me? Or will I stand steady and confident, knowing this is my place, no matter what he says or does?

"That work for you, Harper?"

Heather's question brings me back to the present moment, and I find the table staring at me.

Don't blush. There's nothing wrong with zoning out on your lunch break.

"Sorry, what was that?"

"We go through it once slow, once fast, then Mai, Cleo, and Shelly take a turn, and we see where we're at," Heather explains, no sign of impatience. Probably because her role has her explaining a lot of things to a lot of different people all day. She's used to repeating herself. Also doesn't hurt that falafel is her favorite, and she's got a pile on her plate.

"Works for me." I glance to Shelly, and she nods.

"Me too." The actress might not have the training I do, but she's got an unmatched level of dedication.

Shelly does a few of her own stunts, but they're the smaller, less dangerous ones. The main problem she has is flinching. She'll go through with pretty much anything, but not before that physical tick gives away the fact that she's scared. A fear her character is not supposed to have.

The producers don't want that on film, which is often my cue to step in.

Even though we could likely find a way to train away the flinching reaction, it wouldn't be easy.

And I don't want to change Shelly that way.

The thing about flinching is, it's a survival instinct. And I think it's important that my friend flinches when she thinks she's in danger. That she takes a second to consider if her next steps might hurt her.

Not like me. My eyes find Fred again as he's in the middle of another scan.

No, I see danger, and I jump in headfirst.

Which is why I have so many scars. On the outside and on the inside.

CHAPTER 24

HARPER

Keeping my eyes off Fred while I'm at my job is a struggle. Not that I sit in the middle of the mat and stare at him all day. Sometimes, a full hour goes by without me looking his way. But inevitably, there will be a lull in activity, a break in my work, and my chin tilts, my eyes rove, and eventually, they land on him.

He's not hard to find, forever wearing those gaudy shirts.

Fred always catches me staring at him. The infuriating man will offer a big grin, then move his attention along. Not distracted by me in the slightest.

Which is a good thing. I don't want to distract him while he's on the job.

At least, logically, I don't want to.

Selfishly, I wouldn't mind a slight hiccup of his concentration.

"It's just so … unrealistic."

The deep voice has me grimacing, and I turn to the side, so the speaker doesn't see and cause a fuss.

Since *House of the Huntress* rocketed into popularity, one thing the producers have been working on is sprinkling in a few celebrity cameos throughout each season. Most of the stars they've brought in were super fun to work with. Down-to-earth team players. Most were already fans of the show and were geeking out about the chance to be in it.

Then, there's Gunner Marks. Grammy-winning country artist and pompous ass. He showed up with a cocky swagger, and now, at the end of our first day with him, I've come to the conclusion that there are few men I've wanted to punch more.

"Well, it's a show about hunting monsters, so there is a requirement to suspend disbelief in some areas," Heather explains with more patience than I could manage in her shoes.

"Yeah, but you've got these sweet, tiny ladies battling guys twice their size. How does anyone believe it?" He chuckles and glances around the room, as if expecting us all to be laughing with him.

Read the room, dude.

"Our goal is to present realistic fights on the screen, which is why we tend to focus on fighting styles where smaller opponents can dominate larger ones." Heather, only a handful of inches over five foot herself, could demolish any person in this room. She could knock the singer out with her eyes closed and her dominant hand tied behind her back.

Gunner chortles. "Y'all really do live in a fantasy land. You expect me to believe someone like little Miss Lovegrove could ever take down someone like him?" The singer gestures toward Fred.

When I glance Fred's way, I realize he's frowning. An uncommon expression for the jovial man.

"Of course not," Shelly says, her normally pleasant voice brittle. "Because I, personally, don't have the training. But my character could. The whole point of the show is, she's been fighting since she was a kid. So, someone my size who's been doing that, like, let's say …" She turns toward me with an overly innocent smile. "*Harper*. I bet Harper could take my bodyguard down. No offense, Fred."

"None taken," he offers.

Gunner scoffs. "Don't believe it myself. I bet she couldn't pin ya. Not really."

"How much?" I call out, unable to keep my mouth shut any longer.

The singer shoots me a patronizing smile. "What's that, hon?"

"How much you wanna bet? I mean, I wouldn't want you to think you're tying your name to an *inauthentic* show. So, I'm happy to reassure you and make your pockets a little lighter."

The man smirks. "All right, how about an even hundred?"

"Done." I turn to my former best friend. "That is, if you're willing to have your ass handed to you. Of course, if you're not, maybe Gunner himself would like to step onto the mat with me." I crack my knuckles as I throw out the offer.

The singer laughs, only this time, I think I catch a nervous twinge at the end.

That's right. You're all talk.

"Harper." Heather murmurs my name with a note of warning.

And I know what she's silently saying. *You can't damage the talent.*

And, yeah, I know. But I *really* want to. And I bet Heather wishes she could too.

"Hang on," Fred says.

He crosses to Shelly, and they have a quiet conversation. I see her nod her head, then gesture at Draydon—another bodyguard from Hale Security, who Cleo hired when she started getting death threats mixed in with her fan mail. Fred comes to a conclusion.

"Okay," he says loud enough for the room to hear. "I'm in."

"Now, don't you go easy on her," Gunner calls out with a laugh.

Fred doesn't respond to the guy, just unclips his holster. "Do you feel comfortable holding this?" Fred focuses on Shelly, and she gives him a confident nod. "You're sure?"

"Yes. I feel safe here, and I'm comfortable holding on to the weapon. Now, go show us what you can do."

Fred carefully sets the holster in Shelly's hands and turns to face me on the mat. He toes off his shoes, then strolls toward me, eyes dragging over my body as he approaches.

"Grappling only," he says.

"Don't worry, Freddy. I won't mess up your pretty face," I taunt him with a smirk, my body vibrating at the chance to tangle with his.

"That would be a tragedy."

When we're close enough that I can whisper to him without being heard, I harden my eyes. "If you go easy on me, I'll knee you in the balls."

He grins wide. "Promises, promises."

I strike, going low. He's a decently tall man, and I want to set him off-balance. Fred staggers, but he doesn't go down. Not until he grabs me around my middle and rolls us both onto the floor.

The fight that ensues is different than most I've had in my life. Part of that is because I'm not trying to hurt my opponent. Not *really*. Yet I'm still seeking submission. Domination.

I want Gunner Marks to think twice next time he sees a girl smaller than him and assumes he's more powerful than she is.

Grappling with Fred is like solving a puzzle. He'll get ahold of my wrists, or arms, or torso in a certain way, and I'll figure out the exact way to move my limbs to off-balance him, so I can wriggle free and grab ahold of him in turn.

It's not long before we're both panting and sweating. And I'm grinning because I know if Fred were the same size as me, I'd be the clear winner. I have more skill than he does, but his weight, muscle, and reach make up for his gaps in technique.

Still, the wrestling is invigorating.

Especially when the bodyguard sprawls his body over mine, attempting to pin me to the ground.

What if I let him?

I know how good it would feel. Can still remember the rough scrape of tree bark against my back as his hips pressed me up as he thrust. A year has passed, but my body hangs on to the sensation of being filled by him.

Something of my thoughts must show in my eyes, and when Fred meets my gaze, he pauses.

"Harper—"

Mistake. With a flex of my thigh muscles, I flip him underneath me, twisting my wrists at the right angle to break his hold. I shove up and away, backing across the mat.

Good to know I can get away from him if I need to.

There's a smattering of applause, and I glance around to see we have a small audience. Shelly strolls onto the mat and gives Fred a hand up before returning his weapon.

"That's it?" Gunner calls out, arms crossed over his chest, smirk on his model-perfect lips. "She didn't even knock you out."

What a fucking asshole.

"I'm not looking to give a guy a concussion," I barely keep from snapping at him, my blood rushing in my eardrums. "You wanted proof someone my size could hold her own against a larger opponent? There, you have it. Keep your hundred. I'm good."

I refuse to do a dancing-monkey routine in the hopes of winning the approval of a man I don't care about.

"That was fascinating." Shelly glances between the two of us. "Kind of like a dance. Or a chess game. I could see the call-and-response aspect of it." She hooks her arm through mine. "You're going to have to teach me a few of those moves. Like that last one, where you flipped him?"

As my friend chats, I glance over my shoulder and catch Fred's eyes on me.

And I get the feeling that was only round one of our bout.

CHAPTER 25

HARPER

The neon sign of my favorite sushi place casts a green glow on the sidewalk in front of my parked motorcycle. Normally, I'd dismount immediately and head inside to grab a quick, delicious dinner. But tonight, I linger on my bike, kept in place by indecision.

And residual lust.

Hours have passed since Fred's and my bout, but my body continues to buzz in all the places he touched.

And he touched *a lot* of me.

That match felt like foreplay, and here I am, on the edge, hungry for a release. Or multiple releases.

"You've got plenty of vibrators at home," I mutter to myself.

But the thought of using one to chase an orgasm holds no appeal. I want a body pressing down on me. Someone to wrap my legs around. A set of hazel eyes to stare into and watch glaze over with passion …

"Ugh," I groan and slap my forehead. "Why does he do this to me?"

Luckily, I'm alone in the parking lot for the moment, so no one overhears me arguing with myself. But that doesn't solve the problem of Fred Sullivan and the tight grip he has on my hormones. Just like in Wyoming, I can't ignore this draw between us. All I think about when he's around is stripping his goofy shirts off and leaving scratch marks all over his skin while he gasps my name.

I want to make him beg for me.

My imagination provides scenarios without prompting. Fred on his knees in front of me, gazing at me with as much need as I struggle with. His pupils dilated with desire, his callous palm rough as he handles himself, on the brink of coming just from the prospect of tasting me.

Great. Now, I'm wet again.

With a growl, I stand from my bike and pace beside it. This ache, these thoughts aren't going away. Every day, they get more detailed. Pop up more frequently.

As if denying myself makes the wanting worse.

Spending days around Fred without having him is like edging.

I need the release, or the pressure will keep building.

But I've been through this before. Letting Fred under my skin only gives him free rein to hurt me, whether he does it intentionally or not.

Maybe this time, I could keep things casual. The thought has my agitated steps pausing.

"Just sex."

Saying it out loud helps me grab hold of the idea. I've had plenty of hookups over the years that didn't end in messy, emotional explosions.

Why couldn't we just hook up a few times? Work the tension out?

If the lusty look in Fred's eyes earlier was any indication, he could be up for the arrangement. And it's not like he came out to LA for me. He's got a career to think about.

I doubt he's looking for anything serious either.

"Casual sex with Fred Sullivan."

I don't know if it'll work, but I have to do something before I tear my overly sensitive skin off. And no way will I ask Shelly to get rid of a bodyguard she trusts.

My friend's safety is a priority.

So, one could say that Fred and I sleeping together is the responsible thing to do.

Liking that logic, I pull my phone out of my pocket and start typing a text I hope I won't regret.

CHAPTER 26

FRED

After I finish checking Shelly's home and bid her good night, I pull my phone out of my pocket. The device buzzed about ten minutes ago. Unless it rings repeatedly, I don't check my phone while on duty. But now, I'm off, and my time is mine.

The name on the screen has me pausing before climbing into my car.

Harper Walsh.

She's texting me?

I'm still baffled every time she's willing to talk to me. But that doesn't mean I'll pass it up.

When I tap on her name and open the message, I have to brace a hand against the roof of my car.

Harper: What's your address?

Holy shit. Holy fucking shit.

Harper wants to know where I live. Because?

To send me a housewarming gift?

Not really her style.

To send some thugs to beat me up?

Maybe, but she'd probably do the pounding herself. Also, I felt like we were finding a kind of friendly footing.

So then, why?

In the end, it doesn't matter. I text her back the information she asked for, slide into the driver's seat, and wait for whatever comes next.

Harper: Are you going to be home tonight?

My heart rate picks up, and I reach for the neck of my shirt, kind of wishing I were wearing a tie just so I could tug on it.

Me: Finishing up at Shelly's now. I'll be home in a half hour and there for the rest of the night.

Would take me ten minutes to get home anywhere else, but this is LA.

Harper: I'm coming over. I'll bring food.

Once again, I repeat, *Holy shit.*

Then, I think of the state of my apartment and groan, forehead thumping against my steering wheel.

Forty-five minutes later, there's a buzz at my door. I give my place one last despairing glance, then try to walk at a normal pace to answer.

When I wrench the old door open, perfection is waiting for me on the other side.

"You'd better like sushi because that's what I brought," Harper says by way of hello. She holds up a to-go bag and stares at me expectantly.

But I need a moment.

She's freshly showered—I can tell from the messy, damp bun sitting high on her head. Her cropped tank top shows off her strong arms and a flash of her rib cage. The shorts she has on are some flowy, soft material, begging to be pushed up by a set of hands sliding underneath.

"I like sushi," I say finally after way too long of a silent stretch.

Harper presses the bag into my chest until I reach up to take it, and then she dodges around me. "I was kind of hoping you didn't, so I could eat it all. I'm starving."

I smile to myself as I shut the front door and turn to follow her.

"I can make myself something if you—"

"Fred," Harper cuts me off, and I find her standing in the middle of my living room.

My very bare, *only has a camping chair and folding table and a lamp without a shade* living room.

"When exactly," she asks, turning to face me with puckered brows, "did you become a serial killer?"

I chuckle and set the food down on my kitchen counter. "Oh, you know, I wanted to have a backup plan in case the bodyguard thing didn't work out."

"This apartment is seriously terrifying."

She tosses her keys onto the counter by the food, and I smile at the cute little armadillo keychain holding them together. Harper ignores me, wandering down the hall to the bathroom with the flickering light and yellow-colored tub and toilet.

"No thank you," she mutters and keeps going to the bedroom.

I brace myself.

"An air mattress?" she yells before stalking back to the main room to glare at me. "You are a grown man, sleeping on an air mattress? Please tell me your things are getting shipped and there's been a delay."

I shrug. "I live light." Lighter since the fire in Philly. Then, Roman set me up with a furnished place during my training.

"Light? This is practically off the grid." She stomps up to me and starts aggressively removing food containers from the bag. "Let's make one thing very clear. I refuse to fuck you on an air mattress. I have some standards. Though you might not think it after the tree." She pops a lid off one container and shoves a rice-wrapped item in her mouth.

Meanwhile, my brain has gone offline.

There's an error message broadcasting in my brain waves, consisting of two words.

Fuck me … fuck me … fuck me … fuck me …

"I was kidding," Harper says, crashing me back into the moment so hard that I'm not able to stifle a frown of disappointment. Then, she keeps going. "About eating all of this myself." She shoves a container toward me. "I'm hungry, but not *fifty pieces of sushi* hungry. Help a lady out."

"What was that about fucking?" I rasp.

"That I'm not doing it on an air mattress. The only thing worse is a waterbed. Here, do you still like tuna?" With a deft movement, she picks up a piece of sushi in her chopsticks and holds it out to me. "Toot-toot! Open the tunnel for the food train."

Obediently, I open my mouth and let her place the delicious piece of raw fish on my tongue.

"About the fucking," I say after I swallow.

Harper mixes together some wasabi and soy sauce before dunking her next roll in it. "Yeah. You got me all hot and bothered today. I had big plans of coming over here, fueling you up, then banging the night away. But then … air mattress."

"Don't let that ruin your plans." I try not to sound too desperate as I envision Harper walking out of here without a single bang taking place. "There are plenty of other high-quality surfaces in here."

She glances around, skeptical brow raised.

"For instance"—I stroll farther into the kitchen—"this counter. I sanitize it daily. And it's plenty sturdy." I press on the counter to prove my point. "Great for fucking."

Harper doesn't look convinced as she chews her dinner.

"Or"—I stride into the living room, up to one of the bare walls—"who doesn't love a good old-fashioned wall bang? Can't go wrong with those."

Harper snorts. "I do love when sex is described as *old-fashioned*."

I grin and jog past her to the bedroom, returning a moment later with a thick blanket. With a dramatic flourish, I spread the blanket over the worn carpet in the living room. "There's nothing more old-fashioned than the ground. Let's eat raw fish and bang like the cave people did."

Harper pinches her lips shut, obviously trying not to find me hilarious. I saunter up to her, attempting flirtatious instead of desperate.

"Tell me more about how I made you hot and bothered." Leaning down, I brush my lips along her neck. "Where did you get hot?" I press a kiss to her thrumming pulse. "Where did I bother you?"

"Aren't you wondering why I changed my mind?" Her voice has gone low, husky, and catches on the last words as I kiss the tender skin at the corner of her jaw.

"Purely based off timing"—I trace the shell of her ear with my nose, smelling the peppermint of her lotion—"I assume it was my pineapple shirt. This is my panty-dropper." I catch her hand and stroke her fingers over the aloha button-up I threw on this morning.

"You are the fucking worst." She laughs and shoves at my chest.

I pretend to stumble back a step even though I don't want any space between us.

"Food then …" Harper glances between my three air-mattress alternatives. "Then floor-fucking. You're on the bottom."

Oh shit. Is this really happening?

Suddenly cautious, I return to Harper's side and pick up a piece of sushi, filled with crab and avocado, and pop it in my mouth. Methodically, I work through half a container.

"You went eerily quiet," she points out. "Is this when the murder happens?"

I grin and try not to let on how my body is tight with anticipation. "I've been known to say exactly the wrong thing. I'm trying not to ruin this more than my air mattress already has."

Harper studies me, her head tilted.

"Do you want to do this?" she asks. "Just … hook up sometimes?"

I should be shouting an enthusiastic, *Hell yes!* But the question reveals an aspect of this encounter that digs a painfully deep cut.

What Harper wants from me is only temporary. She's not gone for me, like I am for her. Maybe, one time in our lives, I meant the world to her. But that's over now. I broke it, and this is as much as she's offering.

If this is what I get, I'll take it.

"Whenever you need a good old-fashioned bang, I'm here for you."

CHAPTER 27

HARPER

Fred stares at me from the opposite side of the blanket, his gaze traveling over my body. I don't know what to do with my hands now that I'm not using them to shove food into my face.

I've never done this kind of hookup before. I've had one-night stands, normally where we were both drunk. And I've had relationships where sex was part of our habit. But I've never had another Fred. We have history—some of that is sex, and some is pain, and some is laughter. How the hell do I start this?

"Take your clothes off and lie down," I tell him.

Fred grins wide. "As my lady commands."

His long fingers deftly undo the buttons of his colorful shirt, and he tosses it aside. In the stark light of his bare bulb lamp, I study the way Fred's muscles shift under his skin as he undoes his pants and pushes them off along with his briefs. He's already half-hard, and as I stare at him, his cock lengthens.

"Does my completely acceptable-sized dick pass muster?" he

murmurs, and the thought of our past encounter in the woods has me biting down hard on my lips to keep from smiling.

I point to the blanket instead of answering. But Fred doesn't lie down, like I commanded him. The man steps forward, standing on the blanket a moment before he kneels in front of me.

"What—"

His hot palms come to rest on the backs of my thighs, dragging upward until he cups both of my butt cheeks. "Did I tell you, your ass doesn't quit?" He leans forward, pressing his face against my belly, hot breath creeping through the fabric of my shirt. "Every time you did one of those high kicks today, your ass clenched"—he digs his fingers into the muscle, and hell if they don't do exactly as he described—"and I wanted my hands on you. Wanted to feel your body tensing and relaxing." He nuzzles his face against me until my shirt hikes up and his cheek is against bare skin. "Your ass clenches when you come, you know? And your toes. And your fingers. It's gorgeous." He tilts his head, staring up at me through the valley of my breasts as his fingers sneak to the apex of my legs, teasing against the elastic of my underwear. "You gonna let me see it again? Feel it?"

I'm panting as I fist my hands in his short hair. "You talk too much." *You make me feel too much*, I mean.

He smirks. "Then, shut me up."

Fingers shaking with anticipation, I shove at my shorts and panties, and Fred helps me step out of them. Then, his hands are back on my legs, guiding me down with him. But not toward his erection. Fred reclines on the blanket with me straddling his face.

That's one way to make him stop talking.

Like the hot tub, he laps at me, not concerned about keeping his ministrations quiet. I lean forward on stiff arms, bracing myself and fisting my hands in the blanket as my hips rock. Fred's palms on my backside encourage the movement, and, hell, I know I'm clenching just the way he described.

This is what I've been craving all day. All year more like. Because I might have put physical distance between us, but I couldn't escape the memory of this man who used to know everything about me and, now, somehow still knows enough to wreck me with pleasure.

His tongue dips inside me, teasing and licking, as if I'm delicious and he wants his fill.

My mind struggles with knowing his lips are on the core of me, sliding slick over my folds. He seeks out my clit, and the damn man kisses the bundle of nerves as if my pleasure center is precious. Then, the bastard sucks and keeps drawing me into his mouth with demanding tugs until he drags my orgasm out of me, my body shuddering. Twitching.

Clenching.

"Just like that," he croons to my vulva between licks as I gasp. His hands still cradle my ass, feeling every reaction my body has to his ministrations.

"Fuck you," I mutter, leaning forward until my head presses into the blanket, leaving my butt in the air.

Fred chuckles as he strokes my thighs. He rolls to his side, out from between my legs, and inches up beside me. A heavy, comforting palm settles on my spine, and I shiver as the pressure sets off another round of pleasurable pulses in my body.

"Well, go ahead and stick it in already," I mutter, giving my ass a wiggle.

Fred chokes on a breath, then lets out a scoff. "How the hell am I going to get you addicted to my dick if I just 'stick it in'?"

"That's your goal?"

"Duh." He gives my ass a gentle slap, then presses to his feet. "Catch your breath. I'm going to get a condom."

"You have your own this time? Good for you."

His chuckle is too damn soothing, and as I hear his footsteps pad out of the room, I stretch out on the surprisingly comfortable blanket. The long day of physical activity, belly full of food, and delicious orgasm have me sleepy.

"Did I eat your pussy so good that I knocked you out?" Fred murmurs, closer than I expected.

Maybe I did doze off for a minute there.

"Mmm." I stay lying facedown, my head pillowed on my arms, and spread my legs. "There you go. Have at it."

"Harper." A soft touch on my shoulder feels a lot like his mouth.

Like a kiss. "I'm not going to fuck you when you're half-conscious. Go to sleep. My dick can wait."

"How very gentlemanly of your dick," I mutter.

And I think I hear a laugh.

And I think I feel a soft pillow under my head.

And I think I nestle into a warm body.

But I'm too sleepy to be sure.

CHAPTER 28

FRED

"Freddy?" the slightly sweet, slightly husky voice whispers through my dream.

This is one of the good dreams. The ones with Harper.

"Are you awake?"

"No," I tell dream Harper because I don't want her to go away. Not yet.

Let me dream of you a little longer.

"That's too bad," she whispers to me. "Because I've got this unopened condom and a stiff back from sleeping on a floor. Was hoping a quick morning fuck could loosen up my muscles. But if you're still asleep …"

The events of the night before slam into me, and I sit up so fast that Harper has to dodge to the side.

"I'm awake!"

She's beside me, chest bare, hair loose around her shoulders, grinning in her evil *make me fall for her all over again* way.

"So is your dick. Looks like we're all set."

Glancing at my lap, I realize I do have a case of morning—a glance toward the window shows it's still dark outside—very early morning wood.

"Time for the rise and grind," I declare.

"Please tell me that's not what you call morning sex," she groans but smiles all the while.

In the dim light cast by the glow of my oven clock, I watch Harper rip open the foil packet, and then I moan deep in my chest when she thumbs a bead of pre-cum from the tip of me and uses the moisture to stroke my length a few times before rolling the condom into place.

Harper slings a leg over my hips, ready to sink down, when I stop her with a hand on her hip.

"What about you?" I ask, not wanting her to force herself down on me.

She tilts her head, sending her hair swinging over her shoulder, the strands brushing her hardened nipples. "What do you mean? I'm about to ride your cock."

My gut pulses with pleasure at the words.

"I mean, getting you ready. Foreplay is important," I say in the most educational voice I can manage when my dick is begging to be engulfed.

Harper grins, her fingers playing in the short hair at the back of my neck. "I had a dream where you took me up on my offer last night and plowed into me while my ass was in the air." She grabs one of my hands and presses my fingers between her legs. Her folds are slick with arousal. "Dream Fred took care of the foreplay."

"Selfish asshole," I mutter at the phantom version of myself.

But then I forget him as Harper grasps me at the base, holding me in place against her opening. She lowers herself slow, little noises of satisfaction sneaking out that even biting her lip can't keep them back.

The increasing grip of her body on my length, and knowing that this is Harper and it's been a year since I was inside her, and I don't know if the sun will come up and she'll come to her senses and say this is never going to happen again—it all has me suddenly panicked. My hands grasp her hips then slide down to dig into the muscular meat of her thighs.

Stay with me. I don't deserve you, but please don't leave me.

Harper settles fully in my lap, eyes half-lidded, a smirk of satisfaction on her lips.

"You're about to finish." She snickers. "Aren't you?"

"Excuse me." I affect an affronted tone to cover up the desperate roil of emotions in my gut. "I'm a pro. I can go all morning."

"Hmm. Still, I think you'd better take care of me first." Harper clasps my shoulders and leans back, giving me full access to her clit while she keeps me buried deep.

"Greedy," I murmur as I loosen my hold, sliding a hand around her soft belly and dipping my fingers between us.

I tease over her bundle of nerves but then trace my touch lower, stroking where she stretches around me, fascinated by the heat that radiates off where we're joined.

"Fred," Harper growls, her hips shifting in agitation, sending delicious pulses through my groin. "Do I need to take care of myself?"

"So fucking greedy," I repeat with a grin, then meet her eyes as I fondle her clit, stroking her with firm circles, the way she likes.

Harper moans, her chin dropping to her chest as she watches my hand work. The sight has me panting and eager to please. Like I'm an enthusiastic new employee, desperate to pass my performance review.

"There. There. Keep doing that," she whispers.

Nails dig into my back, though I don't feel a few because some fingers rest on the deadened skin of my burn scar.

Harper must realize this because she shifts her hand away, but before I can feel self-conscious, she has her hand around the back of my neck, pulling me in for a rough kiss that ends in a moan as her body convulses around mine.

There's nothing compared to feeling the grip of Harper's orgasm on my dick. With an arm banded around her lower back, I clutch the stuntwoman to me as she rides out her release.

Then, there's a push. And pull. Rocking.

She's fucking me.

"You're fucking me," I tell her, as if she might not be aware.

Harper chuckles as she straightens in my lap, continuing to roll her hips in a hypnotic motion. "Do you have a problem with that?"

"No. Definitely not. Please, continue. You're doing great. Top-notch work."

I'm definitely going to ruin this.

Harper snorts, then full-on laughs as she twines her legs around my hips and locks her ankles at my back.

"Shut up, Fred."

"I want to. I really do. But I can't." My gaze stays locked on the sway of her hips and how each shift brings on another spark of ecstasy. "You're too fucking good, and I *need* to tell you."

Harper's lips capture mine and stop my words from spilling out. But nothing can hold back my ever-growing obsession with her.

My wanting can't be kissed away.

But soon, my brain goes offline, short-circuiting when she sucks on my tongue and clenches around me at the same time. I mutter curses into our kiss as my balls tighten, then spill.

When my thoughts come back online, I try not to make any sudden moves. Harper has draped herself over me, arms loosely wrapped around my torso, head resting on my shoulder.

We stay there, in the quiet of the morning, lust spent but bodies still connected.

Harper is the one to end the pause on reality.

"I need to get ready for work," she says.

I make a noncommittal noise, then wince when she levers herself out of my lap, my spent dick sliding from her clasp.

I don't want to watch her leave, but I can't stand to take my eyes off her.

"If I get a real bed, will you come by again?"

Harper finishes tugging on her shirt, then pauses to stare at me. The sun has begun to rise, a golden light creeping through my window and illuminating the beautiful planes of her face and the color of her hair.

After considering me for a moment, Harper strides to my place on the floor, bends over, and tangles her fingers in my hair.

"Send me a picture of the bed. I'll see if it passes muster."

Then, after a final hot kiss, she leaves me naked and wanting and planning a trip to IKEA.

CHAPTER 29

HARPER

leeping with someone I see every day at work shouldn't be so easy.

And yet …

It is.

Maybe it's because Fred and I don't actually work together. We're not in constant communication. He's just here. In the building where I work. Mostly paying attention to the world around us, but not me specifically. Even with him here, I can get into the training zone with only the occasional glance his way when I take a water break.

One such time, Fred's scan of the room catches me staring. He flicks his eyes around, and apparently finding no one watching, he proceeds to blow me an overdramatic kiss.

Then, like a lovesick puppy, he waits for me to catch it.

And I know if I don't, he'll keep blowing me more. So, rolling my eyes like his affection is the hardest trial I've ever had to deal with, I make a grabbing motion with my hand, then slap my palm to my mouth. In return, I flip him my middle finger.

Of course, because he's Fred, the man pretends to grab my vulgar gesture out of the air and then clutches his fist to his chest with an expression of utter rapture.

Why am I sleeping with such a weirdo?

Oh well, too late to turn back now.

But even with the occasional silly expression he sends my way, it's clear Fred isn't goofing off either. He's alert, sitting or standing somewhere that gives him a clear view of Shelly and the space we're working in. He makes circuits of the gym. The two of them even have a few hand signals that I'm pretty sure mean things like, *I'm going to the bathroom.*

Then, there's lunch, where we all sit together and joke, and Fred asks us about the behind the scenes of the show and makes friends with everyone, the way he so easily does.

Then, I go back to my place and pretend I'm not waiting for his text to tell me he's heading home. There are nights when Shelly has an event and I don't go over, and I pretend I don't hate those nights.

And there are evenings it would make more sense for him to come to my place, and I pretend it's not weird I never invite him over.

But I can't. There needs to be somewhere in my life he hasn't touched. Somewhere I can retreat to when he leaves. A place that holds no memory of him and is mine and reminds me I don't need Fred to live; he just makes life more fun.

But then there are moments when I can't ignore the proof that Fred is a grown man who's lived a life without me that wasn't all good, easygoing times. Like the first morning I stay for breakfast and he strolls out of his bathroom without a shirt.

A flesh-colored patch on his hip catches my eye.

"Are you quitting smoking?" I point to the tiny adhesive, wondering when that habit started.

We tried cigarettes a couple of times in high school, but luckily, the bad habit never caught on. At least, not for me.

Fred glances down, his hand brushing over the patch. He clears his throat. "Um, no. This is medication. For ADHD."

My mouth hangs open as my mind takes in the new piece of information.

He gives me a smile that has a touch of self-consciousness around the edges. "Yeah. I got a diagnosis a few months back. When I started reading up on it, a lot of things just clicked. Felt like reading a biography of my life."

My knowledge on the subject is limited, but I map the few ideas I have of ADHD over the Fred I knew, growing up. Always getting into trouble, not because he liked causing problems, but he just couldn't sit still for long. Could never focus. Not unless it was something he was intensely interested in.

Knowing that version of him was one of the reasons I was so shocked to find him working for Shelly.

"But it's a problem with attention, right? How does that work? With being a bodyguard?"

Fred nods, leaning back against his kitchen counter with his hands braced at his sides. Tense, but open to me. "I thought I was going to have to drop out of training. But Roman suggested I talk to a professional. Wouldn't accept my excuse that I was a lazy fuckup." Self-consciously, he rubs the back of his neck, muscles flexing with the movement. "When I met with a psychiatrist, they helped me figure it out. Having AHD isn't all bad, and I've been working on how to manage it. The attention part. This seems to be doing the trick." He taps his hip. "Roman put me through the same tests as all his other employees, and I passed." Fred dips his head. "But I get it, if you want to tell Shelly. I know I'm not the prime candidate for her. She should have someone she should trust at all times."

"I trust you," I say without hesitation.

Fred's been on the job for weeks now, and all I see is a man maintaining constant vigilance over my friend. Maybe it's the medication. Maybe this job is something he's passionate about, and so focusing is easy.

Whatever he's doing, it's working.

"You do?" There is something in his eyes when he meets mine—a vulnerable hope—that has me feeling too much.

So, I shove his pants down, and take him in my mouth, and make him groan my name.

Then, I leave before he can ask me to repeat my words.

Do I trust him?

Without realizing how fast the days have gone by, we're suddenly back on set, filming the show. And Fred is there too, keeping a watch over Shelly. There are less random moments of eye contact with so many people moving around and me spending time in wardrobe and makeup. Lunch breaks aren't a group thing anymore, as we eat when we can, then get back to work.

The loss of moments together during the day makes the nights more desperate. Fred passes me a key one day, and when I get to his apartment, I'm surprised to realize there's a couch, and a TV, and a coffee table. In the bedroom, there's a mattress that didn't need to be inflated and a frame that holds it. I shove Fred so hard onto the new piece of furniture that he bounces and topples off the other side, and I end up fucking him on the floor because he's there and I can't even wait the second it would take for him to climb back onto the bed.

"Stay the night," he whispers against my neck every time.

And sometimes, I do.

Sometimes, I force myself to leave, just to prove I can.

Then, it's been two months, and he's still here.

"Roman is flying in tomorrow." Fred leans on the doorway to his bedroom, holding a toothbrush with a dollop of blue paste on the bristles. "I'm going to meet up with him after work."

"Note to self: demand two morning orgasms to make up for not getting any tomorrow night," I say to cover up my disappointment.

This is good. We should spend more time apart. It's not like we're dating. This is just a hookup.

A hookup that happens five to six nights a week.

Totally casual. Totally normal.

"I thought you could come, if you're free," Fred says, his eyes on me. "Maybe Shelly too? Some friends hanging out."

Friends hanging out.

Blarg. Why do those words have me wanting to force-feed Fred dirt?

"Sure. I mean, I'll check my schedule." Even I can hear how weak that last tacked-on piece was.

Fred shoves his toothbrush in his mouth, but not before I spot his smirk.

"What the hell was that?" I demand.

His brows shoot up, eyes wide and innocent.

I argue, as if he replied to me, "I have things in my life that aren't work and you."

Like laundry. And dusting my house. And there's definitely a picture in my closet that needs hanging.

Hell, how did I pass the days before Fred showed up?

Watched more TV and read more books, I guess. And I went on dates every so often.

But not since he got here.

"Of course," he says, the words garbled by the white foam in his mouth.

My skin heats, and a part of me starts to panic.

I'm giving him too much of me. Too huge of a chunk to easily recover when he breaks it off.

"I can't stay actually." I shove off the covers, climbing out of the king-size bed, which requires crawling naked to the edge. Then, I have to go on a clothing scavenger hunt, scraping together most of the outfit I had on before he peeled each piece off of me.

When I stand with sweatpants and a tank top in my hands, a set of strong arms wraps around my waist.

"I'm a greedy asshole," Fred mutters against my neck, sending goose bumps over my skin. "Please don't go." He must have spat the toothpaste out, but the remnants leave a chilly sensation on my skin.

Stay. Stay with him. It would be so easy.

Easy until it's painful.

"I'm going to go," I say, my voice firmer than my resolve. But he doesn't know that.

Fred's arms slide away, the retreat reluctant as his fingers skim over the bare skin on my hips. Before I change my mind, I shove my sweats on and pull the tank top over my head, knowing it's doing nothing to hide my puckered nipples. But if I spend more time searching for my sports bra, he'll wear me down.

When I face Fred, he's smiling, but the expression looks like it took work.

"Will you still see if you can come tomorrow? I think you'd like

Roman." He huffs out a chuckle and scratches the back of his neck. "Or you might kill each other."

I don't fight the twitch at the corner of my mouth.

"I'm interested in meeting him too. I'll let you know."

When I'm at the door, my dorky armadillo keychain in hand, dreading the long drive back to my place, I feel Fred at my back.

Every part of me wants to toss my keys away and say, *Never mind; I'm staying*. Or at the very least, turn and pull his face to mine for a searing kiss.

But I need to stop treating this like a relationship. We've never said that's what this is, and I wouldn't agree if he asked.

"See ya, Freddy." I wave over my shoulder, so he doesn't see how I cringe at the falsely casual good-bye.

"Text me when you get home," he says. "So I know you got there safe."

I don't answer. I just escape to my motorcycle and try to ignore the gut-churning emotions my entire drive back.

After parking my bike in my garage and unlocking my front door, I slide my phone from my pocket and shoot off a text.

Me: Home.

A moment later, I get his reply.

Fred: Good night. Don't forget to tally the orgasms I owe you. Feel free to round up.

When I settle in bed, I toss and turn and silently admit to myself I'd be more comfortable on an air mattress with Fred than I could ever be alone.

And that terrifies me.

CHAPTER 30

FRED

The woman I love is a badass.

I knew this. But now, I *know* this.

Seeing the cast work out and coordinate fights in the gym was one thing. But there were days when Shelly had to be elsewhere, costume fittings and table readings and all the other stuff actresses do in preparation for filming a hit television show. Those days, not being with Harper until the evenings, sucked.

But now, I'm getting to see exactly what she and the other stunt workers were imagining up.

I am in awe.

Today, she's climbed up a drainpipe no less than ten times and jumped between buildings—while on wires, thank fuck—only to land in a roll and crouch, and apparently, tomorrow, something is happening with motorcycles. The film magic plays out in front of me with Shelly delivering lines right up to the dangerous point. She runs through the words sometimes twenty times. Then, Harper steps in, wearing a blonde wig that looks exactly like Shelly's hair, and pulls off some freaky shit that might give me a heart attack.

Tonight, I'm going to demand she soothe my ragged nerves by sitting on my dick. It's the only cure.

"She's amazing, huh?"

Shelly's wandered up to me, holding a plate with two sandwiches. I prefer the days in the gym, where we could all sit down to lunch together. But this is a *eat when you can* situation.

I accept the food offering with a smile and a thanks, letting my eyes rove the room as I take a bite.

Vigilance. That's my job. Knowing where Shelly is at all times and staying aware of who is in the room and making note if anyone seems to be a potential threat. Even with the distraction of Harper doing a series of backflips off a ledge into a foam pit, I don't let myself linger on her. I can admire her for the few seconds I catch a glimpse of her on my scan, but I can't stare uninterrupted.

I'll give her every iota of my attention tonight when I'm off duty.

"She's a great teacher. And I always feel like the real deal after training with her and Heather. But then we get to the set, and she does that." We watch Harper handspring into a backflip. "I know that as good as I could get, she's miles better. Everyone watches the show and thinks *I'm* a badass." Shelly gives a rueful shrug. "Makes me want to shove Harper forward and tell everyone it's her."

"She told me she could never do what you do," I say, not wanting Shelly to discount her own skills. "Harper brings the badass, but you bring the emotions. The personality that Mist Fairshadow"—I name her character from the show—"needs. You two are a team."

Shelly knocks her shoulder against mine. "You're a good friend." She coughs into her hand, and I glance down to see a blush spreading over her cheeks. "I mean, to Harper. Or you're a good … whatever you two are. But we"—the actress hesitates—"I-I know I'm your employer."

Shelly is funny like this, stumbling over words that aren't pre-written for her.

"Just because you pay for me to hang around doesn't mean we can't be friends. And we are. Friends." I grin down at the woman before going back to my room scan.

"Thank you, Fred," Shelly murmurs. "I don't … I don't have a lot.

Of friends, I mean. Real ones, that is." She chuckles, but in a sad way. "Ones that wouldn't sell my secrets to a tabloid. You know?"

I don't actually. I have zero fame, which means that kind of betrayal isn't something I'd ever have to worry about. But I can imagine that's an isolating way to live.

"Well, rest assured, I'm not looking to talk to the press about you." I give her another grin. "And if you don't trust me, just remember, Harper would happily tear my favorite bits from my body if I even thought about it. She's the best friend a person could have." A melancholy cloud drifts over my mind. "Loyal. As long as you don't push her away."

"Is that what you did?" Shelly grimaces after she asks, as if regretting her question.

But I don't mind.

"Yeah." I straighten my spine, determination giving me purpose. "Never going to make that mistake again."

"Good." Shelly picks up her sandwich but pauses before taking a bite. "Because then *I'd* have to tear off your favorite bits, and I doubt I'd be as skilled at it as Harper. Things would get messy."

That has me barking a laugh, and in that moment, I meet the stuntwoman's eyes as she climbs from the foam pit.

Knowing she secretly loves it, I blow the badass a kiss. Shelly giggles at my side, and Harper rolls her eyes.

But she still reaches a hand out to catch it.

CHAPTER 31

FRED

"Are you worried about Roman not being able to find the place?"

I peel my eyes off the entrance to the speakeasy-style bar and glance over at Shelly. She sits farther back in the shadowy booth, cradling an intricate cocktail in her hands, looking relaxed as she sips the drink.

"No. He'll do fine. And he'll either enjoy the puzzle aspect of having to provide a password or he'll think it's childish nonsense, which is fun to hear him grump about." I scan the bar again as I explain the duality of my friend's nature.

"Then, why do you keep staring at the door and tapping your fingers like you're counting the seconds? Am I that boring?"

I jerk my head around, away from the front door, to find Shelly smirking. *Damn, I'm obvious.*

"Would you believe I'm being a very dedicated bodyguard?"

She snorts. "Harper is coming, I promise. She was texting me earlier to get a second opinion on her outfit."

"Outfit? She's wearing clothes?" As soon as the words leave my mouth, I realize exactly how ridiculous I sound.

Only I've mainly seen her in workout gear and the costumes for the show—which are tailored tactical gear and super fucking hot—but nothing like what Shelly is insinuating. Or wearing herself, which is a tight-fitting purple dress.

My charge stares at me, and I feel the blush rising on my face.

"Yes, Fred. Harper is wearing clothes. FYI, this isn't a nudie bar."

"Damn," I mutter, offering a rueful grin. "A man can hope."

She chuckles, and then her eyes flit past me and widen. With a quick turn, I spot who grabbed her attention.

Roman is here.

My friend catches sight of our table and gives me a nod as he weaves his way through the room to us. The guy is a handsome devil, always meticulous about his appearance. Hair cut and styled, clean-shaven, black pants and shirt wrinkle-free.

I also own an iron and ironing board, of which I am very proud.

A thick silver watch flashes on his wrist as he extends his arms, and I push up from the table and give my friend a hug. His stoic appearance belies the fact that Roman Hale is a hugger. At least with the people he's close to.

"Ms. Lovegrove." He nods to my table mate as he slips into the booth across from her.

"Let's go with Shelly. If we're going to drink together." She raises her glass in a toast.

He nods. "Call me Roman."

Any other time, I would have fun, watching the subtle ways Shelly has set my friend and boss off-balance.

But my attention is snagged by another figure in the entrance.

She came.

And, fuck, she has *clothes* on.

Harper and Roman had the same idea, going all black. She wears a tight skirt that reaches her knees with a slit cut on one side, showing off a gorgeous stretch of thigh. Her top is tight, hugging her boobs and ending only an inch below them so I get a thick strip of her rib cage to drool over. I want to trace the edges of the outfit with my fingers. Then with my tongue.

She spots our table, gives a quick wave, then heads to the bar.

Dragging my eyes off her ass, I return my attention to Roman and Shelly. Both watch me with eerily similar smirks.

"So, that's her," Roman says.

"Oh, yeah. He's completely gone over Harper," Shelly announces before sipping deeply from her drink.

"Your bodyguard is obsessed with your stuntwoman. Feel left out?" Roman leans his elbows on the table, focus on Shelly.

"Not at all. Fred is completely professional when he's on the job. And Harper is much less grumpy now that he's around."

"Really?" I ask.

Shelly taps a finger with a glittering nail against her lips and wears a mischievous smile. From the corner of my eye, I spy how my boss's attention follows the subtle movement of the sparkly digit.

"You didn't hear it from me," she whispers, "but Harper hasn't been this relaxed since"—Shelly pauses, her gaze thoughtful—"before the robbery. Of me. When I got robbed." She frowns. "Frick, I'm only one drink in, and I'm talking funky."

"I think you're speaking perfectly well," Roman offers, and I'm about to roll my eyes when Harper shows up at our booth, drink in hand.

The booth is horseshoe-shaped, and there's enough room on both ends for her to choose either seat.

Roman or me.

Harper slips in beside Roman, and I try not to die on the spot from jealousy. Especially when I see them next to each other in their dark outfits. They look like a sinful couple out for a night on the town. Meanwhile, I'm still in my palm tree shirt, which I'm not normally self-conscious about. But I want to be paired with Harper in all ways possible.

"You must be Roman Hale. Freddy's *best* friend." Harper narrows her eyes at the man as she sips from her drink.

Wait. Could she *be … jealous?*

"Is that what Fred said?" Roman flicks his eyes to me, tightening his mouth, attempting to hide his smirk. He fails.

"He did. Still yet to be determined if he's a good judge of character."

Roman spreads his arms in invitation. "I'm ready for your interrogation."

Harper stabs the lime wedge in her drink with the tiny straw. "Tell me about the training you put your employees through."

"You interested in changing professions?"

"Maybe. Can't be a stuntwoman forever. Give me the hard sell."

Roman smiles at Harper, and I hate him a little bit for it while I simultaneously give a silent cheer that they're getting along. I want them to like each other. Just not *too* much.

Roman is only through describing the first part of physical training when Shelly nudges my shoulder.

"Need to use the bathroom," she explains.

"Of course." I slide out of the booth and offer my hand, so she doesn't break an ankle when standing in her deadly heels.

Roman trips over his sentence, and I glance over to see his eyes roaming the length of Shelly's clingy purple dress. He only gets stuck for a moment before shaking his head and returning his attention to Harper. But the stuntwoman caught the lapse, and if it's possible, she's studying him with more scrutiny.

"Be right back, you guys," I say.

Shelly throws me a grateful smile, as if she wasn't sure I would escort her. But despite being included on this outing in a friend-like role, I know I'm still on duty. And this dark speakeasy would be the perfect place to sneak up on someone.

"We'll be here." Harper shoos us, her attention trained on Roman.

And I wonder if I should worry about what's going to be said in our absence.

CHAPTER 32

FRED

Harper gives me a curious look when I return with Shelly from the restroom, but she doesn't say anything. For the rest of the evening, Harper and Shelly entertain us with stories from a movie production they shot in Iceland that seemed to be cursed when things kept going wrong. They finally figured out that the male lead had brought his pet monkey to the set with him, and it kept sneaking out of his trailer and getting into things.

Watching the two women speak with and over each other is a beautiful thing. Shelly, who I'm realizing is shy when there isn't a camera pointed her way, opens up, joy and laughter bright on her face. After a while, I wonder if Roman even realizes I'm still here. He's ensnared by the actress.

Unfortunately for him, I don't think Shelly returns his sentiment. Whenever her head turns his way, I watch that dazzle of amusement hurriedly get tucked away until Harper distracts the actress with another funny memory.

The night ends when Shelly says she needs to head home to sleep before an early phone call, and Roman reluctantly admits he has a morning meeting as well. I can see the suggestion he's silently considering—to be the one to drive Shelly home.

He's far better trained than I am, perfectly capable of acting as her protection detail.

But *where* he got that training is the whole problem.

If he offers, I can see the night ending on a sour note when Shelly turns him down. Best I step in.

"Well, this was fun!" I announce, clapping Roman on the shoulder and pulling him in for another hug. "Text me tomorrow. Let's grab lunch before you leave."

Roman nods before facing Shelly.

"It was good—" he starts.

"So nice—" she says at the same time.

They both stop in the middle awkwardly. Then, Roman holds out a hand for a shake the same time Shelly opens her arms for a hug. Another uncomfortable pause, and then they reverse roles—Roman going for a hug, but getting held up by Shelly's extended hand.

"This physically hurts me to watch," Harper mutters at my side, low enough so only I can hear.

Disagree. I am enjoying myself immensely.

Suddenly, Shelly lunges forward, the act seemingly a fit of desperation to complete some sort of good-bye. She wraps her arms around Roman's neck, the hold intimate with how tight she grasps him. His hands hover, his eyes wide in shock, and just as realization dawns that he's being passionately embraced by the woman he's been captivated by all evening and his arms start to close, she releases the strangle hold and stumbles back.

"Catch you on the flip side," Shelly says. Then, she turns her back on him to face Harper and me and mouths something like, *Oh my God, kill me now*, before striding toward the exit.

"What she said," I add before jogging after my client.

In the car, Shelly immediately turns on the radio, and I take her subtle cue that she'd rather not speak about the awkward departure. After performing my final scan of Shelly's home and wishing her good night, I slip my phone from my pocket, hoping for a text from Harper.

Nothing.

I send a message.

Me: Are you coming over tonight?

My thumbs hover on the keypad before I type another message.

Me: Or I could come to your place?

Harper hasn't invited me to her home, and I'm trying not to let it get to me. But I can't help thinking she's doing her best to keep me on the peripheral of her life. Easier to walk away from when she's done with me.

She doesn't respond to either message.

Then, I enter my apartment and discover Harper waiting for me in her lingerie, and I forget my worries, only concerned I might start drooling. But when Harper sweeps my legs out from under me and pins me to the floor with her hands and her hips, the evil woman finally drops the hammer.

"Tell me about the fire."

Now, I guess I know what she and Roman chatted about when I escorted Shelly to the restroom.

Damn you, Roman.

"I told you—"

"Freddy." Harper has me prone on the floor. At least, now, I have a rug, so there's a touch of softness against my back to offset the hard set in her eyes. "Tell me what happened."

"Why do I get the sense Roman already told you plenty?"

Her lips pinch tight, and her eyes narrow, as if searching for something. "He gave me a rough outline. I want to know what *really* happened. Why it made you want to join his company."

"I didn't start it, if that's what you're asking." I keep the defensiveness out of my tone.

Harper has every right to think I did. It wouldn't have been the first time I'd caused destruction with my thoughtless acts.

Her head jerks back, eyes wide. "That's not what I'm asking. I never thought that."

The shock on her face is a sort of balm.

When I called Phoebe, the first thing I said was, "There was a fire."

And her response was, "Oh God, what did you do?"

While I love my sister, her knowing me so well sometimes leads to her hurting me without realizing it.

And why wouldn't she think that? When shit goes wrong in my life, it *is* my fault. Always has been.

Except for the fire. That was crappy wiring and an old house.

"I wasn't the only one living in the building. I heard Rita—my upstairs neighbor—screaming." My body shudders at the memory. When I heard her, I thought I was too late. "She and her kids were stuck. She couldn't open the door."

"What did you do?" Harper asks in a careful voice.

My gaze flicks to the side, her intense stare hard to hold. "I broke the door down. Didn't take long. It was already on fire."

Harper's fingers clench around my wrist.

"Then what?" Her question comes on a hoarse whisper.

I shrug. "I helped them get out. Rita carried her son, Carlos. He was two, so he was smaller. I carried Camilla. It was smoky, and we had to dodge some things on fire, but really, once the door was open, we were good."

"You saved them."

I close my eyes, not deserving that look from her. Like I'm some hero. How could she ever think that?

"Yeah, well …" I clear my throat. "We all lost most of our stuff. Good thing I didn't have a whole lot to start with." I open my eyes to swing them around the apartment, filled with new purchases. "Nothing like a house fire to give you a good spring cleaning."

"Fred—"

"Rita's parents lived close by." I power on. "So, she and the kids had a place to go. After I got patched up"—and, damn, did burn wound treatment hurt—"I rented a room at a motel. Let Rita know I was okay. Then, a knock came on my door a day later, and it was her dad. And—" My voice cracks, and I clear it. "Well, let's just say, he was emotional. But happy. Happy his family was safe."

And damn me for the asshole I was because, in that moment, a small, selfish part of my heart was jealous. Because when tragedy had struck my family, everyone hadn't come out on the other side.

"He was carrying this cardboard box. He kept saying how it wasn't enough." A chuckle escapes. "I had no idea what was in the thing. But then I popped the lid, and I saw all these colors." Another laugh sneaks out, making Harper bob on my chest. "Mr. Hernandez was a fan of Hawaiian shirts, and he brought me his whole collection because he knew all my clothes were burned up." I meet Harper's gaze now. "He was embarrassed. Didn't think it was enough. But damn if that wasn't the best gift I've ever gotten in my life."

She releases my wrists to smooth her hands over the wrinkled fabric covering my chest, fingering the soft material covered in palm leaves.

"They were a gift," she murmurs.

"And a reminder. That I could do something worthwhile. *Be* someone worthwhile." With my hands free, I let them rest on her thighs, loving how even my long fingers can't hope to encircle her muscular legs. "That's why I went to Roman. I like the idea of keeping people safe."

"I'm sorry I made fun of your shirts. Mr. Hernandez's shirts. God, I'm such a bitch."

"You can make up for it by wearing one," I tease. "Come on. You know you want to."

She glares at me, even as the corner of her mouth twitches. Her fingers fiddle with the buttons, slowly popping each one free.

"You make them look good, you know?" She abandons her task to lean forward, arms braced on either side of my head. "But I don't like that you need a shirt to remind yourself that you're worthwhile."

How can she say that? How can she think that after the pain I caused her in the past?

But Harper's kissing me, slow and deep, and I'm too selfish to ask.

CHAPTER 33

FRED

Harper is going to give me a heart attack. It's hard to believe that when we were teenagers, I would egg her on to do the more dangerous stunts.

Doing doughnuts in her dad's car in the school's empty parking lot until the wheels smoked.

Climbing the rusty fire escape of the abandoned sugar factory a mile down the road from our neighborhood.

Cannonballing off Rick Manning's roof into the pool that was definitely not deep enough for the stunt.

What was I thinking?

Oh yeah. I wasn't.

Now, she's popping wheelies on a motorcycle in front of a camera crew, and I'm ready to remind everyone there's a speed limit here, thank you very much.

"Take a few deep breaths," Shelly tells me, even as she gnaws on her thumbnail while watching Harper's trick driving.

"I'm super calm," I lie. "She's got this." Truth, and yet it only takes away the very top layer of my anxiety.

"She jumped a motorcycle off a flatbed truck last season. I think when the writers figured out how good she was, they decided the motorcycle would be a big part of Mist's character." The actress huffs out a breath. "I pretty much hate them for it."

"Want to tell me where their writing room is?"

She raises her brows, and I give her my most innocent smile.

"No reason. On a completely separate note, Harper and I perfected the stink bomb in high school. The key is canned cat food."

Shelly chuckles, and her shoulders relax. I'm glad I can make one of us feel better. After exchanging a few more creative non-lethal torture methods we could use on the scriptwriters, the director calls Shelly over to film some close-up scenes.

Harper parks the bike on the proper mark, and I watch her double- and triple-check it's properly balanced on the kickstand before she works with Shelly on positioning and gripping the handles.

Since all the scenes Harper is shooting today have her wearing a helmet, she's got her red hair braided tight to her head, and the two of them look badass in their all-leather getups.

Eventually, the stuntwoman struts her way over to me, and I'm proud of myself for being able to maintain my normal scan of the area, even with her hypnotizing hips trying to distract me.

"What do you say, Freddy?" Harper bumps her shoulder into mine. "Want to sit in the sidecar of my bike and ride off into the sunset with me?" She grins, her cheeks flushed with the thrill of her job.

Harper is too damn gorgeous to look at, so I keep up my scan of the crew. Everyone is at least vaguely familiar, and no one appears overly focused on Shelly. Not more than their job requires anyway.

"Who needs a sidecar? I plan on plastering myself to your back and holding on for dear life. What would you say if I admitted I've turned into an unapologetic wimp over the years? No more adrenaline for me. I'm all about Netflix and orgasms now."

Harper hits me with a gentle elbow to the gut. "It's Netflix and chill, you goof. And that's too bad. I was going to suggest we go on an adventurous hike this weekend. Find a nice tree … see what happens."

"Great," I mutter. "Now, I'm going to be hard at work."

"Well, now, you have two weapons in your pants." Harper doesn't sound sorry in the slightest.

"You're the devil," I tell her. "I'm sleeping with the literal embodiment of the devil."

She shifts to stand directly in front of me. "Sounds like you're still a risk-taker after all." Then, the hellion winks and jogs over to where Heather is giving her a wave.

I must be a risk-taker with how I'm putting my heart on the line. Because fuck if I'm not madly in love with Harper Walsh and completely aware that I'm maybe a step above fuck buddy for her.

If that's not a risk, what is?

An hour later, Harper is back on the bike, but at least she's not jumping it off of anything. Seems like they're just filming her driving straightaways. I guess Mist goes off on a lot of lonely rides to contemplate her monster-hunting lifestyle.

Shelly's back at my side, drinking a fruit smoothie and taking a break from wearing the leather jacket she's had on all day despite the heat.

"What else they got you working on today? Want to practice your lines?" I offer.

She doesn't usually need me to respond, and the one-sided conversation is like listening to somebody talk on the phone.

"Nothing else for the day," she says. "Just got to return my getup to wardrobe."

I stifle my regret, well aware I'm here to keep Shelly safe and not to ogle her stuntwoman.

"Sounds good." I turn toward where the trailers are parked, but Shelly waves me to stop.

"Let's watch a little longer. At least till I finish this." She holds up her more than half-full cup of fruit juice mixture.

Not going to argue with that. "You're the boss."

Shelly settles in her classic movie-star folding chair, and I stand beside her. She's offered me a seat plenty of times before, but I'd rather stay on my feet. While the starlet slurps on her straw, we watch Harper gear up at the end of the blocked-off road.

"So, she's just driving a straight line?" I ask.

"At the camera. That's the difficult part." Shelly points down the stretch toward the camera crew. "Looks great when you watch it back—the bike barreling down at you. Then, you can film a completely different event, stitch it on after this, and make it look like whatever it was happened at high speed."

Harper revs the engine, then takes off, shooting down the straightaway, helmet in place to fool everyone into thinking she's Shelly. Or better yet, Mist Fairshadow.

Harper doesn't want the fame or the glory. She just wants the thrill.

And I swear to worship her better than a million fans could.

"Oh!" Shelly's gasp is the first hint something is wrong, and it comes half a breath before the screech of tires.

Harper swerves dramatically to avoid plowing into the camera.

That couldn't have been the plan.

There's no collision, but that's because the bike's turn was so dramatic that it lands on its side. Metal screeches and sparks as the motorcycle slides across the pavement.

The stuntwoman hits the ground and rolls after it.

"Harper!" Shelly screams.

I'm already running, roaring her name, eyes on a body lying limp in the middle of the road.

She's not moving.

Move.

Move.

Move.

The chant pounds in time with my sprinting steps.

Get up.

Please.

I will do anything if you just GET UP.

But even when the paramedics reach her seconds before I do, she lies still.

PART THREE

CHAPTER 34

HARPER

As Fred rolls me in my wheelchair toward the door of my house, I've never been so glad that I live in a single story with no front steps.

"Cute," he says, eyeing the small, almost perfectly square building with its earthy-orange-painted exterior and white shutters. "Just like you."

"I'm not cute," I argue. I've been in a combative mood ever since I woke up a couple of days ago in the hospital and found my body mostly out of commission. "I'm terrifying. And in pain, which makes me irritable and grumpy."

Plus, now, when I look at my adorable little house, all I see are mortgage payments I'm not sure I'll be able to keep paying for much longer.

The production's insurance will cover my medical bills, and I'll still get the paycheck I was promised for this season of *House of the Huntress*. But what then? A stuntwoman can't work with a broken arm and leg. And even when these heal, I'll have been out of the game for months, which can destroy a career. They'll have someone else paired with Shelly, and I'll need new gigs. At twenty-eight, I might be young by the world's standards, but a twenty-one-year-old can bounce up from a fall quicker than I can.

Pissed off at the universe, I glare at the plaster coating my left arm from bicep to wrist and my left leg from thigh to foot. All my career worries manifest in a sour mood that has me snapping at Fred, who is being a downright gentleman at the moment, lugging my incapacitated ass around.

"You're cute when you're grumpy." He gives my ponytail a gentle tug. "Like a little angry troll."

"If you think I can't wrestle you to the ground with only one working arm and leg, you're mistaken," I threaten.

A hot breath brushes against my ear as Fred leans in close. "Don't tempt me with a good time."

I pinch my lips, fighting a smile and a flush.

Great. Now, I'm horny too.

"Now, let's see where Harper Walsh rests her head," Fred says.

Horniness gone.

There's been so much to worry about up until this point that I forgot to consider the reason I haven't invited Fred to my house before. No doubt he thought it was because I was keeping distance between the two of us. Sure, that's part of it. There's a voice in the back of my head that is constantly insisting I need to protect myself from his casual approach to life.

But there's another reason why I've never wanted Fred Sullivan to step foot in my house.

"I think I've got it from here," I announce.

Fred pauses, my keys dangling from his fingers. He looks at me, sitting in my wheelchair that I can't even push by myself because I would only manage to go in a circle. I'm like a rowboat with one paddle.

He has the grace not to point out exactly how ridiculous what I just said is.

"Why don't I get you inside and to your bed?" he offers.

I grit my teeth and try to smile.

"No. It's fine. My mom should be here soon." By soon, I mean, in over twenty-four hours.

As soon as I realized I was going to need help to function in my day-to-day life, I called her in Ireland and asked her to do something she hadn't done in over a decade. Come take care of me.

I love my mom, but I am *not* looking forward to relying on her for everything.

Fred stares at me, then glances at my door, then back at me. "You don't want me to go in your house."

Oddly, for Fred, there is no emotional inflection in his voice. No sign of hurt.

But somehow, I still know it's there. And despite all the persistent aches in my body, this is a new pain and, in a way, more overwhelming.

I'm hurting Fred. Maintaining this wall between us is hurting him. This is different from my play threats or my wrestling or my creative insults. By shutting him out from a part of my life, he is experiencing pain.

He did the same to me all those years ago, and I'm still struggling with the healing of that wound. I could be petty and follow his example now. Leave him on my front porch with no explanation.

But then I wouldn't have him. And as much as I hate to admit it, right now, I need him.

I want him.

And I'll deal with the consequences.

"Fine," I grumble. "You can come in my house. On one condition."

"Anything," he says without hesitation.

That word leaves open so many doors that I am tempted to make him do something ridiculous. But I hold on to my maturity with an iron grip.

"You cannot comment on my decoration choices."

Fred stares at me, his brows ticking up with each second that passes with no further explanation from me.

He breaks the silent standoff. "To get this straight, you don't want me coming into your house because you think that the man who slept on an air mattress for months is going to pass judgment on your decoration choices. Do I have that right?"

Just because he says it like *that* doesn't mean I don't have a reason to worry.

"Correct."

Fred grins so wide that I'm pretty sure his jaw is about to topple off his face.

"That does it." He bends over in front of my chair and steals a kiss before murmuring against my mouth, "I *cannot* leave until I see the inside of your house. I hope you know that now."

"That didn't sound like a promise to me." I try to maintain a warning glare in the face of his glee.

He shrugs. "I don't like to make promises that I can't keep."

"Asshole," I mutter.

Fred stands and saunters toward my front door, still wearing a wide smile. If I was being honest with myself, I knew this was going to happen. It's impossible to keep him out of my life. Eventually, Fred was going to end up here, at the entrance to my home. Can't keep the guy out of anything, can I?

At least injured, I'm assured the mockery will only last so long.

The click of the lock is a warning tone. Fred cracks the door, then opens it all the way.

I duck my head and brace for the reaction, my body going tight, as if expecting a blow.

But I hear nothing. When I glance up, I find his eyes on me. Fred has opened the way into my home without looking. Restraining himself just that bit is weirdly comforting.

Fred knows he's going to find something odd inside, and he knows he's going to laugh and make fun of me. But he's not prioritizing that. He's putting me first as he returns to my side, circling behind my wheelchair and grabbing the handles before pushing me forward.

"Whatever it is, I'm gonna try not to be too much of an asshole," he whispers directly into my ear again, causing a shiver to go through my battered body.

Then, we cross the threshold, and I hear him choke on his own breath.

"Oh. My. God."

CHAPTER 35

FRED

Armadillos.

Armadillos everywhere.

The creatures claim almost every surface in Harper's house. There are knickknacks, rugs, throw pillows, lamps, and framed paintings on the walls ... all of the armored mammals.

Directly in front of me, hanging above her key rack, is an illustrated image of an armadillo wearing a cowboy hat and a speech bubble that says, *Howdy! Welcome to my home-adillo!*

"Harper—"

"Shut up."

"I never knew—"

"Shut up."

"That you loved—"

"Shut up."

"Plants."

The most adorable woman in the world gives me a seething look, and I somehow keep a straight face as I point to a tiny cactus on her windowsill.

In an armadillo-shaped flowerpot.

"Just say it," she grumbles.

"Say what?" This is too much fun.

"You know what, asshole."

"Oh." My grin hurts my face; it's so huge. "You want me to address the giant … armadillo in the room?"

"Fuck you."

I wander into the living room, doing a slow rotation to take in the glorious discovery of the woman I love. "Where do you even get all of this? I never knew there was so much armadillo decor in the world. And *armadillos*? When did this secret love affair begin?"

"You know, I think I'm good," she announces. "Why don't you head out?"

Then, the poor woman tries pushing her wheelchair one-handed and only manages a ninety-degree turn, followed by a frustrated growl.

"I'm sorry. I'll stop." Striding over, I come to my knee at her side. No more armadillo talk. For now. "What do you need? Hungry? Want to hang out on the couch and watch some TV?"

Harper frowns at her lap, and I can see her teeth grinding just from the way she clenches her jaw. This healing process is going to suck. Weeks with only the full use of two of her limbs. Months away from her job.

This is a certain kind of hell for her, and I vow to do my best and not take any harsh comments to heart.

Harper in a wheelchair is a grumpy goose.

Note to self: don't call Harper a grumpy goose if you don't want to be bitten by said grumpy goose.

"I feel gross. I want to shower, but I know I *can't* shower."

"Sexy sponge bath it is." I return to the handles of the chair and guide her down a hall that is thankfully wide enough to accommodate the wheelchair.

There's an armadillo shower curtain.

"My mom got me all of it." Harper sits on the closed toilet seat as I arrange towels and washcloths and body wash on the sink.

"Got you what?" I sniff the body wash. The familiar peppermint has me smiling.

"The armadillo stuff," she explains. "Soon after we moved to Ireland, I saw this armadillo keychain in a store and thought it was so random. They don't have armadillos in Ireland, you know. And it made me laugh and think of the US, and so I bought it. When Mom asked why I liked it so much, I didn't want to make her feel bad about the move, so I just told her armadillos were my favorite animal." Harper grimaces. "She took that as the go-ahead to get me armadillo stuff for every birthday and Christmas. Easter baskets no longer had plastic eggs and bunnies. They were filled with armadillos." Her expression softens. "It's ridiculous. But I can't seem to give any of it away."

"I'm an asshole," I mutter, guilt picking away at me for mocking the sweet gifts.

She smirks. "Only some of the time. But all is forgiven if you can make me feel like I've had a proper shower."

I grin to cover up my shame. "Challenge accepted."

We start with her clothes. With her left arm and left leg in full casts, Harper has on her loosest shirt and shorts. I go for the top first, helping her slip her right arm and head out before maneuvering it over her immobilized arm.

Then, I take a moment to steady myself.

Her entire torso is a bruise. There's barely a quarter's worth of flesh that's not some shade of black, purple, or sickly yellow.

"Lucky," the doctor said in the hospital. "She was lucky."

This doesn't look like luck to me. This looks like the edge of devastation.

"It looks worse than it feels." Harper plucks at the drawstring on her shorts. "Just wait till you see my ass. Worse spanking of my life."

I force a chuckle at her joke, then lean over her so she can grab around my neck and lift herself enough for me to slip the shorts over her hips and butt before resettling her and easing the material down her legs. In the hospital, Harper said underwear was too much of a hassle, so she's bare now, except for the casts.

She's still beautiful, only this version of her terrifies me.

So close to losing her. If she'd gone a little faster or turned a second later or not been able to shove away from the bike before getting caught underneath it, I wouldn't have this battered but beautiful woman in front of me.

One faulty gear mechanism kept the camera from rolling out of her way, as planned.

A small mistake, and she almost died.

My throat clogs with emotion as I focus on wetting and soaping a washcloth.

Don't cry. You're here to help her, not have her comfort you.

I silently pass the terry cloth to Harper, and she drags it over her neck, torso, and the top of her exposed thigh. She offers the cloth back to me.

"Gonna need some help with reaching the rest."

I re-wet and re-soap the material, and then, as if polishing a priceless glass artifact, I run the washcloth over her back, along her shoulders, up her mostly uninjured arm, then down her unbroken leg. Harper twitches as I clean between her toes.

We repeat the process with a wet-with-no-soap washcloth, and then I wrap my bruised stuntwoman in a thick towel.

"Bedroom is down the hallway." She points. "Next door on the right. Shirts in the second-to-top dresser drawer, shorts in the bottom."

"Got it."

"Don't pick out anything weird," she warns me.

I grin, and wink, and don't let the jovial expression fall until I'm out of the bathroom, where she can't see. The tears come a moment later, and I hurry into her bedroom, pressing my shoulders against the wall to keep from sliding to the floor.

She's alive. She'll be okay.
She's alive. She'll be okay.
She's alive. She'll be okay.

The same chant I repeated to myself as I drove Shelly to the hospital and the two of us sat in the waiting room for hours. It was all that kept me from breaking down.

The words keep me from collapsing right now.

So many bruises. That fast, she could've been gone.

I know what it's like to have someone disappear from my life without even a moment to say good-bye.

Please, never let me live through that again. I'm not sure I'll make it. Not if it's Harper who disappears.

Dragging in a deep breath, I wipe the moisture from my cheeks and stride to the dresser and grab whatever is on top because now that I've had my minute to break down, I need her in my sight again. Need to be sure I wasn't lying to myself about her being okay.

Harper waits for me on the toilet, where I left her, towel around her shoulders.

"Let's get some clothes on you," I announce in too chipper of a voice.

She sees through my cheerful mask, giving me a hard stare.

"Were you just crying?"

Great. Probably have puffy red eyes giving me away.

"Me? Never." I kneel in front of her and unfold the shirt that reads *University of California Cheerleading*. "Don't know how."

Harper is silent for a stretch, and I can see her struggling not to wince as I help her dress. When she's covered and flushed from pain, I take a fresh washcloth, wet it, and wipe the sheen of perspiration from her forehead.

"You can cry in front of me, Freddy. I won't make fun of you."

My insides tighten at that. "Not even a little?"

Her nose wrinkles with her smile. "Okay. Maybe a little. But it'd be a very caring and understanding type of mocking."

I kneel between her spread legs and lean in close. "Noted."

Then, I kiss Harper Walsh because she's alive and I can.

CHAPTER 36

HARPER

"Oh. You … kept them all."

Maggie Walsh stands in my living room, having just arrived from Ireland on the first flight she could get after I called her. That—asking my mom to drop her life and come baby me while I heal—was not an easy thing. But the tasks I can do for myself are greatly reduced, and I refuse to let Fred take time off work on my account. Any more than he already has.

I'm not his responsibility. We weren't even dating really before this went down.

Who in the world has their fuck buddy nurse them back to health?

So, Mom it is. Mom, who is suddenly judgmental of the decor *she* gave me.

"What do you mean, I kept them all?" I follow her stare to the armadillo coasters on my coffee table. "You gave them to me. As gifts."

"Yes. Well …" She clears her throat and fails to smooth away a grimace. "They each seemed charming individually. But seeing them crowded into one place like this …" Her attention lands on me, where I lie, sprawled on my couch. "Dear, it might make people think you have an obsession."

You've got to be fucking with me.

"Really?" I say instead of dropping an F-bomb or two. "I thought it was giving off a modern vibe." I try to keep the words light, even as the throbbing pain radiating through every inch of my body has me wanting to fight with everyone and everything within my eyeline. I set the ice pack on my chest to the side and grit my teeth as I sit up to properly greet my mother. Sitting is the best I've got on my own.

"Maybe if you rearrange some things, it wouldn't all appear so … overwhelming."

"Mom," I groan. "Please don't move my stuff. I'm going to have a hard enough time getting to things when I know where they are. If I have to search for things, it'll be impossible."

Mom looks at me then—*really* looks at me—and her face pales. When I sat up, the blanket I had over myself fell to my waist, leaving me in only a sports bra and shorts and putting the mess of my body on display.

"Oh, Harper." She hurries to my side. "I didn't realize it was this bad. Look at you. Bruises all over. Those are the largest casts I've ever seen." Her hands hover just over me, a tremor in her fingers. "How bad does it hurt?"

I shrug and try not to wince with the movement. "I can handle the pain. It's the mobility that's the problem."

"You were right to call me." She settles on the coffee table in front of me. "I'll take care of you."

"Between the two of us, you'll be back on your feet in no time." Fred enters through my open front door, carrying Mom's suitcases. "That cab driver was a chatty fellow. Nice guy. Says he does food delivery in the area too. Bet we'll get to know him over these next few weeks." Fred smiles in our direction, but I can't help thinking there's a strained note to his jokes. "I'll just put your bags in the guest room, if that works for you, Mrs. Walsh?"

"Yes. Thank you, Fred."

I glance at my mother, noticing she also has a pinch to her mouth.

Maybe I should've warned her about my and Fred's situation.

Honestly, I didn't think about it. It's not like he's a new person in her life that she needs to be introduced to. I figured it would be a quick catch-up with the two of them and she'd be as happy as Mrs. Sullivan was to see me.

But I could see the shock on Mom's face when Fred was the one to greet her at the door. It was only then that I remembered how despondent I had been as a teenager after he cut off contact. How my mother must have seen the devastation on my face for the months following him ghosting me.

She might even blame Fred for my wild teenage antics I got into once he left my life. The staying out late, getting into fights at school, messing around with drinking and drugs. Anything to forget about all I'd lost. My dad and my home and my best friend.

It's a miracle I maintained decent enough grades to get accepted into college. And lucky I squashed the most self-destructive habits once I was stateside again, deciding I didn't want to entirely torpedo my life.

Still, maybe Mom will see Fred has matured some. I'm coming to terms with that fact too. Yeah, he's still a charming goof. But he's also turning out to be devoted. And reliable. And responsible. And most of all, caring, as demonstrated by him returning to the room, heading to the freezer, and pulling out a cool pack to replace the one at my side that's turned room temperature.

"Did you have a good flight?" Fred asks, voice polite.

Don't like *that* change though. His overly careful tone gives me the creeps.

"Yes. Thank you." My mother smooths the blanket on my lap, then stands with a brisk jerk. "No need to order food in. I'll cook tonight. Where are your keys? I'll go to the market."

I point to an armadillo-shaped key holder by the front door, not bothering to argue that I have food in the fridge. My boxes of takeout probably aren't the ingredients she's looking for.

"Don't forget to drive on the right side of the road," I warn her.

"Remember who the mother is around here," she chides, leaning in to press a kiss to my forehead. "I'll make your favorite tonight. Be back soon."

As my mother heads out, giving Fred a nod of good-bye, I wonder what she thinks my favorite is. When we moved to Ireland, I lived a strangely separate life—where, at home, I tried to make my mom happy in any way I could, and out in the world, I did all the dangerous things that helped me forget my constant sadness.

This has now left me with a house full of armadillos I apparently didn't need to keep and a mother who might not know as much about me as she believes.

"Is this her first time back in the States? Since you two moved?" Fred asks, settling beside me on the couch.

"No. She came for my college graduation. So, this is her second time." With a sigh, I relax into his chest. "But I think it stresses her out. And this isn't helping." I wrap my knuckles on my cast.

He slides a hand under my hair, gently massaging the muscles at the base of my neck, one of the few places on my body where I'm not bruised.

I'm only half-embarrassed of the purr-like noise I make.

"Do you …" He hesitates in a non-Fred-like way. "Do you want me to go? With your mom here?"

Oh God, no. Please don't go, my mind shouts.

"You don't have to stay," I say out loud, which is the truth. He doesn't have to.

Fred shifts, so he can press his forehead to mine, cupping the back of my skull in his hand. "Let's put it this way. I'm going to keep coming over here, and when you get tired of me hanging around, just say, *Fred, get the fuck out of my house*. And even then, you might need to call an exterminator to truly get rid of me."

He seals the declaration with a kiss.

With his mouth against mine, I let out a laugh of relief.

Maybe not everything in my life is a mess.

CHAPTER 37

HARPER

I haven't taken a proper shower in weeks, my body aches, I can only dress in my loosest and most unflattering clothes, and still, somehow, I'm horny.

It's all Fred's fault.

The evil son of a bitch is always taking his shirt off in front of me—to change, he claims.

Bullshit.

He knows what he looks like, unbuttoning those gaudy floral shirts, slowly revealing his chest that's hard with bodyguard muscles. Seriously, it's like someone told him a six-pack could stop a bullet.

It can't, but it does stop my breathing in a not-so-healthy way.

The torture has reached a pinnacle.

I've made a decision. I'm on a mission.

Tonight, the horniness will be dealt with.

At bedtime, I'm lying on my back, like usual. Can't lie on my left side with it plastered up and can't lie on my right because then my casts weigh like bricks on my body. I used to love sleeping on my back.

Fred made fun of me the first time he saw. He said I looked like Dracula in a coffin with my arms resting on my chest. Then, he tugged my vampire body into his and snuggled me like the clinging octopus he is.

Now though, I miss the freedom of easily rolling over. Especially when Fred slides under the covers at my side, carefully and quietly, as if he thinks he might wake me.

But I'm fully conscious and ready to cure the only problem of mine I can at the moment.

"Let's have sex."

Fred jerks, rocking the mattress with the startled motion, then rolls —with no effort, damn him—onto his side to stare down at me in the dark bedroom.

"What was that?"

"Sex. Let's do it." Reaching with my uninjured arm, I stroke his bare chest, scratching my nails in the scattering of hair on his pecs.

Fred leans down, and my whole body clenches in anticipation, ready to be ravished.

But instead of doing dirty things to my mouth with his tongue, the bastard kisses my forehead.

"You're adorable. But no."

Disappointment and frustration tag-team my excitement, beating the crap out of the bit of hope. Before the accident, he would've been inside me already. Now, I'm like a grouchy child he feels obligated to care for.

I *hate* it.

He's right here, looking so fucking scrumptious with his messy hair and evening scruff and caring eyes.

And, damn it, I want some dick!

Fred, meanwhile, thinks I'm *adorable*. Even that is too kind of a description. I'm a mess.

"It's because I stink, isn't it?" The words come out in a whine.

His brow quirks. "Harper—"

"Just admit it. I'm a bitch, covered in smelly plaster, and your dick wants nothing to do with me." Yep, definitely. Grouchy child.

He huffs a breath and shifts closer, torturing me by pressing his body flush against mine. Then, I realize there's a distinct hardness poking my hip.

"My dick wants to do *everything* with you." He growls the words. "I'm an asshole, getting a hard-on while helping my injured girlfriend get dressed. Never doubt that, if I'm alive, I want you."

He thinks of me as his girlfriend? Never mind. Bookmark that for later.

"Perfect." I tangle my fingers in the short hair at the base of his neck and try to pull him to me. "Time to sex me up good. I need a dose of Fred."

The sexy asshole resists.

"Half your body is in a cast," he argues.

"We'll be careful."

"Harper …"

"I won't even move," I promise. "I'll starfish and let you do *all* the work."

Fred's hand creeps across my stomach as his eyes go hot and flick to the low neckline of my tank top and back to my face. "That shouldn't sound as appealing as it does."

I think I have him, and then the shifty man gives a small shake of his head.

"Your mom is in the next room."

I stifle a groan, not giving up hope when I feel his thumb slide under the cotton of my shirt.

"I'll be *so* quiet." My nails tease along his pounding pulse, pleased at the speedy rhythm. "I won't say a word. Won't moan or anything. People will think you're *terrible* at sex."

"Fuck, that's hot." Fred grins, his teeth bright in the dark room, and the sight of his laughing face makes me want to cry because I want him so much.

So much that I can't tease anymore.

"Please, Freddy. *Please*. Don't tell me no because you're trying to be responsible. I need you." I'm begging, and I don't care. He's worth humbling myself. "Please," I say again on a desperate whisper.

His lips cut off any more words, pressing against mine, giving me sweet and dirty kisses, the way only Fred can. My skin tingles and heats as he slides his palm up to cover my boob and pinch my nipple.

"You let me know if anything hurts." The command is fire against the side of my neck, where he drags his mouth to lick and bite my skin.

"Okay." I breathe the word on a pleased gasp.

Fred rises above me, a stern frown on his face. "What happened to not saying a word?"

So, that's how we're going to play it?

I mime locking my lips and tossing the key to the side. Which means that Fred immediately picks up the imaginary key and makes a show of swallowing it, and I want to tell him he is the ultimate dork, but my mouth is locked, and his hand is on the waistband of my athletic shorts. I've taken to not wearing underwear because the leg holes aren't stretchy enough to fit over my cast.

Fred sneaks his fingers past the waistband, tugging at my intimate curls before sliding his fingers lower.

"Let's see how strong that lock is, huh?" His whisper is husky, dragging along my nerve endings.

Another time, I might give him a snarky smirk in challenge, but I'm too busy biting hard on my lower lip as his callous fingers stroke on either side of my clit, then massage a firm circle, just the way I like.

I keep my promise as long as I can. As he teases his fingers through my arousal. As he strips off his briefs, then carefully removes my shorts. Even when he guides my legs wider, being so delicate when arranging my casted leg.

The care batters at the walls I've been trying to keep erect round my heart these past few weeks.

When Fred finally settles his hips against mine and sinks inside me, I forget my promise and moan from the relief and slow torture.

"Harper," he scolds, voice tight, even as he grins.

He wants this as bad as I do.

"Faster," I demand.

"No." He softens the refusal with a lingering kiss and a slow and steady stroke.

"This is not how we have sex," I complain softly between gasps as he works himself in and out at the speed of a drunk turtle.

"How do we have sex?" Fred's voice is pure teasing, which only makes me needier.

"With a touch of violence and witty insults," I say. "Asshole." I tack on that last bit as an example.

The evil man chuckles, and the shake of his body against mine does something beautiful inside me and makes my muscles shudder. There's an ache in my injured arm and leg, but I can ignore the twinges for more of *this*. Even if this is so slow that I probably won't finish until all my bones are healed.

"It's good to try new things." Fred kisses along my collarbone. "I'm going to do something new right now, okay?"

"Fine." My attempted mutter comes out as a breathy mumble.

He lifts his head, grinning down at me. "You ready?"

"Yes, all right." I try my best to sound put out when all I want to do is beg for more, more, *more*. "Do your new thing."

Fred buries himself deep in my body, then teases his nose against mine in a playful gesture before dropping his head to the side, lips brushing my ear as he does his new thing.

"I love you," he whispers.

"What?" My gasp is hoarse.

"Mmm," he hums happily, continuing his deep, glacier-speed thrusts. "I love fucking you."

Oh. Okay. That's okay.

"I love sleeping next to you."

Oh no.

"Fred—" I break off on a groan as he alters his angle, his pelvis pressing against my clit.

"I love waking up with you, and eating with you, and living with you." With every listed item, he drives into me. "I love you when you're laughing and when you're pissed off. I love when you threaten me."

His hand reaches down, confidently guiding my uninjured leg to wrap around his hip so he can go deeper. But his words are already at the center of me.

"I love you when you hate me," he whispers. "And I love you when you tolerate me."

"You don't." *Please do. Don't take it back.*

Fred lifts his head, smiling wide as he gazes down at me. "I do.

And I love you when you come. Wanna see? Wanna see how much I love you?"

"Fuck you," I say as tears leak from the sides of my eyes, and he lifts himself enough to sneak a hand between us.

"Anytime. Anyplace," he whispers with a smirk, working my clit just right until I'm shuddering through an orgasm in my prone state as the man I shouldn't let have so much of me watches with love shining from his eyes.

CHAPTER 38

FRED

There's an extra car clogging up Harper's driveway when I arrive after dropping Shelly at home. The actress mentioned she planned to drive herself over here later, but there's no way she could have beaten me. Not without a magical tunnel that would have transported her around the solid wall of traffic I just sat in for an hour.

Laughter drifts from inside, enticing me to turn my walk into a jog. Harper tries not to let the lack of mobility get to her, but she's been in a surly mood.

Good thing I think she's adorable when she's mad and mopey.

"Look who finally made it home," a familiar voice greets me as I step through the door.

"Phoebe."

My sister sits on the floor next to the couch where Harper lies, sprawled. The stuntwoman looks unbalanced with half her body lax while the other is held rigid by her casts.

"Hello, dear brother." Phoebe tosses her phone to the side and crosses her arms, hitting me with a withering glare. "When exactly were you going to share about your new job? When you told me you were moving to LA for work, I thought you meant being a delivery guy or bartending while you tried to convince Harper to give you another chance. Not bodyguarding. I would've guessed you'd sign on to do porn before that. I mean, you're *staring* at people all day while holding a *gun*."

"You paint a beautiful picture of my life with your words."

After tossing my keys in the armadillo-shaped bowl by the door, I stroll up to the women, giving Phoebe an affectionate pat on the head, then lean over to press a kiss to Harper's forehead. I try to be subtle about the fact that I'm breathing in her peppermint shampoo. Her hair is damp, which means someone else helped her bathe.

Don't be a jealous asshole. You're not the only person who cares about Harper's happiness.

But I'm on edge after last night. I told Harper I love her in a lot of variations. Sure, a small, secret part of me hoped she'd say it back, but I wasn't surprised when she didn't. What I'm most worried about is getting kicked out of her house and her life for moving our relationship into more serious territory.

But, damn it, I want everything with her, and I don't want to lie about it.

"And that." Phoebe points between us. "That's new. What's the deal? Where do I sign up for the Fred Sullivan newsletter, so I can keep track of what's happening in your life?"

With a groan, I settle on the floor beside my sister, leaning my head back until I feel the hard press of Harper's cast against my skull. "This okay?" I ask.

Please tell me I didn't fuck everything up.

"Yeah." The fingers of her not-plaster-covered hand tangle in my hair and scratch my scalp in a soothing drag. "Now, give your sister the rundown before she explodes. I can only distract her with videos of baby goats doing parkour for so long."

"I've seen enough tiny farm animal daredevils. Tell me about your life, you dirty, rotten fiend."

Letting my eyes close, I allow my body to relax as I walk Phoebe through the parts of my life I kept from her for more than a year.

Meeting Roman, the true extent of the fire, my training to work at Roman's company, my suggestion for him to reach out to Shelly, and how I ended up on her security detail.

"But you're ..." Phoebe trails off, and I think she's trying to find a nicer way to say *a fuckup*.

"Fred's really good at it." Harper puts in. "He's always aware, and he has eyes on Shelly. She feels comfortable around him, which is a big deal for her. I think he's found his calling. I mean, he hasn't had to take anyone down yet. But I think we know he can handle that." Her finger lightly sweeps over the bump on the bridge of my nose.

Well, shit. I swallow a time or two, keeping my eyes closed to stop them from watering.

But, fuck, it means a lot to hear Harper say she believes in me.

"My brother. A bodyguard." Phoebe's tone is still one of disbelief.

I don't blame her. This version of me—the responsible one—is just over a year old. She's got twenty-some years of the other version to contend with in her mind.

Phoebe pops up and faces me, then crouches in an attack position with her hands out. "Show me some moves. I'm a terrifying threat. Take me down. Strike fear into my heart."

I don't leave my spot, not wanting to lose Harper's hand in my hair.

"There are bears in California," I say.

Phoebe straightens from her crouch, eyes flying to the window. "No, there aren't. You're messing with me."

"You told me to strike fear into your heart," I point out.

"Not with bears!" She shivers. "You were kidding, right?"

"There's literally one on the state flag. Your lack of awareness about bears is em-*bear*-assing."

She huffs. "You are the worst brother. Now, I have to stock my car with bear spray."

My pillow bounces, and I realize Harper is laughing.

Fuck, I love that sound.

Our bear banter gets cut off when the door opens, and I try not to stiffen when Harper's mom walks in, Shelly close behind her.

"Look who I found outside," Mrs. Walsh practically sings, grinning at the actress before facing the room. "Oh! Phoebe. I-I didn't realize you were coming."

"Hi, Mrs. Walsh. Long time." My sister strolls up to the woman from our past and wraps her in a tight hug. "I can't wait to hear about Ireland. Or talk about anything really. Just want to hear that accent of yours." Phoebe holds the shocked woman at arm's length. "I'm taller than you! Look at that. Weird, right? And don't worry; I have a hotel room, and I'm only in town till tomorrow. Not here to crowd up the house. Ooh, is that Thai food?" The sight of takeout bags gets my sister to stop rattling off random thoughts.

"Y-yes," Mrs. Walsh says. "But I'm not sure it'll be enough."

"I brought tacos." Shelly holds up a bag with a hopeful smile. "And I got a lot. Thought leftovers might make your life easier."

Shelly, Mrs. Walsh, and my sister go about setting out the food on the table and arranging plates. Phoebe keeps up a run of questions, never letting a silence stretch.

Meanwhile, I face Harper. "Full house."

My stuntwoman smiles. "At least I won't be bored tonight."

"I'm uninteresting, am I?" My fingers lace with hers, fiddling with the callous digits. "You wound a man."

"Fuck off," she mutters with a smirk, and I chuckle.

"Getting to the table"—I tilt my chin in the direction of the group—"do you want the wheelchair, crutch, or to be romantically carried in my impressively strong arms?"

"Why do I feel like you have a preference?" She smirks, but then her lips tighten. "I need more practice on the crutch. Help me up?"

Gently hugging Harper under the arms, I lift her until she's balanced on her uninjured leg. She grasps my arm for balance while slipping the crutch under her armpit.

"Got it." Her short trip from the couch to the kitchen table isn't graceful, but she manages it with only a few mild curses.

"Have you considered a motorized chair?" Shelly asks, piling tacos on Harper's plate.

My woman grimaces. "They're expensive. And this isn't a long-term thing. Besides, I *want* to move. If I sit all day, I'm going to murder someone. Probably Fred because he's always within reach."

"She's doing great." Mrs. Walsh leans over to clasp Harper's arm in a comforting embrace that has me smiling at my plate. "She and I are managing everything that comes along."

My expression freezes, but I force my face to relax and not react to being excluded.

"And Fred takes the night shift. Remind me to punch your time card," Harper adds, her right hand squeezing my thigh under the table.

Normally, I'd make a joke about putting in overtime to get a bonus, but I've been trying to tone down my outrageousness when Mrs. Walsh is around.

I know she'd rather I spend the nights at my own place. That she'd be more comfortable if I wasn't around.

And I get it.

But no matter how guilty I feel about the discomfort I cause Harper's mom, I can't leave when the woman I love wants me close.

For however long that lasts.

CHAPTER 39

HARPER

I wait until Fred and I are alone in my bedroom to ask the question that's been bothering me for weeks now.

"What's up with you and my mom?"

Tonight, at dinner, I couldn't explain it away anymore. Something about Phoebe and Shelly being here made the tension visible to me. There were moments I swear the other two woman glanced between my two caretakers with curious expressions. They saw it too. I know they did.

But I don't want to ask them. I want Fred to tell me. To be honest and open with me.

Fred stares at me from beside the bed, where he was in the process of arranging the covers so I can slip in easier with my casts. His strong fingers dig into the soft blanket, but he lets a smirk tug up the corner of his mouth.

"You trying to set me up? Sorry, I've already got my eye on a snarky stuntwoman."

"Ha-ha." My voice stays deadpan. I'm not looking to joke about this. But is it possible to get a straight answer out of Fred? "Seriously.

You two act like you think the other is carrying a bomb. What's going on?"

His attention goes to his hands, as if the bedcovers were more important than this conversation.

"You guessed it. We're playing bomb chicken. She's going to crack; I know it."

"Fred," I snap.

"Harper." He shoots me his silly smile, but he doesn't meet my eyes.

And I know I'm right. He's not telling me something.

Hell, that hurts.

Maybe another time, I'd fight and push and demand he fess up. Put him in a headlock until he relented.

But tonight, I … can't.

What he said last night, what he did, broke something open inside me, and I feel like my heart is sitting on the outside of my rib cage, ready to be torn to shreds with the slightest wrong touch.

Fred took away my shields, and now, he's got his up.

"Fine," I mutter and hobble my way down the hall and into the bathroom with my crutch, managing to close the door behind me.

I twist the lock, needing a moment to myself.

When I plop down on the closed toilet lid, my leg cast knocks against my cheap shelf of towels, sending a sharp ache through my leg, which still hurts less than the one in my chest.

"Shit," I hiss, watching the rolls of terry cloth topple to the floor, unrolling in a mess I won't be able to fix on my own.

Looks a lot like my life.

"Harper?" Fred calls out, close to the door.

"I'm fine!"

I'm not fine, but apparently, we're lying to each other tonight.

All I want to know is what's up with the tension between him and my mom. At first, I thought I was imagining it, but after these past few weeks, the way they stiffen up around each other is blatantly obvious.

But he won't tell me.

It feels like the beginning of the end.

Maybe Fred loves me, like he claimed.

But last night wasn't the first time Fred Sullivan said those words to me.

That day in the airport, when I was flying out of his life, Fred growled the sentiment, as if his love would somehow convince me to stay. And I wanted to, more than anything. But I didn't have control of my life back then, so I left.

And his love didn't last.

This won't either.

Saying *I love you* and actually *loving* a person—sharing all of yourself with them—are different things.

Maybe it's selfish to expect Fred to divulge his secrets. But he's the one bringing love into this. He's the one who left me without a word all those years ago and still hasn't told me why.

My body hurts, my heart aches, and once again, I realize I *still* haven't forgiven him.

My eyes feel swollen with misery, and tears spill down my cheeks.

Don't fall in love with him. He'll only hurt you in the end.

But, damn it, I don't think I can help myself.

"Harper?" Fred calls to me again, and the doorknob rattles.

"Just give me a minute." I choke on the words.

Maybe I should tell him to go. Leave now before I rely on him so much that I'm permanently damaged when he decides caring for a woman whose life is falling apart is too serious for him. When his fleeting love runs its course. When whatever secrets he's keeping from me drive him away again.

"Are you crying?" There's no humor or teasing in his voice now. The knob twists harder this time.

"The door is locked," I snap. "Stop trying to come in."

Give me some space to break down without your sweet smiles and silly jokes to convince me there's nothing to worry about, I want to say.

"I'm sorry." The barrier muffles his response. "Just ... let me know if you need me."

I do. Damn it, I do. But that's the whole problem.

Furious, I glare at my injured half. Before the accident, I had control over this. I could keep my distance from Fred. He was close, but not too close.

Now, he's everywhere.

"I'm still strong," I mutter, low enough that I'm only speaking to myself. "I'm still me, with or without him."

To prove this, I roughly swipe the tears from my face and decide I'm going to get through my nightly routine on my own. And then I'm going to leave this bathroom and tell Fred he can start sleeping at his apartment again.

But when I move to stand up, everything goes wrong.

CHAPTER 40

HARPER

My cast catches on the towel rack, my precarious balance goes wonky, and the next thing I know, I'm toppling to the floor, barely managing to get my good side under me before I hit the tiles.

"Fuck!" The word is part-shout, part-growl, but mostly sob.

Was I not miserable enough? The universe decided I needed to sink deeper into a pathetic state by firmly wedging my broken body between the bathtub and the toilet?

Damn past Harper for not cleaning these corners thoroughly.

I can already feel a cobweb in my hair. Add that to the new bruises and overall humiliation, and this might be one of the lowest moments of my life.

"Harper!" Fred's voice rises with anxiety. He must have heard my shout. "Please let me in."

"I can't," I moan, trying—unsuccessfully—to lever myself off the floor.

"You can. I won't ask any questions or even talk. Please, just let me in."

"No, I mean, I literally fucking cannot let you in because I'm stuck under the goddamn toilet!" Anger and panic and embarrassment turn my voice shrill, and Fred doesn't deserve this version of me, but it's the only one there is at the moment.

A pause.

"Are you clear of the door?" he calls out.

Oh no. "Why?"

"I'm going to break it down."

"Don't you dare break my door, Fred Sullivan!" But what else do I expect him to do? It's not like this is something that will get better with time.

When he doesn't respond, I brace for the crack of wood.

Nothing happens after the count of ten, and I relax. But then I panic all over again because, now, I'm sure Fred has peaced out, tired of dealing with my cranky ass. Soon, Mom will check on me, realize what's wrong, and call the fire department, and *they'll* break down the bathroom door. Why couldn't I have just let Fred do it?

"Oh shit. Hang on, Harper." Fred's voice sounds as clear as if he were standing in the room.

Have I been fucking a ghost who can walk through walls?

"How the hell did you get in here?" I ask the porcelain side of my tub, unable to see any more of the room.

"I'm not in yet. I'm at the window." He grunts, and I hear a shuffle.

The bathroom window is a small, frosted rectangle of glass set high in the wall. In theory, it's large enough for someone to fit through, but I doubt the maneuver is easy.

"Forget what I said," I tell him. "You can break down the door."

"No need. Already halfway in."

There's a clatter and an oof, and then the next thing I know, strong hands slip under my torso and shoulder.

Oh-so carefully, Fred lifts me, freeing my body from the wedged position that felt like a prison moments ago.

The relief, and humiliation, and lingering devastation all crash down my throat, forcing out a pathetic wail.

Which is how I end up sobbing in Fred's lap as he cradles me against his chest, rocking us both while he sits perched on the toilet seat.

"Let it out. That's good," he murmurs, hand rubbing a soothing circle on my back. "It's all going to be okay."

"No, it isn't." I hiccup, unable to stifle my fears when I'm in pain and I have a clear view of this man walking out of my life.

"What's wrong? Tell me, please."

There, in his voice, I pick up a hint of panic. As if he's just as afraid as I am.

"Why can't you tell me?" I throw back at him. "I know something is off between you and my mom. But you just shrug. And you joke. And you avoid my eyes. Just tell me. *Please*."

Now, with tears streaming down my cheeks, puffing my face into a mess, I stare into his hazel eyes and watch as pain clouds there.

"Harper …"

"Please, Fred. Please."

He grimaces, and then with a world-weary sigh, he answers, "I expect your mom can't look at me because I'm the reason her husband is dead."

All the air leaves the bathroom at once, and I choke on a gasp, my tears cut off at the complete absurdity of the statement.

"You're fucking with me," I manage after a moment.

Fred ducks his head, but not before I see the torment in his eyes.

"What the hell are you talking about?" I say. "You weren't even in the car with them!"

"But I'm the reason they were going through that intersection." Fred's face is pure devastation as the confession spills out of him. "They were on their way to pick *me* up. From goddamn detention. I just couldn't keep my mouth shut in Mr. Hayfield's class that day. I knew he was strict, but I was bored, so I kept wandering around the room and throwing out jokes, and he got tired of it and gave me detention. Your dad went to the hardware store with mine, and then they were going to swing by the school to pick me up. Because my selfish fuckup ass was in trouble. Again. They never would've been on that road if I'd just kept my mouth shut and stayed in my seat in class. And now, they're gone because of *me*. My dad's gone. Your dad is gone. The love of your mother's life—" He stumbles over his words. "Hell, I don't know how you can even be in the same room as me."

Raw emotion fills his twisted logic, contorting his handsome face.

This might be the most honest he's ever been with me. Maybe anyone.

Oh, Fred.

More than a decade.

He's thought this for more than a third of his life.

Taken the blame for our fathers' deaths on his shoulders, silently letting the weight of guilt crush him.

"It wasn't your fault."

He doesn't respond.

Cradling Fred's chin in my hand, I force his eyes to meet mine. "They went to the hardware store to get a light fixture for my bedroom. Was it my fault?"

Fred's eyes widen. "No. Shit, Harper, that's not—"

"You didn't call your mom to pick you up because she always worked late, right? Was it her fault?"

His lips tighten, and—sucky as it is—seeing his self-loathing does wonders to clear up my own anxiety. I lean in to press a gentle kiss against his firm mouth.

"I got detention three times that same year. We were kids. We messed up. But it wasn't your fault that some random, shitty thing happened. You weren't the guy who fell asleep behind the wheel and ran the red light. There were a thousand small decisions our dads made that day that put them in that intersection at the worst time. You can't predict stuff like that. You did nothing wrong, Fred. Nothing at all. And if my mom blames you for something, then *she's* in the wrong. But I never have and never will."

"I always seem to fuck things up, whether I'm trying or not. I never want to be the reason you're hurting," he rasps. "If I were a better man, I'd tell you it's best to leave me in the past. But I can't let you go, Harper."

You did once, I almost tell him. But I hold the words back when I realize how counter they go to what I just claimed.

He was a kid then. He messed up.
"Don't let me go," I say instead. "If you do, that's when I hurt."

CHAPTER 41

FRED

I've been leaving Harper to go to work every morning for close to three weeks now, and it still sucks every single time. The past few days more than the rest after the talk we had in the bathroom.

Also known as the horrible fucking day that I made the woman I love cry.

I try to focus on the forgiving words that she said to me. Logically, her points made sense. I wouldn't blame anyone else for what happened to our dads. But it's still hard to separate what I did and what happened to them. Maybe with time though, I could start to feel the way that she does about it. Maybe in time, it won't weigh so heavy on me.

"It's weird, being on set without Harper." Shelly walks beside me as we head back to her trailer.

Production has continued, even with my stuntwoman laid up for the foreseeable future. There's another woman who's taking her place, and even though she seems perfectly nice and good at her job, the sight of her doing the work that Harper should be doing gives me a sick twist in my stomach. Harper has made comments that let me know she's worried about her career and the future. But I also know it's not my place to talk to Shelly about her and Harper's business relationship.

Which is why it eases a touch of worry in me to hear Shelly say what she just did.

"Harper misses it too. She appreciated you coming by the other day. She's getting antsy in her house. If I don't show up to work one morning, it might be because she murdered me." I offer the actress a rueful smile. "But a very loving murder."

Shelly gives a sad chuckle and leans against the side of her trailer. We've established a series of steps when entering a new place. I scan the area outside to make sure that no unsavory character is lingering around, which is what I do now. Coast is clear. Then, it's my job to go into the trailer and give that a once-over before Shelly comes inside.

Maybe it's over the top, but even months into our working relationship, Shelly still agrees the extra steps give her a needed comfort. And I am happy to take all the extra measures to make her feel safer.

"Let me take a look. Be right back."

The trailer door has a lock on it that Shelly sticks her key in and twists before stepping back. Even though I've been doing this for weeks now, I try to treat every time as if it were the first and not get complacent.

Which is why I don't let my surprise show when I enter the bedroom section of the trailer and find a man sitting on the mattress, looking disheveled.

Maybe the unkempt appearance is how he normally looks, or maybe it's because he climbed through what seems to be the smashed open window in the back of the trailer. Either way, I wouldn't care if he were a clean-cut kind of fellow.

He's not supposed to be here.

"Hey, buddy," I greet him, as if there were nothing wrong with this situation.

There's something about this person that gives me a sense he's not completely with it. One hint might be that he broke into a trailer that's not his. But he also doesn't immediately threaten me or demand access to expensive goods. The guy doesn't come off as a robber. He just stares at me, looking both perplexed and annoyed.

Deescalate the situation. Try to keep violence off the table if it's not already there.

With Shelly outside, I have options.

I keep my voice friendly. "I think you might have gotten turned around. This is a private trailer."

Even if this is a confused individual who didn't mean to be here or who doesn't mean Shelly any harm other than showing up in her life in a very invasive way, I still rest my hand on my hip, close to the holster tucked in the back of my pants.

"Where is she?" he says in a perturbed voice.

"Fred?" Shelly asks from the open doorway, thankfully not coming inside.

The guy's face fills with ecstasy. "My Shelly," he whispers.

Okay, yeah, we definitely have a fan who has committed way too much to this parasocial relationship.

"Just having a chat," I call out to my client. "Why don't you stay outside?"

I hear the sound of footsteps pounding the pavement as Shelly runs away. On her way to the closest security station, just like we planned if I ever told her I was chatting with someone.

Good girl.

The man's face crumples. "Did she leave?"

"She's got a busy day," I explain, keeping my voice friendly. "Probably couldn't hang around. Why don't we go out to the set, and we can see if we can find her?"

Once we're out of the close quarters, I'll have more room to overpower the man, or the studio security can take over if Shelly gets them here fast enough.

The guy stares at me, his brow scrunched, as if deep in thought. I don't know what's going through his head. How many of his thoughts are rational. I'm just hoping his drive is to get to Shelly and my promise to do that can keep him complacent enough to get us both out of here without any injuries.

"I've got access to this whole set," I tell him. "Anywhere you want to go, I can take you there."

Reluctantly, he nods and stands from the bed. Keeping my eyes on him, I back up through the trailer, my muscles relaxed, face smiling.

"Let's head on out." I wave toward the open door.

The man nods and sets his foot on the first step.

Just then, two security guards come sprinting around the corner. The sight of the burly men pounding toward him spooks the guy, and he whirls my way. I'm set to grab him.

The knife he slips from his pocket is unexpected.

Silver flashes, and I block his wild swing at my chest, shoving his arm to the side. This close, I don't want to reach for my gun, so I concentrate on his hand. He seems more intent on getting away from security than going after me, but I'm in the way.

He throws himself at me, and I use my larger size to wrap him in a crushing hold that pins his arms to his sides. I manage to hold him like that until reinforcements climb into the trailer and pull the guy away from me, kicking his knife out of reach and zip-tying his hands behind his back as he cries out for Shelly.

The scene is scary, and sad, and hard to concentrate on when I realize there's an aching burn in my side.

And that's when I spy the red stain growing on the carpet beneath me.

CHAPTER 42

HARPER

"I will murder this spoon, this soup, and the entire food pyramid!" I shout the threats at my kitchen table, my seething glare directed at the dribble of chicken and noodles down the front of what was—only moments ago—a clean shirt.

"You're not supposed to kill it. You're supposed to eat it." My mother tsks from the stovetop, where she fills a bowl with her own lunch.

"Why did I have to break my left hand? If I were a righty, I wouldn't be such a mess." I bemoan one more of the tiny issues that comes with half my body being out of commission.

"Think of this as a learning experience," she offers. "Training or something like that."

"Stop trying to make me feel better," I grumble. "I want to complain. I want to soak in my surliness."

"Fred might find that cute, but I'm not here to let you mope. Try again, and I'll help you change after we eat."

Scowling at my soup, I attempt another mouthful, this time managing to get most of it past my lips. I also try to forget how Fred fed me ice cream last night. He had a fun time telling me to open the tunnel for the train to pass through. Then to prepare the runway for the plane to make a landing.

Then to open the vagina for the frozen penis to penetrate.

I refused to open my mouth for that last one, so he smeared the ice cream on my lips and licked it off.

Then, we had slow, *I think my heart might burst from intense eye contact* sex. Again.

As much as I loathe being out of commission, I'm finding it surprisingly bearable to be babied by Fred. I think it's because I know the moment I have full use of all my limbs, he won't try to keep coddling me. Fred is giving me what I need in the moment. He's good at that.

When my bowl is empty, I've only spilled two more spoonfuls on myself. The yellow stains on my Red Cross Halloween Blood Drive T-shirt mock me.

"I'm going to have to do another load of laundry." Feels like I just did one yesterday. "Maybe I should just live in a bra."

Problem is, I prefer sports bras, but I don't have any with clasps, so they're a bitch to get on over the cast. If I wasn't so worried about my savings account dwindling, I'd go online and order some new, easy-to-wear clothes.

"I was planning on doing a load today. I can put yours in with mine." My mom picks up my bowl and heads to the sink.

I sigh through gritted teeth. I love her—so much—and am eternally grateful that she flew all this way to help take care of me. But when Fred does it, he makes everything fun. When my mom does, I feel like she's trying to tuck me back into the crib as she reorganizes my life.

She's already shifted things around in my apartment. And not in the *let's put them on a lower shelf to make it easier for Harper to reach* way. She alphabetized my bookshelf even though I preferred the colorful disarray. She relocated plates and cups in my cabinets, so even when I *do* manage to heave myself up to them, I can't find what I'm looking for before my balance starts to tilt. She even moved pictures and paintings around on my walls to *better fit the room* despite me specifically asking her not to.

If I wasn't so worried about getting stuck between the tub and the toilet again, I might start gently nudging Mom toward booking a flight back to Ireland.

Still, while she's here, I'm going to attempt to show her I'm not helpless despite what my food-spattered appearance might convey.

"That's okay. I've got it. I think Fred's got a pile in our room I can toss in with mine." I reach for my crutch, determined to lever myself up all on my own.

Mom sets the now-clean bowls in the drainer, then faces me as she dries her hands with a dish towel.

"*Our* room, is it?" Her focus stays on her hands. "He still has his own place, doesn't he?"

And here it is again. The tension that hovers between the two of them.

Could Fred be right? Does my mom truly blame him for Dad's death?

I know for a fact that my father never would have. The only person at fault was the truck driver who nodded off behind the wheel and ran a red light at exactly the wrong time.

"Yeah," I say, "he has his own place. But he's been sleeping here for a month now."

Shrugging, I grip my crutch with my good hand. Luckily, all the physical fitness I had under my belt before the accident comes in handy. Moving around without the help of one side of my body is hard, but not impossible.

"If you need a break from him, I can help you at night," Mom says.

I snort and slide to the edge of my seat. "More like *he* would need a break from *me*."

The guy is a saint for wearing a smile through all my surliness.

"It's just," she continues, a determined note in her voice, "I understand … how hard it must be. To spend so much time around him."

I pause before easing myself out of my seat, her cryptic words starting up an ominous churning in my gut.

"Fred is a good man." The description sounds cold. Inadequate. *A good man?* More like kind, funny, sweet, sexy, handsome, caring, infuriating in all the best ways.

"I know." Mom steps toward me, a concerned smile on her lips as wrinkles form at the tight corners of her green eyes. "But being around him … it brings up all those memories. You shouldn't put yourself through that. You don't need to. Best leave him in the past."

My fingers go numb.

Then my hands.

Wrists next. Arms, shoulders, chest, legs, neck, head.

The only bit of me with feeling is my heart.

And it hurts.

"Best leave it in the past," she said.

"Best to leave me in the past." The words sounded weird on Fred's lips, and I know why now. They weren't his.

"What did you do?" I rasp.

Maggie Walsh flinches, shock showing at the sudden venom in my voice.

But I can't help it. This is too important. Too devastating.

"Wh-what do you mean?"

"Why did Fred say almost *exactly* what you just did? *Best leave him in the past.* When did you say that to him? Why?"

My mother's face goes white as she clutches the dish towel against her chest, as if she needs to protect herself.

"Dear—"

"Tell me," I growl. "Tell me what you did."

Her eyes water, and her lower lip trembles. "It was only … you were so heartbroken. Crying every time he called."

Oh God. Oh my fucking God.

"We moved to get away from all that," she says, voice desperate. "To try and leave the sadness behind. But you wouldn't let go. Not when he kept calling."

The cast on my arm must have grown like a living thing, encasing my chest, to the point where my rib cage can't expand. I can't breathe.

"What did you do?" I wheeze the question without air.

"I only talked to him. Just a short call."

As if a small number of words she spoke to him couldn't have devastated a grieving boy.

"What did you *say* to him?" My throat burns with unshed tears.

Mom twists the towel in her fingers, staring at the faded kitchen tiles beneath her feet.

"I told him the truth," she confesses. "How you cried when he called. And you couldn't make a life in Ireland if he clung to you. If he kept bringing up bad memories. I said … it was best to leave it all in the past. To leave"—she chokes on her words now—"him there as well."

I couldn't stand now if I tried, the world reeling and tilting, set off-balance by the betrayal.

My mother took my best friend from me. Shoved him away with her innocently cruel words.

I've been thrown through a glass window, bucked off a horse, hell, even dragged along asphalt by a motorcycle.

This hurts worse.

"How could you say that to him? How could you do that to *me*?" I sob. "Fred was the only thing keeping me from drowning. I couldn't breathe without him!" I'm struggling to breathe now, just thinking about that time in my life. "Do you know what I did to cope when he stopped talking to me?"

The drugs. The fights. Hooking up with random people just to feel like I wasn't alone for a few moments.

"Harper …" Her eyes go wide, horrified.

She doesn't know. I kept it from her. And I always thought I was a shitty actor, but I guess I finally managed to pull off the role of not-emotionally-devastated daughter pretty well.

Fury surges through my body as I stagger to my one good foot, hand braced on my kitchen table.

"Maybe that was what *you* needed to deal with Dad's death—to forget everything and everyone who knew him. But it wasn't what *I* needed. You had no right to push Fred away from me. You can't do that shit to someone you love!"

My heart is as messed up as my body, and I want to pace and rage, but I can barely stand on my own. The restriction only increases my furious frustration.

Grief has me desperate for an outlet. I hobble-hop out of the kitchen.

"You can't *do* that, Mom. Damn it!" I stumble into a neatly organized shelf. "And you can't fucking rearrange the books." I start ripping titles off the shelf, tossing them to the floor in a crash and tear of damaged pages. "And you can't put the cups in the cabinet to the left of the refrigerator." A mountain of battered books forms at my feet, jostling my cast and threatening to trip me if I try to move again. I keep tugging and tossing. "And you can't put the coffee table armadillo on the bathroom shelf. It's not a fucking *bathroom* armadillo!"

I don't even know what I'm saying anymore. All I know is, the person I love most in the world did something horrible to me, and I want to yell and rage and make her feel horrible too.

But I also don't because I love her and she's all I have left.

It's just that I can't figure out how to make my insides stop hurting.

So, I throw more alphabetically organized books on the floor as tears drip down my face.

"Harper!"

My mom's sharp shout has me jerking around and grabbing hold of the now-empty shelf to keep from slipping and falling onto the evidence of my devastation.

She stands just outside the perimeter of destruction, arm reaching toward me, my phone in her hand.

I get the sense she's said my name more than once.

"They keep calling," she says, and I don't understand until I see all the notifications on my screen. Multiple missed calls and texts from Shelly. Same with Phoebe.

Speaking of the woman, her name lights my screen up again.

I snatch the phone and answer, fighting off another wave of dread.

"Harper. Finally." The normally cheerful woman's voice is tight with panic. "Fred's in the hospital."

CHAPTER 43

FRED

My side throbs and burns in waves that match my pulse. Every beat of my heart attempts to push blood through skin that used to be connected fine, but now, there's a long gouge with a neat row of stitches. I grimace as I try to sit up on the bed.

"Careful. You don't want to tear out the doctor's hard work," a nurse scolds me as she strolls into the room.

"I feel great." I offer my most charming smile. "I'm ready to run a marathon."

The nurse frowns.

"But I won't," I assure her. "Promise. Are my pants here somewhere?"

They put me in a blue gown that opens in all the weird places and doesn't have pockets, which means I don't have my stuff. I want my phone. I need to check on Shelly and let Harper know what happened, so she's not worried when I don't show up at her place after work.

"Remember, sir, we had to cut your clothes off when you were admitted. The doctors needed a clear view of your wound."

The nurse checks my machines, and I try to work through what she said. Which is more difficult than it should be. My mind feels like it's running on a delay, and I struggle to fill in gaps of my day.

"Am I on something?"

"You were given a painkiller," she explains. "And the anesthesia from your surgery is still wearing off."

"I was in *surgery*?" Now, the weird gown makes more sense. And why there are stitches in my side even though I don't recall getting a needle stuck in me.

She offers me a small smile a babysitter would give her charge. "Yes, sir. The knife cut into one of your muscles. When your head clears a bit more, the doctor will explain everything."

"I need my phone." *Does Harper know I was in surgery?*

"Okay. Lie still. I'll find your phone for you."

"It was in my pants."

"All right, I'll—"

A shout from outside my room cuts her off.

"I don't want a fucking wheelchair!"

The familiar voice cursing brings a grin to my face. Then, I frown.

"Why's Harper in the hospital?" I ask. "I took her home weeks ago."

The nurse glances between me and the open doorway, where a furious, flushed stuntwoman appears, clutching tight to a crutch.

"Fred!" she wails as she does an awkward jump-shuffle toward me.

"Hey." I try to sit up again, but my arms are too loose to manage the maneuver, and my side aches fiercely when I tense my stomach. "Ow."

"Don't move," the nurse tells me in a commanding voice. "And you"—she points at Harper—"he's doing fine. Let me get you a chair." The woman arranges a seat next to my bed and helps Harper settle into it. "The anesthesia is working its way out of his system, so don't expect to have a coherent conversation for a bit. I'll be back around to check on you."

The nurse disappears, but I don't notice much other than Harper looking at me like I'm something she needs.

"Oh God." She clutches my hand with the one of hers that's not in a cast. "What were you thinking?"

"You're wearing one of my shirts."

It's the blue one, covered in tropical fish. My eyes trace over the colorful pattern until I lose track and return to Harper's face. Her eyes are puffy, her pale cheeks blotchy.

Oh shit. She's been crying.

"Hey." I squeeze her hand. "Don't be sad. The shirt looks good on you."

Harper half-laughs, half-sobs, pressing my knuckles against her forehead. She's so warm, and I realize how cold my skin is. I shiver.

"I love you."

"I love you," I say back to her.

Back to her.

Wait.

She said it first.

"Hold up. You love me?"

"Yes. And it's all your fault," she growls at me, even as she smiles, and tears run down her face.

"Wait. Wait, wait, wait." I shake my head, trying to clear the fog from my brain. "I'm on drugs, Harper! Why are you telling me while I'm on drugs? Quick"—I poke her cheek—"record it. So I'll remember later."

The gorgeous love of my life kisses my palm as she laughs. "Does voice mail count? Because I left you one along the lines of, 'I love you, you fucking asshole. If you die before I can tell you, I'll fucking carve it into your gravestone and then resurrect you as a ghost and fucking kill you again.' Or something like that."

"Oh good." I love watching the way her teeth dig into her lip whenever she says *fuck*. "Yeah, I'll save that with the others."

"What others?" She rubs her cheek against my hand.

"The other messages. That you left when you were in Ireland."

"You … you saved those?" Her lashes are wet with tears I want to kiss away, but I can't sit up, damn it. "All this time?"

"I've loved you," I explain. "All this time."

She presses another kiss to my palm. "I know this isn't the moment.

Because you're on drugs. But when you're sober, we're going to talk about what my mom said to you. She was wrong, you know. I'm not better off without you. Never have been."

Harper smiles at me, her nose wrinkling and chafed red.

"You're *so* hot," I tell her.

And she busts out laughing, which is better than any painkiller this hospital could give me.

CHAPTER 44

FRED

Eventually, my mind recalibrates, and I can appreciate what Harper said to me, no matter how pissed off her tone was when she spoke those beautiful three words.

Also, I'm able to feel thoroughly guilty because she dragged her broken butt across town just to make sure I wasn't dead or dying.

Note to self: tell someone to text Harper I'm alive if I'm ever in a hospital situation again.

Add Phoebe and Mom to that list.

"Stabbed!" My sister huffs, not for the first time, as she glares at me through the phone screen. "Who gets *stabbed*?"

I raise my hand, and she rolls her eyes.

"Do they give you time off work?" my mom asks, tone worried.

Ah, the American work ethic. Unless you're dead, you'd better show up on Monday.

"Yeah, Mom. I get leave during my recovery period."

"He'll be hanging out with me."

Harper hobbles her way into the frame, and I try not to wince when she jostles my shoulder, which shifts all of me, which has my side screaming.

"Shit, sorry."

"S'okay," I gasp.

"You two are a mess," Phoebe informs us.

"But we're a mess together," Harper says, grinning wide at the other two women in my life.

"And Harper told me she loves me. But she did it while I was on drugs," I add, just to hear her grumble of chagrin.

A throat clearing at the doorway to my hospital room has us both glancing up. At the sight of Mrs. Walsh, I automatically try to sit higher in my seat, which leads to another wince of pain.

"Stop hurting yourself," Harper scolds and scowls at me as she tries to fluff my pillow with one hand.

"You need to sit down," I throw back at her, not liking all the hopping around she's been doing. I half-expect her to rip off that leg cast and start running through the hospital on a broken bone.

"You sound like an old married couple," Phoebe chimes in.

"I'll call you later. Love you. Bye." I rush them off the phone, spying the discomfort on Mrs. Walsh's face and recalling another piece of information Harper brought up when I was under the influence.

She knows why I ghosted her.

"Mom." Harper's greeting is stiff. Defensive, as if she's readying for an attack.

"I'm glad to hear you're doing better." The woman from my childhood offers me a smile full of regret. She takes a step closer. "I hoped I could say something. Apologize."

"You don't need to," I tell her.

In the end, the decisions and mistakes I made were mine.

"I do though." Maggie Walsh stands at the foot of my bed and holds my stare with a set of green eyes that are much like her daughter's. "Saying what I did to you all those years ago, that was unfair. I don't blame you for what happened. I never meant for you to think that. It's only … eleven years later, and the life I had here with Harper's father … it still hurts to think about. And you were tied up in that life. I thought it would hurt less if everyone went their separate ways. Maybe ... I still think that way." She swallows. "But I shouldn't have made that choice for Harper. For you and Harper. And I'm glad you two found your way back to one another."

Never knew a stint in a hospital bed would bring on so many emotional conversations. And no matter what Mrs. Walsh thinks, it was still my decision to cut off contact with her daughter.

Remembering that time now, I think I was looking for a way to punish myself. To pay penance in the role I took in our fathers' deaths. Giving up Harper was the highest price I could imagine. The worst punishment possible.

But I'm not looking to pay for past mistakes anymore.

"Thank you for saying that," I say. "It means a lot."

Mrs. Walsh's smile is tight but seems more genuine than the ones she's managed to direct my way these past few weeks.

I never wanted Harper to find out what her mother had said to me because I knew what could happen. Harper's body is tense where she sits beside my bed, and she wears a lost, betrayed look in her eyes as she avoids her mother's searching gaze.

"Harper—" Maggie starts.

She cuts her off, "I'm going to need time, Mom. It wasn't just back then. You've been pushing me away from Fred *now*. When you've seen us together. Seen how amazing he is." Her ponytail swishes against her shoulders as her head shakes. "I just ... I need time."

"Of course." The woman's body droops. "I'll make my way back to your house then. And you call me when you need a ride home."

When she's gone, Harper sags in her chair and throws me a hopeless glance. "I don't know what to do. I love her, but I'm so angry with her."

Carefully, I extend my hand, and she twines our fingers together.

"You've got time to figure it out." I run a thumb over her knuckles. "And I'm here to listen and help. And to come up with inappropriate ideas that will make you want to headbutt me."

Harper lets out a damp chuckle and presses her lips to my knuckles.

"That's all I could ever ask for."

CHAPTER 45

HARPER

"Let's go to the mountains."

Fred and I sit on the couch in my house and stare at Shelly as the world-famous actress paces in front of us. My casted leg rests on Fred's lap, and he's wearing only a pair of sweatpants, leaving his bandaged side on display.

We're each a mess, but we're a mess together, which somehow feels perfect.

"Uh, sorry, Shells," I say and tap my knuckles on my plastered leg. "I'm not really up for a hike."

She shakes her head. "Hear me out. I found a house in the mountains I want to rent. Phoebe was telling me about your trip last year, and it sounded so … relaxing." Ever since the group dinner at my house, Shelly and Phoebe have become texting buddies. "I need something like that in my life. And I think you two do too."

My mind goes back to that trip. Before my abrupt departure, it was lovely.

But it was also full of hiking and climbing and a few more movements I can't exactly manage at the moment.

As if hearing my thoughts, Shelly adds, "The house has a bedroom on the ground floor and beautiful views, and I'd make sure the fridge is fully stocked. There's a hospital not too far, in case you need to check in. But I thought we could just, you know, get away while you all heal."

Fred and I share a glance.

Something is up with her. I convey with a frown.

Want to help? says his raised brow.

Duh. I roll my eyes.

Mountains sound cool. He smirks.

"What about *House of the Huntress*? The rest of the season?" I ask.

Fred and I might be out of commission, but Shelly is still in working order and expected to film a TV show.

"I have another week, and then my scenes are done." Her hands clench and release at her sides.

Clench and release.

Clench and release.

The playful note left over from my silent communication with Fred evaporates when I think about Shelly on set without us.

The stalker fan who broke into her trailer was apprehended and is in a psychiatric facility. But this is the second violent event Shelly has been at the center of in barely over a year.

Looking at her now—*really* studying her—I can pick out the frayed edges of her normal reserve.

Fred and I might require physical healing, but Shelly has some mental recovery that needs to take place.

"How is Manuel working out for you?" Fred asks, probably picking up on the same nervous energy that I am.

"Oh." Shelly smooths her hands over her thighs. "Great. Good. Really capable."

I twist my lips to keep from grimacing. Shelly must still see something on my face.

"He's fine," she insists. "Really. He's just ... Roman called to brief me ... he's former military. And I said that's okay."

But it's not okay. Shelly might be safe from another attack, but now, she's dealing with internal dangers. Scars from her past.

"Doctors said I'll be good to return to work in a few weeks," Fred offers.

"That's great. I ... that will be great." Shelly settles on the coffee table, facing us. "But I think we could all use a break. And I don't want to take another job before you're better, Harper."

Her thoughtfulness warms my heart.

"I'm all for a change of scenery, Shells. But I'm going to be out for a while longer than Fred. Don't wait on me." This hurts to say and do, but she shouldn't sideline herself for me. "There are lots of great stuntwomen out there."

Shelly's already shaking her head, blonde hair brushing her cheeks.

"But you're *my* stuntwoman. I have in my contract that you have to be offered the job before anyone else, and I don't plan on changing that unless you leave the business."

"You what?" *I'm in her contract?*

Shelly reaches out and takes my uninjured hand. "I've told you a little about my past, but not everything. I trust you, Harper. You don't know how much that means to me. It's the most important thing."

If I could hug her without five minutes of shuffling and rearranging, I would.

"For what it's worth, I trust you too." My voice is wobbly, and I blame my vulnerable state. "So, the mountains, huh?"

A grin splits her face. "Fred said you liked them." She glances to the man at my side.

He rubs my bare shin but keeps his focus on Shelly. "You should still take protection out there. Harper and I won't be much help if someone were to bother you."

Some of her joy falters, but she nods. "I'll talk to Roman."

Fred's hand on my leg pauses, and a slow smile unfurls on his sexy mouth that promises sneaky business. "You know, I think Roman has been putting in a lot of overtime. He might need a mountain vacation too."

Shelly straightens, face thoughtful. "There's enough room. A few extra bedrooms. Do you want me to invite him?"

"Why not?" Fred's question is casual, but I see a glimpse of his sister's plotting ways in the gleam of his hazel eyes. "A hobbled stuntwoman, a stabbed bodyguard, and a sought-after actress obviously need an overworked grump. Sounds like a complete set to me." Fred chuckles.

Shelly glances my way.

I don't know exactly what my man is up to, but I believe Fred has only good intentions.

I shrug. "Go for it. Not many people can put up with twenty-four/seven Fred. Might be good to have someone we can pawn him off on."

"Exactly," he agrees.

"Okay." Shelly stands, and the cloud of anxiety she entered my house with seems to have thinned. Though not evaporated completely. "Thank you."

"Damn," I grumble.

They both look at me, and I can feel the blush heat my cheeks.

"What's up?" Fred asks.

"Nothing. Just … I realized I won't be able to go in the hot tub. Assuming there is one."

"There is," Shelly offers. "Sorry."

My gaze clashes with Fred's heated one, and I know he's remembering our last time, like I am.

He wears a rueful grin. "I guess we can comfort ourselves, knowing at least we won't be bear soup."

EPILOGUE

FRED

"I say this with all the love in my heart"—I turn my head to address Harper over my shoulder, where she's riding my back—"but I have to put you down because you're too heavy."

Harper fists her fingers in the short hairs at the base of my neck, tugging my head back so she can give me a proper glare. "Seriously?"

"Seriously." I try to keep a straight face and not groan in ecstasy at the way she manhandles me. "You're, like, pure muscle. Do you know how dense that shit is? Look at me. I'm sweating."

She's fighting a smile. I know it by the way she sucks her lower lip into her mouth and chews on the tender skin.

Mmm. I want to do that.

She lets go of her lip and my hair at the same time. "You would make a terrible Prince Charming. The absolute worst. Dropping princesses in the wilderness left and right. Daring rescues only half-complete."

"I never said I was *abandoning* you," I argue. "Just taking a short breather. A quick break, so I can stare at you adoringly."

Her cheeks flush darker than her hair. "Don't try to sweet-talk me out of being lazy. The doctor said you're basically healed. I seem to recall you hauling your mom around, no problem. If I didn't have this cast on my leg, I could carry you for *miles*."

Two months out from the incident with Shelly's stalker, and my side is knitted back together with only the occasional twinge. If the blade had hit organs, I would've been bedridden for a lot longer, but muscle and fat took the blow.

Still, carrying Harper half a mile on a mountain trail wears on a man.

"Oh, really? Well, I can't wait. I'm over walking on my own. The second your leg is back to normal, I'm clinging to your back and never letting go."

At least she's been able to downgrade her cast size on both limbs. Now, she's only got her forearm and lower leg encased.

Even that much restriction has her antsy.

But that's not why I brought her to this overlook.

"Fine. You can put me down. But only because it's pretty here."

Harper loosens her hold on my neck, and I crouch so she can easily slide off my back. She keeps ahold of my shoulder for balance, putting all her weight on her uninjured leg. My eyes trace down the muscular limb to her single yellow Converse. The sight of the worn sneaker has me smiling.

For a moment, we stand quietly side by side on the rocky outcropping I've brought us to. The overlook gives us a beautiful view of a sprawling mountain valley. Trees stretch out before us, the colors shifting with the beginning of autumn. Yellows and reds weave into the greens of pines, and a touch of chill tangles in the air, kept at bay by the sunny day.

Shelly found a beautiful rental in the Colorado mountains, and she's given no sign of wanting to return to California. We're happy to stick by her side as long as the invite remains, but I know, eventually, we'll leave this place and go back to LA.

As much as I've enjoyed it here, I'm looking forward to that. Living a normal life with Harper Walsh in her armadillo house.

But there's something I'd like to do before we leave this gorgeous setting.

As if reading my mind, Harper turns a sardonic glance my way. "You're trying to make this some grand romantic gesture, but let's be honest."

I fight a smile at her suspicious tone. "Enlighten me."

"You wanted to get away from that stifling sexual tension as bad as I did."

I groan out a laugh. "I've been trying to figure out if Roman will fire me if I tell him to take Shelly on a long hike in the woods and fuck her against a tree." As I talk, I help Harper sink to the ground, the two of us settling on the sun-warmed rock.

"Well, don't get *that* specific." She rests her butt in my lap and leans back against my chest. "Then, you'll sound like a weirdo who fantasizes about his friends going at it."

Great. Now, I have that image in my mind.

"This really isn't the way I meant for this conversation to go," I mutter, hand tapping my pocket.

"*This* conversation?" Harper glances up at me, her green eyes shaded by a baseball hat. "You had a specific topic in mind?"

"I did. I do." Unable to help myself, I steal a quick kiss. "Stop distracting me."

"I'm so sorry." She smirks, not sorry at all. "Please continue. I'll sit here quietly, like a well-behaved lady."

"Hmm." Nuzzling my nose behind her ear, I draw in a deep breath that smells of peppermint. "Don't like that either. Can't have you getting ideas about being well-behaved. Those poison a young lady's mind. Next thing you know, she's following the rules. Then, she stops cursing. And a well-behaved lady would never even consider spending the rest of her life with a fuckup like me."

Despite the confidence I imbue in my voice, my hands are sweaty, fingers shaking as I pull the ring from my pocket and hold the gold band between us.

Harper doesn't even look at it. She cups my face in her hands, holding me so our eyes are locked, the rough material of her cast brushing my clean-shaven cheek. "We talked about this."

"Getting married? Well, yeah."

After arriving home from the hospital, I brought the possibility up as something I wanted her to think about. We both know how short life is, and we already lost too much time.

Harper's response was, and I quote, "Yeah, that makes sense. Not like I can get rid of you."

"But I was sneaky," I say, "and made you think I wouldn't ask for a while. Maybe years."

She shakes her head. "You know what I mean. You're not a fuckup."

Oh. That. We have had some late-night discussions about me being nicer to myself.

"The joke landed better if I said I was." My voice is strained, anxiety about her lack of an answer getting to me.

"Say it to me straight, Fred." Harper's voice is serious, all teasing gone. "We'll joke for the rest of our lives if you say it to me straight this once."

Those words give me the strength and the safety to be vulnerable.

"I'm not a fuckup," I whisper. "I'm proud of the man I am. A man you love. Whatever happens, I'm here for you. Forever. Will you marry me, Harper Walsh?"

"Hell yes." She crashes her mouth against mine, laughing and crying into our kiss.

I hold her close, giving back everything in equal measure.

"The shirt," she groans, pulling away enough to stare down at my button-up. "*This* is why you wore it?"

My cheeks ache with my grin. "Wanted to look my best. Give you every reason to say yes."

She pinches the material, trying to scowl and failing, her nose wrinkling adorably. "Where did you even find a Hawaiian shirt with armadillos on it? Please tell me that's not custom-made."

"Fine." I kiss the corner of her jaw. "I won't tell you that."

Because the cast makes Harper's fingers swell, I slip the gold band on her right ring finger, then keep making out with her while she straddles my lap. If I could stay here, like this, for the rest of my life, I'd die happy.

But life intrudes in the way of a buzzing phone.

Harper is faster than I am, slipping the device from my pocket.

"*What did she say?*" she reads off the screen. "From Roman. Your *best* friend."

Her attempt to sound put out when her lips are plump from my kisses is adorable.

"Still salty about that, huh?" As I tease her, my hand sneaks to the front of her loose shorts.

"Of course not." Then, Harper sets my phone aside, tangles her fingers in my hair, and tugs my head back until I'm staring straight up at her, held unmoving in her iron grip. "Because now, I'm your fiancée. Which means *I'm* your best friend again." She nips my lower lip. "Right?"

"Does it count if I say it under duress?" *Or with a raging hard-on?*

"This isn't duress." Harper strokes a thumb over my cheek. "This is loving encouragement." Her hold tightens, to the point of almost being painful. "Now, say it."

"I love you," I groan out, my eyes on her mouth, wanting to taste her again more than anything. Breathe her in as she whimpers my name.

"Duh." She rolls her eyes, all sass. "I know that. Now, say I'm your best friend."

"Fine. You're my best friend in the whole fucking world. I need you. I love you." My touch slips past her waistband. "Now, *please*, can I finger you on this rock?"

Harper grins in triumph.

"Of course, Freddy. What are friends for?"

The End

***

Thank you so much for reading FALL BACK INTO ME. I hope you enjoyed Harper and Fred's love story! If you did, please consider leaving a review to help other readers find this book. Reviews mean so much to independent authors like me, and your kind words are an important part of the bookselling process. Thank you for being one of my readers!

Want more romance? Check out the following steamy contemporary stories about some reformed bad boys and the awkward women they can't help falling for!

RESCUE ME
Forget the Past Book 1

Dash Lamont is out on parole, working at an animal shelter, and focused on living life by the rules. Number one on the list: avoid temptation. But that's hard to do when Paige Herbert parks in the middle of Dash's well-ordered life, demanding his attention with her offbeat conversation and sinful curves.

READ ME
Forget the Past book 2

Cole Allemand visits the library for the books, but he stays for the librarian. Summer Pierce is as bright and warm as her name, and he's been crushing on her for months. Cole is determined to get Summer to fall for him before she finds out the secrets of his past. The ones that could drive her away.

Keep reading for a sneak peek of *Rescue Me*, Book 1 in the Forget the Past series. Join Paige as she deals with losing her job, fiancé, and home by adopting a pit bull and convincing a hot rescue worker to train her dog…

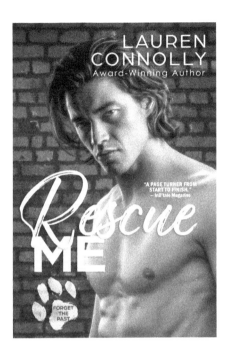

RESCUE ME

PAIGE

One of these houses is mine. I'm just not exactly sure *which* one.

A sigh pushes out, weighty and exhausted, from deep in my chest. The sun set hours ago, back when I was still on the highway. Trying to read the tiny print on each of these mailboxes isn't easy after staring out the windshield for the past two days. My eyes practically crackle, begging me to close them.

Sleep. Just go to sleep.

"That one! I…I think."

I pull up alongside the curb, letting the heavy engine rumble on as I flip through photos on my phone. Martin sent me a picture two weeks ago, a selfie of him with a large tan house behind him that looks like the one I've stopped in front of. Unfortunately, the homes on either side of it are mirror reflections.

Normally, Martin's preference for uniformity doesn't bother be. Tonight, though, I wish he had picked a weird bungalow with daisies painted on the siding and a turquoise front door. Just so I know, without a hint of a doubt, that I am parking in front of *my* house.

And I am definitely parking because I need to pick one of these clone homes before I drive myself mad puttering around this neighborhood all night.

As I shut down the engine, the whole car settles as if she's ready to sleep for the night.

"Enjoy your rest, Penelope," I mutter to the steering wheel.

I need a bed bad. A pounding started in my temples way before I even crossed the Louisiana/Mississippi border. The headache comes courtesy of long hours in the car paired with my hair being pulled up into a high, messy bun. I'd let the heavy mass down if I wasn't terrified of its condition. Two days' worth of greasiness has built up. I doubt removing my hairband would even do anything. The hair would likely continue sitting on top of my head, permanently reshaped.

My priorities have changed: before a bed, I need a shower. The vision of scrubbing a thick lather of shampoo into my scalp plays in my brain like a porno. I can imagine the transformation of the knotted mess into its normal smooth cascade.

"Butter on bread," my mom always says when she affectionately tugs on a strand.

Not sure I approve of being compared to a boring slice of white bread, but I take comfort in the fact that she's simply referring to my complexion and hair color rather than my personality.

When I push the car door open, the heavy New Orleans air embraces me. It is almost as warm and wet as an actual shower but nowhere near as refreshing. The humidity sits on my skin, weighing me down as I trudge up the front walk of a house that I hope is mine.

The easy solution would've been to just call Martin on Friday night when I decided to change my travel plans. That way my fiancé would be waiting out on the porch, ready to wave me down.

Instead, I chose the surprise method. I'd like to convince myself that this is a romantic gesture.

I just couldn't stay away from you for two more weeks!

In reality, my silence arises from shame. Whenever I let my thumb hover over his number, I couldn't even imagine how the conversation would go.

"Hey, honey! Guess what? I lost my job!" I whisper under my breath and pause with my foot on the bottom step leading up to the elevated porch.

Well, I guess I *could* say that.

Now that I'm here, potentially a few steps away from Martin, the words don't seem so inadequate. Depressing? Yeah sure. But I can clearly envision his face, how his blond brows will dip in the middle as he scowls. Not *at* me but *with* me. I can taste the glass of red wine he'll pour me as he rages over the unfair treatment.

That's when I realize why the need for surprise. I don't actually want to *talk* about how I got fired from my dream job. All I want is to see my anger reflected in the face of my partner. To feel connected to him in a way I haven't in a while.

With the moving plans, and Martin preparing to start his residency down here, and me trying to finish up all my large projects before going remote, we've barely talked. I can't even remember the last time I looked him in the eyes during a conversation. We usually just shout to each other from opposite rooms.

And sex? Well…it's been some time.

As I knock on the mystery door I hope is mine, I make a resolution. Whether I find Martin in this clone house or the one next door or the next street over, when I finally locate my fiancé, the first thing I'm going to do is stare deep into his eyes. I'll hold his gaze until our connection is firmly reestablished. Then—after a shower—I'm going to jump his bones.

Light spills into the dark night from around the edges of the curtains. At least that means whoever lives here, hopefully Martin, is still awake. After the polite taps of my knock ring out, the steady pad of footsteps sound behind the door. I brace myself, ready to stare my fiancé down.

Only, Martin doesn't open the door.

A small slim woman dressed in a robe stands before me. She is adorably petite. I could practically fit her in my pocket. Her bare feet peek out from under the floor-length robe, and her long brown hair lays in a damp mass over her shoulders.

Envy spikes hard through me. Clearly, this woman has just taken a shower. My greasy strands weep in envy.

Also, her appearance makes it clear my navigation skills have failed me. I am no closer to my own glorious shower, having no idea which one of these houses Martin bought for the two of us to live in.

"Sorry. I thought this might be my house. Do you know a blond man? About so tall?" I hold my hand a few inches above my head like the sleep drunk idiot I am.

I'm ready to continue describing my fiancé out of pure desperation when I notice the woman's face. With a stranger knocking on her door at midnight, I would expect confusion or annoyance. But if I had to guess, her slack-jawed, wide-eyed stare is closer to horror.

Apparently, my need for a shower is even direr than I knew.

"I told you I'd get it..." The familiar rusty voice drifts from behind the stranger as my fiancé trots down a set of stairs visible just over her shoulder.

The showered girl shuffles back, so I have a clear view of Martin, clad in only a pair of gym shorts, his hair just as gloriously damp from a recent cleaning as the woman in front of me.

Our eyes meet. His top half stops, but his bottom half doesn't get the memo. Instead, one of his bare feet slips on the wooden step, and he lands hard on his ass, shocked gaze never leaving mine.

So, this *is* the right house.

It's just everything else in the world that is wrong.

Whatever way I might want to interpret this situation is made impossible when I flick my eyes back to the stranger, who I now realize is wearing *my* green, cotton robe. Red splotches scorch along the tops of her cheekbones, and guilty tears pool on her lashes.

Something dark and sickening rolls in my stomach, but I flash freeze it. After one last look at the boy I've loved since my senior year of high school, I turn to the girl he chose to hurt me for.

"You can keep the robe." Reaching out, I clasp the doorknob. "And the man." I wrench the door closed on the most devastating scene of my life and sprint back to my sleeping car.

Penelope revs to life, more dependable than any man could ever be.

I shift into first gear and tear down the street, not caring who I wake up. With the roar of my sweet girl's engine, I can't hear Martin shouting.

But I can see him. In my rearview mirror, he sprints down the street after me. I skid around a corner and lose sight of him.

And he loses me.

Keep reading Rescue Me

Sign up for my newsletter for book news and freebies! All subscribers get a FREE copy of the enemies to lovers college romance LOVE AND THE LIBRARY.

Get my free book!

ABOUT THE AUTHOR

Lauren Connolly is an award-wining author of contemporary and paranormal romance stories. She has lived among mountains, next to lakes, and in imaginary worlds. Lauren can never seem to stay in one place for too long, but trust that wherever she's residing there is a dog who thinks he's a troll, twin cats hiding in the couch, and bookshelves bursting with the stories written by the authors she loves.

Lightning Source UK Ltd.
Milton Keynes UK
UKHW010743200123
415680UK00001B/30